refund

STORIES

Karen E. Bender

COUNTERPOINT PRESS

F
Ben

Library of Congress Cataloging-in-Publication Data

Bender, Karen E.
[Short stories. Selections]
Refund : stories / Karen Bender.
   pages ; cm
ISBN 978-1-61902-455-7 (hardcover)
I. Title.
PS3552.E53849A6 2015
813'.54—dc23

2014034079

Cover design by Faceout Studios
Interior design by Domini Dragoone

Counterpoint Press
2560 Ninth Street, Suite 318
Berkeley, CA 94710
www.counterpointpress.com

Printed in the United States of America
Distributed by Publishers Group West

10 9 8 7 6 5 4 3 2 1

To Robert, Jonah, and Maia, with love

Contents

refund

Reunion

Anna Green could not afford the tickets to Surfview High's twentieth reunion, but she walked into the Mercury Ballroom, anyway, to meet her classmates. She had seventy new business cards in her pocket, and she wanted to hand one to everyone here. The ballroom was crowded, and glossy green balloons, shaped like palm trees, stretched into the dark spangled light. She passed the boy who called himself Johnny the Weatherman; he was describing the weather across the world. Johnny used to run around the high school clutching maps and telling people detailed weather reports—he received thunderous applause at graduation, as though people were both paying tribute to his efforts and perhaps grateful that they were not him. He was now almost forty, older, angrier, but still standing in front of the crowd with, surprisingly, the same map. "There is snow in Denmark and a drought in the Midwest, and fires are raging across Mexico," he said, gesturing to the map with a pointer. No one appeared to be listening; the room roared.

She had not intended to come. The gold postcards had been arriving in the mail for months: Surfview High 20th! Buffet dinner, dancing, tickets, $50 each. She threw the cards out, or her husband Howard did. And then, two weeks before the reunion, she picked up the phone: Tiffany Mann, former vice president of the student body, exclaiming: "Anna Green! You sat behind me in bio! We dissected a frog together. Hey. We want you to come."

She listened to Tiffany, whom she barely knew. Anna longed to stand beside her in a sequined dress; she was also aware of her own deep sense of shame. "I wish I could, but I just—"

"You must! You must! For you, our special discount. Thirty!"

She swallowed. How did Tiffany know? "I wish I—"

"I know! Hard times for all. No worries. Twenty! You can bring business cards."

Anna paused. Tiffany sighed.

"Tough customer," said Tiffany. "Okay. Free! We need guests! I have to see you, hon, I do."

Her husband had said, go, hand out business cards, just go. "Connections," he said. They had no idea what would work. When she was getting lots of calls for her business repairing appliances, they bought a foreclosed house in the Inland Empire, 1,400 square feet, enough for them and their two children; they behaved as though they were middle class, but the money rushed in and out for nothing, it seemed, and with a few skipped paychecks, a car accident, a broken roof, they were on the edge of ruin. It was 2009, and some days the phone was silent, and now Anna sometimes woke before dawn; she jumped up, her heart like a silver bell in her chest.

Her classmates gathered in the ballroom's dim haze. Anna listened to them describe their lives. There were free agents, the childless, the ones living abroad, the briefly famous—there were those who were unaccounted for, there were those who were already dead—but most were, at this point in the continuum, employed and organized into the strict nations of family. There was Tiara Hanson, the popular girl who loved reunions because she was in her glory for four hours once every ten years. Her hair was abundant, her teeth perfect and unmarked. "Anna!" she said, placing her hand on Anna's shoulder. "You look fifteen! Don't we all." There was Stuart McKenzie, who had been an avid collector of baseball cards and now served as a statistician for the achievements of his children, holding out photos of them engaged in myriad activities: "Benny was first clarinet in his school orchestra," he said. The children stared, imprisoned by their father's desire to have something to love; they peered out, wanting to run across streets, to drive cars.

Many of the people who made it to the reunion had done well. There were photos of recently purchased objects: summer homes, gazebos, giant TVs. Anna hugged, shook hands, pressed her cards into one palm after another. Her classmates held the cards to the light, tried to see who she had become. "Appliance Doctor?" Yes. She walked into the homes of strangers to fix their washers, dryers, refrigerators, their Kenmores, Maytags, Frigidaires—she liked to see their wallpaper, the arrangement of their furniture, the hopeful attempts to claim their right to the world.

"I go anywhere in the Southland," she said, trying to press down the eagerness in her voice. "My prices are better than Sears, Walmart. Always. Give me a call."

She talked at length to Deirdre Hoffman, who rented out four houses in West Covina and thus had a number of appliances that could break down at any moment, and she learned about whom Deirdre had seen at the supermarket last week, and finally Deirdre pocketed her card and leaned toward her. "Sounds good," she said. "But . . . what I want to know is what happened to that guy Warren Vance?"

Anna didn't know. After Deirdre moved off, she stood beside the pale glasses of champagne and wondered about Warren Vance, whom she had loved first, before all this. He had been a skinny, swaggering boy with an overconfidence that was thrilling then, as though every adult's failure was a conscious and unfortunate decision. He was going to become a congressman, a TV news producer, a real estate tycoon. Sometimes she caught him muttering the inaugural address in his sleep. He wet his hair with his palms in the morning and brushed it so it looked like Donald Trump's.

She met Warren in high school auto shop, junior year. Warren was casing the class, looking for who would help him pass it. He had trouble standing in one place. But while she fixed the engine, she could sense him pausing, absorbing what she was doing, and when she glanced up at him, his face twitched; it was the one time she saw he was afraid.

The first time he touched her face, it was as though he were cradling a piece of crystal in his palms. They dated for two years; he left when, at twenty, she did not agree to marry him. "No one will love you the way Vance will," he said, and he vanished. It took her years before she stopped believing she saw him on the street.

Now as Anna walked through the sequined sea of her classmates, Johnny the Weatherman brushed past her shoulder. "Screw everything," she heard him mutter. "Hell's bells."

"What?" she asked, startled, but he had moved on.

"Anna Green," a voice said.

She looked up.

An enormous man stood, blowing smoke out of his mouth. It was Warren; he looked as though he had been inflated, a large balloon. He weighed probably close to three hundred pounds. His hair, which had been lush, shining ribbons of brown, was now all gray. His blue gaze was familiar—fierce and bright, as though he had been trying all his life to peer through walls.

"It's your true love," he said. He laughed and placed a large, heavy hand on her shoulder; his palm was cold.

"Warren?" she said, carefully, trying not to seem too shocked.

"Life's been treating you good," he said.

Her legs felt unsteady. "How are you?" she asked.

"I've been fab." He was a little out of breath. "Vance does this, Vance does that. He gets tired."

"You, tired?"

"Arlene," he said. "My wife. Other wives break you for diamonds. She loves gold. Vance's dream house went to her earrings, her necklaces. Now we're renting a one-bedroom, no pool. Now her arm looks like Cleopatra's. Who's happy?"

"You?" she asked.

He blew out a puff of smoke. "This could have been yours," he said. He lifted his arms. His suit fell around him like the dark wings of a bat. "Vance was a millionaire," he said. "Twice over. He built a hotel in Vegas, he sold limos. Don't underestimate him. He's going to make his fucking third million by forty."

A waitress passed carrying a tray of tiny hamburgers. "No smoking, sir," she said.

"Give me one of those, honey pie," he said. His eyes darted around the room. "So what are you up to?" he said.

"I'm married, living in Inland Empire. I have two kids. I repair home appliances," she said.

"Well, hurray for you," he said. He drained his drink and crushed the plastic glass with his foot. "Vance needs another drink," he said, and he thundered back to the bar.

She stood, watching him walk away.

Johnny the Weatherman pushed by her.

"Move," he growled.

"Hey," she said. He had always moved slightly off-center, like someone had pushed him, but now he stumbled to the center of the room with a surprising aggressiveness. He stood, watching the crowd swirl around him for a moment. Then he shoved his hand into his red sports jacket and brought out a gun.

She blinked. The gun looked like a toy. She noticed that his hand gripped the handle in a way that seemed too comfortable; she stepped back.

"What's the weather?" Johnny yelled. "Hey! What's the weather?"

He pulled the trigger, and the bullets zoomed up and hit the ceiling, their explosions trembling through her throat.

A waiter scuttled toward the kitchen, holding his hand protectively over miniature quiches. Classmates hit the floor.

"Did it rain in Ohio?" Johnny yelled. His face was slick with sweat. Anna crouched on the maroon carpet. It was a movement new but also oddly familiar, as though she'd been secretly figuring out how to do it for years.

He began to shoot. She touched her thighs and arms and realized, with surprise, how deeply she loved her body. A wineglass exploded on the floor beside her foot. She cried out and pressed her face into the musty carpet. She saw Warren Vance hunched under a table. The flat carpet bristled against her face.

The bullets were still coming. When would they stop? The wounded cried out for help. Others crawled away, like animals, in their finery. Some bent to help others, and some fled; Anna's mind was gray, static, and she did not know where to go. She saw Warren crawl up from under the table, and he caught her gaze. His head nodded toward a side door. There was a way out. He turned and stumbled down the hallway, and she scrambled up, kicked off her maroon fake-suede heels, and ran after him. She rushed down a bare beige corridor, the linoleum cold on her bare feet, past the hotel kitchen, the oddly domestic sounds of pans clattering and water rushing into a sink; she ran, the sound of screams fading behind her, pushing through the side doors into the parking lot, and she kept going until she got to the edge of it and then stood there, in the black night. Below her, traffic streamed down on the highway. The light glowed, a pale mist, off the speeding cars.

Sirens sounded. Emergency personnel leapt out of red trucks. Her clothes held the odor of champagne and smoke, of a celebration, not a crime. She walked to her car, past the sign in the parking lot: *GO OTTERS! WELCOME CLASS OF '84.* Her classmates stumbled out of the hotel, clutching key rings imprinted with photos of themselves as young people; they stood around weeping or fled into the night. She did not realize she was trembling until her hand could not fit the key through the lock in the car. The night air was light and cool on her arms. She looked around for Warren Vance. She wanted, urgently, to run to him, to kiss him, to thank him for showing her the right door. She walked slowly around the parking lot, looking, but he was gone.

SHE DROVE HOME, TWO HOURS DEEP INTO THE INLAND EMPIRE where she lived. Her family resided in a community splashed onto an area that should have remained desert—pale stucco houses pushed aside rattlesnakes and coyotes, and the newly made streets burned with a glaring heat. It was late, and on the freeway she passed a man shaving in his car with his interior lights on, a pickup truck full of drunken teenagers, a driver of an oil rig listening to Italian opera. Everyone drove with a giddy foolishness, obeying the traffic rules. She had to think carefully to remember to grip the steering wheel, to press the gas. Was she, in fact, alive? How did she know? Had she, in fact, been hit by a bullet, and was she now dying on her way home? Then she realized she could not be shot because they could not afford to fix her. She pressed the hard, ridged pedals with her bare feet. The dampness of the vinyl steering wheel came off on her hands.

It was almost midnight when she returned. She opened the door quietly and crept upstairs. Everyone was awake. She heard the monotone voice of her husband reading to the children. For a moment, unnoticed, she watched. Her husband appeared to be reading nursery rhymes to the stale air. The girl, who was just two, was wearing a pink ball gown, and her face was smeared with red lollipop. She was climbing to the top of her brother's bunk bed and diving off it into a single pillow. The boy had emptied hundreds of cards he was collecting—Pokémon, Yu-Gi-Oh!, baseball and football heroes, idolatry of all persuasions—into the middle of his room and was organizing them feverishly. The children were so tired they looked drunk.

Her husband's family had divorced bitterly when he was seven, leaving him to be raised by his grandmother, and he had become a social worker, to help others with their sorrow. She and Howard had met when she installed a dryer for him, and he had, like the others, asked for her ID. "Anna," he read, matter-of-factly; she had not realized until then that the suspicion of her customers caused her pain. She would stand at the door, and the homeowner would look at her, as though she were wearing a costume of a repairperson and that she could not do what she did, and a part of her enjoyed tricking them, seeing their expressions turn from concern to relief. But with Howard, there was no suspicion. He told her about his clients, who were struggling with prison and bankruptcy and child care and runaway teenagers; she listened to how he helped them with small steps: getting a driver's license, a new apartment, an order of restraint. Sometimes these steps moved his clients along, sometimes they did not, but she loved the way he looked into the chaos and tried, with a form or a phone call, to find a way out.

They were married; one child came into their home, then another. The children sat in their pink and blue onesies, smiling, toothless, but she was aware that the hats with the puppy ears, the outfits decorated with trains and cats and roses were useful in distracting parents from noticing the darkness; from the breathless, gasping love the children elicited and that made the parents sit up in the middle of the night, listening. They were always listening; there was always a simmering fear.

So here they were, in their late thirties, perplexed but trying to get on with it, and recently, the girl had developed a problem going to sleep. It seemed sparked by nothing: the sight of a witch on a video, an awareness of the end of herself as a baby. She now refused to go to sleep at night. She rejected all offerings of comfort—toys, juice, songs—and stood in the dark light, screaming.

"We have to just let her cry," she had told him one night.

"How?" he said to her, to anyone who advised him to do this. "It's how she tells us how she feels." Recently, he had turned thirty-nine, the age his parents had been when they divorced. Now, every night, he crawled into the little girl's bedroom. He lay on the carpet while the girl fell asleep in her bed. For months, Anna had woken alone in their bed to find him curled up on the carpet of their daughter's room; he said he wanted the child to wake up to his face, as though to the sun.

But it was ruining him. He staggered up at dawn and sat at the kitchen table; when he left the house one morning, he drove the car into a tree. Then he began loaning money to his clients, for groceries, for textbooks. He waited for them to pay him. They waited. The girl stood in her crib and screamed.

Now it was 11:45 PM, and she watched them; she wanted to rush in and gather them in her arms and feel the sweet thrum of their bodies—but she could not. She was afraid something inside her might crack apart, and her weeping would frighten them. She stood, instead, silent, dim, in the hallway, trying to remember that she was real.

Then she stepped into the room.

"They're still up?" she asked.

The girl looked at her and shrieked with joy. The boy jumped up. "Did you get me a toy?" he whispered, seductively, into her ear.

"Oh," said her husband. "I thought you were staying for the whole thing—"

"Something happened," she said.

"She took my Harpie Lady card!" yelled the boy.

"She didn't take it," said her husband tiredly. "She found it."

"She stole it!" yelled the boy.

"Welcome home," said her husband. He looked like he had endured a brawl. "Good night." He stood up, zoomed into the bedroom, and collapsed onto their bed.

"Daddy, no!" screamed the girl.

"Please, God," he muttered, hoarsely, into the bedsheets.

Anna lifted the kicking girl into her crib. "Time for bed."

"Daddy, help me!" screamed the girl. "Help!"

Her rage was awesome, tremendous. Anna closed the windows so the neighbors would not hear her screams. Anna touched her hair, softly. She did not know what to say to the child. "Please," she pleaded with her child. "For God's sake, please." The girl glared at her mother until her father crawled in and stretched out on the carpet. In all of the lit homes, were parents making similar pleas of their children?

"You also need to sleep," she said to her husband.

"No," he said. "Sophie, I'm here." The girl stood in her ball gown, clutching the bars of her crib, beaming.

The boy was hurling the girl's stuffed animals at the wall. "Look what she did!" he yelled. He opened his fist. There was a tiny shred of crumpled card in it. "Look!"

She smoothed his hair and guided him to his bed. "I'm sorry," she said.

"Get me more for my birthday," he begged. "I want to get fifty. Sixty. Please!" He rolled over and fell asleep.

SHE LAY AWAKE IN THE DARK WHILE THE OTHERS FELL INTO THEIR dreams. Was it strange that Johnny the Weatherman had begun to shoot? Or was it stranger that Tyra Johnson, a beauty, had gained one hundred pounds and moved to Modesto, or that Brian Horwitz, the class clown, was president of his synagogue, or that Laurie Stone, who had held her hand tenderly as they walked into kindergarten, had been indicted for embezzlement at a local bank? She looked out the window, and all she saw was determined innocence—the bullish SUVs parked in the driveways, testament to dreams of safety, of endless oil; she looked at the houses of her neighbors, flocking here, to the edge of the desert, the only place they could afford in Southern California; she saw the development vanishing violently in a wildfire, in a terrorist attack. Her own childhood home in Granada Hills was bulldozed for a luxury condo complex, her parents retired, taking medicine for their hearts, her father a math teacher now bagging groceries at Ralph's for extra money, both of them praying that Social Security would hold up. The sight of her father, a man of six feet, gentle but bad with money, carefully guiding groceries across the parking lot made her ache with useless love. She could not save him. The houses were slapped together with drywall and paste.

When she finally fell unconscious, she dreamed of Warren Vance. She dreamed that Warren bragged that he spent $800,000 on a day trip to the moon. She saw him standing on the moon's white surface in his cheap suit, smoke trailing off the end of his cigarette. "Vance wants you," he said, and he pulled her toward him.

HER HUSBAND WOKE FIRST AND WENT DOWN TO MAKE BREAKFAST; Anna hurried to the front lawn and grabbed that day's paper. The shooting had made the front page; eight classmates had been injured in the shooting, two were dead. Her throat felt cold as she read about the dead: Tiffany Mann, Harry Waters. She had just glimpsed them in the ballroom. Their high school faces smiled from the front page.

Her husband was standing in front of the stove making breakfast. The hearty smell of bacon filled the air.

"Read this," she said, handing it to him.

He glanced at the newspaper. The pale desert light poured through the windows, as though shoveled from a mine of diamonds. Her husband looked up at her quickly.

"Two dead," she said. "People were injured—"

He looked at the paper and then at her and then lifted strips of bacon from the grease to a paper towel. His hand trembled.

"Are you okay?"

"I think so."

"What did you do?"

"I hid under a chair."

He blinked.

"Did you think of throwing something at him?"

"He had a gun," she said.

He looked dissatisfied. "Did anyone try?"

"We were afraid," she said.

"My God," he said. He clutched the handle of the pan, trying to will all of them into an ordinary domestic scenario. Then he stepped forward and hugged her. They clung to each other, their hands grasping but awkward, as if touching these bodies for the first time. The girl hurled her bacon to the floor.

"Hot!" she announced.

"Don't throw your bacon!" shouted the boy, joyfully. He slapped her arm. The girl shrieked and whacked him with her spoon.

"Stop, everyone!" Anna said, pulling them away from each other. The girl threw the spoon across the room, where it hit the monthly calendar; it slid down. "Stop now!"

"Have more," said her husband, piling more bacon onto their plates.

The sun made the children's hair gleam. She felt the boy's arm twitch, slow. The children resumed their breakfast. Her husband looked at her; he wanted to ask more.

"Was there blood?" he asked.

It was not what she had expected him to ask.

"There was," she said, and they waited for this to answer something. They were all balanced, barely, on the fragile sheath of linoleum.

"More bacon!" yelled the boy. "Now."

SHE HAD FOUR APPOINTMENTS THAT DAY, AND SHE STRAPPED HER-self in the car and set off. Her car joined the flood of others on their daily missions. Anna knocked on doors, looked at circuit boards, listened for unusual noises; tightened, aligned, cleaned, lubricated parts; brought out her RF leakage detector, her thermistor vacuum gauge, her hex wrenches; she turned machines on. She lingered in homeowners' kitchens, chatting with them about warranties, prices, but really, she was looking around. There was the precise cleanliness of the floors, the proliferation or absence of family photos. She pretended to be checking a dryer to make sure it was running, but she was listening to the way the customers talked to people on the phone while she worked; she needed to compare the tenor of their fear to her own. They all were afraid of something, big or small—the shoddy work of a contractor or being too shy to wear a certain dress, or the results of a biopsy or a child's bad grade on a test or the thought that the cat had spoken or the weird sound the refrigerator was making. And on and on.

In the car, returning from the day's work, she remembered Warren Vance as a young man. She remembered the first time they had sex, the frantic way he pulled her toward him, the way they both cried. He had lived in a tiny, dark apartment with his aunt, for his father was dead; his mother was in institutions sometimes, sometimes not, and his aunt worked as a telemarketer fifty hours a week, and the house was covered with a thin sheen of dust. Warren's room was always very clean. It was plastered with cutout pictures of famous leaders who had risen from difficult circumstances. The apartment was a shoddy, barely furnished place, but it seemed holy with them in it. He did not have a particular career goal but wanted to assume the top post of various organizations: the head of Coca-Cola, the governorship of California, the presidency of the United States.

She saw the cars lining up in front of her. Now she was here; she had made it to this life. She clutched the steering wheel so hard her hands ached.

Her cell phone rang.

"Hey, Annie," Warren Vance said, in a soft voice.

SHE MET HIM, TWO DAYS LATER, A HUNDRED MILES AWAY. SHE told the babysitter she would be working late; it was absurdly easy to arrange. She would meet him at his work—he said he wanted to talk business.

The sky was white with smog above the freeway, which cut through San Bernardino, City of Industry, passing superstores selling electronics, discount clothing, sporting goods; she passed parking lots shimmering like dry lakes, warehouses containing patio furniture, used tires, drugs, mirrored cube office buildings, palm trees with thick furry necks. Fast-food franchises loomed off the freeway, hawking fried chicken and burgers and fries with bright orange and red signs. The freeway stretched on and on; she could see forever and she could see nothing. She turned off into an industrial area, aluminum warehouses lining the empty streets. Vance's office was located in a storefront in a crumbling mini-mall. It was a treeless block, and the sky above the street looked infinite. His office was bordered by a Subway sandwich franchise and a Family Dollar store.

When she walked into Vance Real Estate, she noticed that he had a steel desk balanced on a tennis ball on one side, a glass coffee table with a crack in it, and that the ventilation between this office and the Subway store was so faulty that the room smelled of salami and sliced ham. Taped on the windows were posters of palatial homes perched in glamorous destinations: Beverly Hills, Paris, Monaco.

He was sitting in his chair, which was made of a maroon material that resembled leather. "Anna," he said, standing up. "How are you?"

He stood, towering over her, and shook hands firmly. She felt her hand vanish into his. She was encased in the moment, perfectly still. Then he released her, and she felt the cool air again surround her hand.

"This is where you work?" she asked, concerned.

"Temporary," he said. "Renovations at the main office."

He was a little out of breath.

"How are you?" she asked. "Since the reunion, I mean."

"Fine. Vance is always fine," he said.

"Thank you," she said.

"For what?" He strode over to a poster of the Eiffel Tower that was starting to peel off the wall and tapped it down.

"You told me where to go."

He shrugged and adjusted a big silver watch around his wrist.

"Did you hear about Harry? Tiffany?" she said. The room was silent. Nothing was the right thing to say. "Sandra Scone lost an eye," she said. "They don't know if Carl Blandon will ever walk again—"

"Eh," he said, shooing something in the air.

"Don't you care?" she asked.

"They got in his way."

"What do you mean?"

"Vance knew better," he said, proudly.

She looked at his face, the pores of his skin mottled like the peel of an orange. "You don't really think that," she said, wondering.

He swept his hand through his hair. "Vance doesn't think too hard."

"Weren't you scared?"

He shrugged. "Fear's a luxury," he said. He clapped his hands. "You've got to move. Margie," he called. "Bring some coffee for my first love."

A girl with yellow hair so dull it looked gray came out of the back. She had the overly obedient manner of someone who had recently been released from something: mental hospital, jail. Smiling, she held out a Styrofoam cup with some instant coffee.

"Margie's been with me—two years," he said.

"Usually I work at the Subway," said Margie.

"Ha, ha," he said, clapping his hands together loudly. "It's been too long. Sit down. Glowing. You define the term—"

"Oh, please," she said, wanting him to go on.

"Others—not so good. Georgia Haring? Sun damage. Looked like a leather suitcase. Brian Smith? Bald as an egg."

This appeared to be unchanged, his certainty about others' failings, as though that hostility gave him a clear view of humanity. His confidence amid the bareness, the dirty windows, calmed her.

"What do you do here?" Anna asked.

"Vance is a real estate agent," he said.

"For what?"

"Glamour properties. Lots. From bitter divorces. No money

down. Good deals. Why should only the rich live like kings?" He set some brochures out on his desk. She picked one up: a half acre, beachfront, near Santa Barbara.

"That's a good one," he said. "Rock star caught with seven assistants, quote unquote, wife sues him for every penny, he's trying to get rid of this lot before she learns about it. Quick. Worth ten million dollars, he's unloading it for five. From heartbreak comes opportunity."

They sat across from each other in the milky fluorescent light. Warren's voice was hoarse with the same excitement it had as a young man. The sameness of his voice, its stubborn ignorance of the passing of the last twenty years, was somehow touching. How had he not aged like the rest of them? It seemed a supreme, thrilling force of will.

A voice in the adjoining room cried out for a turkey sandwich. Warren lined up photos of beaches, vineyards, mountain lakes on his desk like cards in a deck. "How long have you been married?" he asked her.

"Eight years," she said.

"I've been hitched for fourteen," he said.

"Oh," she said. "How is your wife?" she asked, lightly.

"Great. Hot. We're off to Cozumel. Next week." He whipped out a wallet and handed her a photo. She had expected to see a thin, glamorous starlet type, but the woman was perfectly ordinary, with a Dorothy Hamill haircut, purple sweat suit.

"Why did you marry her?"

"She said yes." He howled with laughter. "We went to the Riviera last year. A dream, Anna, my life is a grand dream—"

"How did you know where to go?" she asked.

"Hard work," he said. "Vance turned down no offers, he shook hands—"

"No," she said. "Out of the hotel."

"Oh, that," he said. "Instinct. Vance keeps his eyes open. His mama taught him that by not giving a fuck about him. I saw the door, and I ran." He paused, slightly out of breath. "Anyone can do it."

She did not know why she had followed him. Talking to him now, it seemed a questionable choice, but at that moment it had been correct. He was gazing at her, squinting, his eyes bright and his mouth just smiling. He leaned across his desk. "I have a secret," he said. "Don't limit yourself. Reach. Grab what you can."

"Like what?" she asked.

"Move, Anna Green. Don't just sit. That's how Vance got out of there."

She listened. Move. He knew, somehow, how to say what she wanted. There was the faint, sad blast of a truck's horn on the freeway. The walls rumbled. Warren Vance tilted back in his fake leather chair and lovingly examined a photo of a cliff overlooking a pure blue sea. "Wouldn't you love to live here? Malibu. Fall asleep to the sound of waves."

"Someday," she said.

"What if we had been here, Annie. You and me?" he murmured.

The husky intimacy of his voice intrigued and frightened her. She looked at her watch; she had a two-hour drive home.

"I've got to go," she said.

"Wait," he said. He stood up. "Hey. Call anytime. Been too long!"

She walked slowly to the door. When she turned, he was standing like an enormous, discarded boy, arms dangling; her heart rose with sympathy.

"I'll think about it," she said, and she drove the hundred miles home.

TWO HOURS IN THE TRAFFIC'S WHITE GLARE MADE HER HEAD FEEL light. When she returned home, she felt blurry, unreal, the way she had when she returned from the shooting, but now she was also embarrassed. She hurried inside to find her husband at the kitchen table with the children. They were digging into a frozen pizza. The ceiling lamp cast a stale glow upon them. She walked into the room briskly, holding out presents she had purchased earlier for the children.

"Hello!" she said. She said to the boy, "Hey. I got you a new pack of Yu-Gi-Oh! cards."

He looked at the pack and said, "I don't collect Yu-Gi-Oh! anymore. Only Pokémon." His facial expression had become slightly condescending, as though he had finally, after much searching, made a crucial decision. He threw them to the floor.

"Oh," she said. She turned to the girl. "And here, I got you . . . a pink pony!"

The girl violently slapped the pony away. "I hate pink! I want yellow!" she declared.

The children's faces appeared more fleshy and solemn in the kitchen light. They had changed over the course of the day. It was something she generally noticed over weeks, months, the way their faces, arms, legs became larger, the way they acquired skills, but now Anna noticed the small, precise shifts that had happened just that afternoon. Carefully, she took her seat at the table.

"You want cheese or pepperoni?" her husband asked. There was a new streak of gray in his hair.

"Cheese," she said.

"Did you know," said her son, as though lecturing to a college class, "that Earth is mostly water?"

"Really?" she said.

"It is true," he said, and he bit off a large piece of pizza.

She did not know what to say. Their faces looked so innocent—of the trip she had made that day, of their own march to adulthood, old age, their passing—she was overcome with tenderness toward them. Her helplessness—at their growth, at her tumble toward Warren Vance—overcame her, and she began, quietly, to cry; then, embarrassed, she pretended that she was coughing. Her family stared at her. They proceeded with their pizza. The girl jumped up, climbed into her lap, and said, "I'm sorry."

"She learned it today," her husband said.

"I'm sorry," the girl said, over and over, delighted with the word.

THE NIGHT FELL UPON THEIR NEIGHBORHOOD. THE SKY FADED; THE golden hills rising beyond the development turned blue with dusk. The houses around them, identical with slanted red roofs, glowed with light. The children were bathed, dried, their teeth brushed, and eventually it was time for them to settle into their beds. Already the children were formed, moving into their lives with distinct approaches and confidence. The boy pored over his new cards as though they would tell him everything about his future and then abruptly fell asleep. Anna read a story to the girl and kissed her and placed her in the crib. The girl clutched her wrist and looked up at her with accusing eyes.

"I want juice," she demanded.

This request was filled.

Then: "I want my blue pony."

"Lion."

"Pink bear."

Her husband tried to fill all requests—first kindly, with a soft voice, and then, by the thirty-minute mark, with the silence of a slave. Finally, he settled himself in a corner of her room. Anna watched her husband sitting there, pretending to look at a newspaper, to appear occupied, but it was futile, as there was no light.

Anna crawled in beside him.

"You can't just sit here forever," she said.

"You want her to sit in the dark, screaming?"

"We'll tell her we're here."

"What if we gave her everything? What if she felt so loved she wasn't afraid?"

The girl's pastel ponies and kittens and bears regarded them from their perches.

"But you can't sit here your whole life," she said.

He looked at her with a sharp expression. "Sometimes I think you don't know anything about me," he whispered. "What am I thinking right now?"

"Who still owes you money."

He rubbed his hand over his face. "Okay, okay. They needed something. I helped."

A sheer curtain lifted and fell with a breeze from the window, as if it were trying to breathe.

"Our children can be president if they can just shed their fear," he said. "I know it."

"But we can't be with them every day," she said. "Every minute."

"So?"

"So they still have to learn to fall asleep," she said.

He sighed, sharply. "And then what?" he said. "How long can you listen to her scream? Five minutes? Ten? Thirty?"

She looked away. "I don't know."

She thought, suddenly, of Warren Vance's naked body. He was not only wide but also surprisingly tall, his head almost touching the ceiling. Warren wrapped his arms around her and began nuzzling her neck. She closed her eyes, trying to get the thought of him out of her head.

She looked at her husband, his long legs stretched in front of him. She understood that they married not only to love each other in the future, but also to remedy the past—to give each other what they had not had as children.

"I don't know what to do," he said.

"I know," she said.

They sat, frozen, beside each other. The girl was finally asleep. Anna reached over and clasped his hand. She felt the pulse of his heart in his palm.

THREE DAYS LATER, SHE WAS MAKING DINNER WHEN THE PHONE RANG.

"Annie," said Warren, "You never call. You never write."

She stood against the counter; she felt pinned, even though she was the only one in the room.

"Been thinking about you," he said. "Been thinking about that girl in auto shop who could take apart a carburetor faster than any of them. Remember her?"

The children were in the living room, watching the television as though they wanted to eat it. "I guess," she said.

"That girl should be standing on a cliff watching the sun set on her personal slice of the Pacific," he said. "Would you believe five grand?"

She could taste his voice in her mouth. "I don't know," she said.

He cleared his throat. "What did you think of Vance, Anna? Be honest."

"Why?"

"Should Vance have had children, Anna? Tell him. His wife didn't want to. Should Vance have gone to business school? Maybe Vance should have learned Russian. Arabic." He was short of breath.

His anxiety alarmed her.

"Do you know that I am the fattest man in my zip code?" he said, sadly. "I like all cuisines. I hate nothing."

It was dusk. The windows glowed. She moved from the refrigerator to the microwave, defrosting meat. She held the phone to her ear.

"Tell me what you used to tell me," he said. "After."

Her heart jumped. "What are you talking about?"

"You know."

She remembered when she was eighteen years old and lying naked beside him, the experience of love so new that she felt she had been taken apart and reassembled. She closed her eyes and spoke to him, a soft, obscene endearment.

"Say it again," he whispered.

She did. The moment was clear and full.

"You say it," she said.

He said the word to her. She closed her eyes and breathed.

"Thank you," she said, solemnly.

She was frightened. The kitchen looked drained of light.

"I have to go," she said.

"Wait," he said.

She clutched the phone and listened to his breath.

"Let me get you a deal," he said, softly.

She laughed. Hearing this, a business offer, after she spoke to him the way she had twenty years before, was so absurd it was a relief. "Oh, right," she said.

"Grab what you can," he whispered. "Just a little money down. Five thousand. Investment in the future."

She barely heard him. She thought of herself, her family standing on a cliff together looking at a sunset. Her guilt at speaking to Vance so intimately made her want to buy them something. A plot of land.

"I can even take credit cards," he said.

She read him her Visa number, slowly, and he wrote it down.

"Thank you," he said. "You've made the right decision. Vance will call back in a couple days." He hung up.

Two days passed, then three. She did not tell anyone about her sudden purchase of a beachfront lot. She picked up her phone quickly whenever it rang. She had been so captivated by the idea of her family and the sunset, and the idea of this, a promise, a deal, she had not considered the obvious: they didn't have an extra five thousand dollars.

A week went by.

She did not hear from Warren Vance. The credit card bill arrived. She had allegedly purchased $548 worth of gourmet steaks from Wisconsin, $1,234 worth of airline tickets via Orbitz, and $3,284 worth of watches at Cartier.

She stood, trembling, reading his longings. Then she tried to call him, but the number was dead.

The next day, she told the babysitter to stay late and sped out to his office. The sky was blue and empty of clouds. She drove too fast, past the palm trees, the superstores, the blue-silver chaparral on the golden hills, the giant parking lots—they were all bleached by the white light, as though they had all, in some crucial way, been imagined, and she gripped the steering wheel with the same fierceness she had when she had come back from the reunion.

She turned the car into the parking lot where his office had been. A couple young, bulky men were carrying mattresses into his office. She ran toward them.

"Where's Vance's Real Estate?" she asked.

"This here's Ed's Beds. No one here by that name."

Panic fluttered through her. She ran into the Subway outlet. Margie was at the register, her hair now arranged in a net.

"Where's Warren Vance?" Anna asked.

Margie's eyes flashed, as though the name woke her up. "The fucking jerk. He said he'd give me forty bucks for saying I was his secretary, bringing coffee, smiling, et cetera, and then one day he didn't show. Where is he? Do you know?"

Anna rushed out of the store into the parking lot. The sky was so bright and hot her eyelids hurt. She started to type a number into her cell phone; then she stopped. She stood under the hard blue sky and watched the workmen bring in mattresses to Vance's former office, one mattress after another, and she watched a few customers come in and out of the Subway.

The phone rang. She lifted it to her ear.

"Yes?" she said.

"Can she eat peanut butter? I forget, a lot of kids can't eat peanut butter," the babysitter asked.

"Yes, she can eat peanut butter," Anna said.

"Okay, thanks! See you soon," said the babysitter, and she hung up.

Anna felt the weight of the cell phone in her hand; she slid into the car, set it on the seat beside her, and began to drive home.

That night, she called the credit card company to cancel the card. "You didn't purchase the steaks, the tickets, the watches?" asked the customer service rep.

"No, I did not!"

"Aha. Well. Unfortunately, I see that you never purchased the customer fraud insurance plan, just $8 a month, so we can't guarantee all will be returned—"

"Are you serious?" she asked.

"You could purchase it now," the customer service rep said, cheerfully.

It took her three more days to show the bill to her husband and inform him about the absence of the fraud insurance plan. They sat at the kitchen table, and she put the bill in front of him. He read it, and then he stopped.

"Five hundred dollars of steaks?" he said. "Did he eat a whole cow?" He paused. "And watches? Who are we subsidizing here?"

She realized that she was drawn to his moral quality because she was always waiting to be judged.

"It was an accident," she said.

They looked at each other. He leaned forward and touched her arm.

"What's going on?" he asked.

She closed her eyes. What? She remembered the musty odor of the hotel carpet, the sudden, surprising beauty of Warren Vance. She thought about how she had hunched under the chair, listening to the bullets, the cries as people were hit, the sound of people diving for the floor, running out. She thought of the way he nodded toward the door, and how she ran through the hallway, following him, her footsteps echoing through the empty corridor until she got to the parking lot of the Mercury Hotel, and stood at the edge of it, looking at the freeway, the cars a pure ribbon of light.

"I was almost shot," she said.

She heard each word as she spoke them. She did not look into his eyes. She felt the sweet presence of his fingers on her wrist.

"What did you think about?" he asked. "During?"

She had had no thoughts. The chair leg, the carpet. The taste of salt in her mouth. She remembered a sense of urgency in her arms, a trembling. To move.

Then she ran.

"I'm not sure," she said.

"Did you think about the children?" he asked.

She paused. "No."

"Your parents?"

"No."

"Did you think about me?"

She paused. "No."

He leaned back. "Why not?"

"I thought about myself," she said.

That was true. There had been the thunder of bullets, the carpet against her cheek. The slow pulse of her breath. And when she had run outside, there had been this gladness, her chest full of cool air. She was here. The asphalt was warm, crumbly under her bare feet. The light from the cars lifted off the freeway. She surveyed it all, wanting it, wanting to reach out and feel the light in her hands.

They sat in silence for a moment.

"I would have thought of myself, too," he said. "I know it."

How perfectly could they recognize each other's sadness? It was the imperfection that they had married and pledged to care for. She leaned toward him and kissed him. His hand grabbed her shoulders as though they were both floating, moving without gravity through the air.

THE LIGHTS WENT ON IN ANNA'S HOUSE EACH NIGHT, AS THEY WENT on in the other houses on their street. The houses clung to the arid hills, temporarily finding a foothold in the brush. One night, Anna told her husband they had to tell their daughter good night and then leave the room while she fell asleep. He looked at her and closed his eyes for a few moments; she did not know what he was thinking. Then he opened them and agreed. Anna kissed the girl's hair. The girl stared at them, her eyes dark and burning.

The girl screamed for twenty-three minutes and then fell asleep.

The next morning, the girl stood up in her crib. "I awake," she said. Her tone was matter-of-fact. She stood in the fresh light, gazing at Anna eagerly. Anna stumbled toward her and lifted her out. The girl kicked softly in the air.

"You did it," she whispered to the girl. The girl was bored; she wriggled in her arms, looking for her toys. The morning spread out, glazed and damp and blue, outside the windows. Anna clutched the girl's soft, living weight against her chest.

The boy abandoned all cards to focus his attentions on soccer. The girl decided to eschew princesses to become a witch. She sat at the dinner table wearing a pointy black hat.

Anna and her husband lay in their bed. Her husband's arm came over her body at night, and she held it. One night, she whispered to him the intimacy she had spoken to Warren Vance, so softly she did not know if he heard it. He said the word back softly and pressed his face against hers. They huddled in this island of time together before they would all separate again.

Theft

G inger Klein held all the cash she owned, which came to
$934.27, in an envelope in her red velvet purse. As she waited
in line for the first dinner seating on this cruise to Alaska, she fingered the muscular weight of the bills. The ship's ballroom was a
large, drab room, tricked into elegance with real silver set out on the
linen, sprightly gold foil bows on the walls, white roses blooming
briefly in stale water. The room was filled with couples, friends, tour
groups, glittering in their sequins, intent on having a good time. The
guests greeted each other, their faces gilded by the chandeliers' silver
haze. Gripping her purse, Ginger watched them and tried to decide
where to sit.

Until a few months before, Ginger had been living in a worn
pink studio apartment on Van Nuys Boulevard, storing her cash
in margarine containers in her refrigerator. She was eighty-two
years old, and for the last sixty years, she had sometimes lived in
better accommodations, sometimes worse; this was what she had

ultimately earned. On good days she sat with a cup of coffee and the Los Angeles phone book, calling up strangers for contributions to the Fireman's Ball, the Christian Children's Fund, the United Veteran's Relief. Her British accent was the best one; with it, she could keep confused strangers in Canoga Park, Woodland Hills, Calabasas on the phone. "Congratulations for being the sort of person who will help our cause," she told them, and she heard their pleasure in their own generosity. She cashed the checks at different fast-cash stores around the San Fernando Valley, presenting them with one of the false IDs from her bountiful collection.

One day, she took the wrong bus home. She looked out the window and was staring at a beach that she had never seen before. The water was bright and wrinkled as a piece of blue foil. Surfers scrambled over the dark, glassy waves. Ginger felt her heart grow cold. She had succeeded for over sixty-five years as a swindler because she always knew which bus to take.

She had actually intended to pay the doctor if the news had been good. He asked her a few questions. He held up a pair of pliers, and she had no idea what they were. She returned to the office twice and saw more doctors who wore pert, grim expressions. The diagnosis was a surprise. When he told her, it was one of the few times in her life she reacted as other people did: she covered her face and wept.

"You need to plan," her doctor said. "You have relatives who can take care of you?"

"No," she said.

"Children?"

"No."

"Friends?"

His pained expression aggravated her. "I have many friends," she said, because she pitied him.

She listened to him describe the end of her life and what she should expect her friends to do for her. Then Ginger had to stop him. She told the secretary that her checkbook was in the car and left the office without paying the bill.

SHE TRIED TO COME UP WITH A GRAND SCHEME THAT WOULD PAY for her future care, but her thoughts were not so ordered, and each day, she lost something: the word for lemons, the name of her street. Peering out her window at the lamplights that pierced the blue darkness in her apartment complex, she imagined befriending one of her neighbors, but her neighbors were flighty college dropouts, working odd hours, absent, uninterested in her. Ginger did not want to die in a hospital or an institution. Dying in this apartment would mean that she would not be discovered for days; the idea of her body lifeless, and worse, helpless, was intolerable.

She was watching television one evening when she saw an ad for a Carnival cruise. Many years ago she had sat with a man in an airport bar. He had been left by his wife of thirty-six years and was joking about killing himself on a cruise ship. "Someone finds you," he said, on his third bourbon, "A maid, another passenger. Quickly. It's more dignified. You don't just rot."

He was on his way to the Caribbean, desperately festive in his red vacation shirt festooned with figures of tropical birds. "What an interesting idea," she had said, lightly, deciding that it was time for a game of poker; she got out her rigged cards. When he stumbled off two hours later, she was $150 richer and certain she would never be that hopeless.

Before she went on her cruise, she wanted to buy a beautiful purse with which to hold the last of her money. Three public buses roaring over the oily freeways led her to the accessories counter at Saks. The red purse sat on the counter like a glowing light. It was

simple, a deep red with a rhinestone clasp; when she saw it, she felt
her breath freeze in her throat. The salesgirl told her that it was on
hold for someone.

"It's mine," said Ginger, her fingers pressing so hard on the glass
counter they turned white.

Perhaps it was the hoarse pitch of her voice, or the pity of the
salesgirl toward the elderly, but the salesgirl let her buy the purse.
In it, Ginger put her cash and also two bottles of sleeping pills. The
Caribbean was sold out this time of year, so she spent most of her
remaining money on a cruise to Alaska.

SHE WOKE UP EARLY THE FIRST MORNING OF THE CRUISE, RESTLESS,
trying to remember everything she had ever known. The facts of her
life flurried in her head: names of hotel restaurants, the taste of bar-
becue in Texas versus Georgia, the aqua chiffon dress she had worn
at a cocktail party in 1959. She sat at the table scribbling notes on a
pad: *Fake furs on Hollywood Blvd., 1966 cloudy, blue fur hats from the
rare Blue Hyena from Alaska, lemon meringue pie at the cafeteria on
W. 37th St., New York, 1960s, the seagulls flying on the empty Santa
Monica beach at dawn, how much money I made a year, $37,000 from
Dr. Chamron in 1977—*

Magnolia in Los Angeles, she wrote. She remembered the scent
of magnolia as she and Evelyn stepped off the train in Los Angeles
when she was fifteen years old. She remembered her sister Evelyn's
walk—Evelyn just seventeen then—her walk her first successful con;
stepping hard onto her feet, shoulders lifted, she tricked Ginger into
believing that she knew what to do. It was 1936, and they walked off
the train into Los Angeles, two girls alone, armed with an address
for an aunt they would never meet.

Finally, Ginger's hand ached and she put down her pen.
Scribbling her room number on a paper, she put it in her purse and

walked to lunch. She went carefully around the naked ice sculptures of David or Venus that rose, melting, out of bowls of orange punch. Table Sixteen was empty so she sat down, and a silver domed plate floated down in front of her.

She began to eat her salmon when a young woman slid into the seat across from her. Her hair hung down in long, straight sheets, as though flattened by the heat of her own thoughts.

"Darlene Horwitz," she said, holding out her hand for Ginger to shake. She was young, ridiculously young, with the glossy, unmarked skin of a baby. "This is my first cruise."

"Ginger Klein."

"My parents sent me here," said Darlene. "They had enough of my moaning." She looked at Ginger. "Have you ever been on a cruise?"

"In the past," said Ginger.

The girl unfolded her napkin onto her lap. "Are you retired? What did you do?" asked the girl.

Ginger leaned across the table and whispered to Darlene, "This is what I do. People have dreams that I want to be part of. I say I can make them come true. One gentleman expressed a desire to sample gelato in Italy. Then *I* just did it for him, but on his dime. That man was in the field of advertising. I thought of him sitting behind his desk, eating a bag lunch, a little sweaty, and I thought he'd be grateful that I could taste that gelato for him."

This was Evelyn's philosophy, really; she had believed that swindling was generous, as it allowed the suckers a moment to dream. Ginger pushed her seat back slightly. She unfolded her napkin and spread it on her lap.

"I don't understand," said Darlene.

Ginger coughed. Then she said, slowly, "I'm a swindler."

"Oh," said Darlene. She rubbed her face with her hands. Then she laughed. "Should I be hiding my purse? Are you going to steal money from people?"

"No," said Ginger. "I don't need to anymore."

Darlene seemed to want to steer the discussion back to more familiar territory. "What does your family think of your job?" she asked, carefully.

"I haven't talked to them in over sixty years," Ginger said. They had lost their parents suddenly, their mother to illness, their father to lust—when their mother died of tuberculosis, their father left Brooklyn to pursue a stripper in Louisiana. He left a note with some train fare and an address for an aunt in Orange Hills, Los Angeles.

They tried the first phone booth on the street. When the number didn't work there, they tried another. By the fourth phone booth, they realized that there was no neighborhood called Orange Hills and there was no aunt. At the time, the girls had between them $43.

"You want to know why I'm here?" Darlene asked. She looked a bit dazed. "His name was Warren. One minute we were finishing each other's sentences. The next minute he was packing his bags. Now I'm twenty-two years old and afraid I will never find the one."

Waiters came out carrying ignited Baked Alaskas. Sparklers on the desserts fizzled, and a faint smoky odor filled the air.

"I went to my parents' house," said Darlene. "*Big* mistake, they packed me off to the glaciers, to meet people and have fun—"

Ginger did not want to spend one moment of this week comforting someone else. She folded her napkin, stood up. "Well," said Ginger, "I hope you have a grand time." Then she turned and walked across the room. The ship was approaching the first glaciers. Sliding down the mountains the ice was rushed and utterly still. The glacial ice was pale blue, and huge pieces drifted by, like the ruined bones of a giant. She watched the pale ice float by her and wondered when she would forget her name.

Her awareness had been her great gift: of the best hour to meet the lonely, of the hairstyle that would make her look most innocent, of the raised eyebrow that indicated a person's longing, and of course, of the moment when she knew that what a person owned would belong to her. Sitting on a train she would feel the money, a roll wrapped around her hip, as she listened to the click of the wheels along the tracks. She wanted to be the imposters she claimed to be: the lost cousin, the secret aunt, the high school classmate, the one who had loved from afar. Glancing at herself in the dark train windows, she sometimes thought she had become this other person; her heart lightened for a while as she imagined what this person might feel.

THERE WAS A KNOCK ON HER DOOR AT 10:00 AM. IT WAS THE GIRL from lunch. "Remember me?" she said. "I'm your seatmate. I wanted to go to the chocolate buffet." She clutched her own hands fiercely. "Who wants to gorge on chocolate alone?"

It was the tyranny of the normal, the attempts of regular people to energize their lives. It was ten in the morning, and she could hear the rapid footsteps of the other passengers as they rushed to fill their mouths with sweetness. The girl was insistent, and Ginger found herself in the long winding line. All of the passengers appeared to have risen for this experience. To maintain order, a waiter walked through the crowd, doling out, with silver tongs, chunks of milk chocolate to eager hands. Another waiter, dressed as a Kodiak bear, was offering cups of hot chocolate spiked with rum. There was a radiant excitement in the air.

Darlene was chatty. "After this I go on a diet," the girl said. "A major one. Celery and water for weeks . . ."

Ginger knew that she herself would never go on another diet. She pressed her hands to her waist, her hips. She wanted all of the chocolate, now. She moved quickly, placing truffles, chocolate-dipped potato chips, macaroons, chocolate torte, mousse, fudge on her tray. She was so hungry she was in pain.

When they sat down, she looked at the girl and she wanted to convince her of something; she wanted to shout into Darlene's ear.

"I've had better than this," she said. "1959. The Academy Awards party at the Sheraton. Truffles everywhere. I said I was a waitress. I said in my off-hours I was working for Cary Grant's father, who I said was dying of cancer, and could they please contribute to a cancer fund—" She paused. "They were a nice bunch. Generous. I actually have a high opinion of mankind—"

"Did anyone get mad at you?" asked Darlene.

"Mad?" asked Ginger.

"When they realized that you had taken their money—"

Ginger rose halfway in her seat. "Why would I care?" asked Ginger. "Look. You go to a regular job. They tell you what you're worth. Or you love him and he leaves you and you feel like you're nothing at all. Darling, I don't have to tell my worth to anyone."

Darlene looked down. The longing in the girl's face was like a bright wound.

"What was so good about him anyway?" asked Ginger.

"He said my eyes were pretty," Darlene said. "He also liked listening to the Cherry Tones. He liked to put his hands in my hair—"

This was the material of love? "So fool him into loving you."

"How?" Darlene stared, desolate, at slices of chocolate cake so glossy they appeared to be ceramic.

"What did he want? Pretend to be it," said Ginger.

"He wanted a million dollars."

"So say you've won the lottery," said Ginger. She bit into a truffle.

"But I didn't."

"No one knows what they want until you show them."

Darlene's face was flushed, excited. "But I want him to love the real me—"

"Who do you think you are?" said Ginger. "No one. We all are. That's what I do, notice no ones—"

"I'm not no one," said Darlene, huffily. "I come from a nice suburb of San Diego. My father is a successful pediatrician—"

"So? That's all temporary," said Ginger. "But the noticing, that's yours."

Ginger had never allowed herself weakness, never told anyone how it felt to walk into a new city, how she chose her new name just as the train slowed down. Everyone rushed by, gnarled and worn down by the burden of thwarted love; she was free of that, new. She would wash up in the station bathroom and walk out, erased of her secrets: the fact that everything she did with a man was faked, so the only way she could feel pleasure was to give it to herself; the fact that her broken right hand had healed crooked because she couldn't afford to see a doctor to fix it; that she often ate alone on holidays. In empty coffee shops on Thanksgiving, Ginger looked at the food on her plate, and she knew a strange, burning love for the things the world offered her, real and surprising, again and again.

EVELYN AND GINGER RENTED A ROOM IN A SALVATION ARMY, AND Evelyn began to weep. She curled up on the hard, stained mattress and cried so hard she screamed. Ginger sat beside her sister, a hand on her shoulder. Sometimes, she had an urge to laugh. Other moments, she wished she could put her hands around Evelyn's throat and strangle her. She was shocked by the private nature of her emotions. Evelyn seemed to believe she was comforting her, and Ginger was surprised that she could.

During the day, they walked down Hollywood Boulevard,

trying to decide what to do. Their breath smelled, darkly, of bananas. In the light, Evelyn talked rapidly; they both listened with hope to the sound of her voice.

"We will be cigarette girls," Evelyn announced one afternoon.

They walked into sixteen bars before they found one that had jobs for both of them. Every night the two of them strode in wearing black tights and rhinestone loafers, selling cigarettes to heavy, sad-looking men with liquored breath.

Once, Evelyn told Ginger that she tried not to be afraid for five minutes a day. Ginger was impressed that Evelyn could identify when she was afraid, for her own fear floated just outside her skin, like a cloud; she experienced nothing but a heavy numbness. She watched her sister closely, trying to catch her in those precious five minutes when she was clearly not afraid. In those five minutes, Evelyn owned something mysterious, and even the claim of strength made Ginger ache to experience it, too.

At home, Evelyn's grief metamorphosed into a bloodthirsty envy of the loved, the parented. She wanted their expensive possessions: the jeweled brooches, the feathered hats.

One night, she leaned close to a man clad in a velvet jacket and said, in a husky, unfamiliar voice, "I have a baby at home."

Ginger, walking by with her tray, stopped.

"He is sick," Evelyn said. "Bad stomach. He needs operation. Look. Please." She brought out a wrinkled photo of some stranger's baby. His mouth was open in anguish. "I need just ten more dollars—he cannot eat—"

"All right," he said. He dug into his pocket and handed her a bill. His face was haughty with a perplexing pity, and Ginger stared at it, awed.

Later, Evelyn walked with Ginger down the sidewalk and smoothed the bill, like green velvet, in her hands. "I have a baby at home," she said, laughing. She looked at the people walking, lifted her hands, and said, almost gently, "Fools."

THE NEXT MORNING, GINGER SAT IN HER CABIN, LOOKING THROUGH the nine photographs that she owned. They were souvenirs from fancy occasions, set in cardboard frames so old they felt like flannel. She had kept them because she liked the way she looked in them, as though she had been enjoying herself.

She heard a knock at the door. It was that girl again. "I wondered if you wanted some company. Can I come in?"

Darlene was dressed in imitation of a wealthy person. She wore a sequin-trimmed cashmere cardigan that Ginger believed she had seen in the cruise gift shop and a strand of pearls. Her shoulders were thrust stiffly backward, giving her the posture of a rooster. The girl's earnest quality shone through her outfit like the glow of a lightbulb through a lampshade.

"Who are you?" asked Ginger.

"I am his dream."

"No," said Ginger. "Don't try so hard. Wear your usual and add an expensive piece of jewelry. Make him guess why."

Darlene shrugged off her cardigan and stepped forward too purposefully, like a salesgirl trying to close a deal.

"I can buy you a Rolls-Royce," she said, her voice too bright, to the air.

"No, no! Just hint that you went on a trip to—Paris. The four-star hotels have the best sheets. Nothing he can prove," said Ginger.

Darlene looked at the photos laid out.

"So who are these people?" asked Darlene.

Ginger stood up and picked up a photo. "Here I am on New Year's Eve, 1959," said Ginger. "The presidential suite of the Beverly Hills Hotel." She still could see the way the pink shrimp sat on the ice beds, as though crawling through clean snow. "I lit Frank Sinatra's cigarette," said Ginger. "I lent my lipstick to Marilyn Monroe." She remembered the weight of the sequined dress against her skin, the raucous laughter. "Don't I look happy?" she asked.

"I would be happy," said Darlene.

Ginger's mind moved in her skull, and she felt her legs crumble. She grabbed hold of a chair and clung to it.

"Whoa! Are you okay?"

She grasped Darlene's hand and felt her body move thickly to the bed.

"What happened? Should I call a doctor?"

"No," said Ginger sharply. "No."

She let Darlene arrange her into a sitting position, her feet up on the bed. Her arms and legs fell open in the obedient posture of the ill. The girl got her a drink of water from the tap, and Ginger sipped it. It was sweet.

"Thank you," Ginger said.

They sat. Ginger picked up another photo. "This was when I met the vice president of MGM and had him convinced I was a duchess from Belgium—"

Darlene frowned. Ginger realized that it was the same picture she had just described. "They were all at the party," she said, quickly. "Sinatra and Marilyn and duchesses. It was in Miami. Brazil. The moon was so white it looked blue—"

Darlene looked at her. "I wish I could have been there," she said. She reached out and briefly touched Ginger's hand.

Ginger looked down at the sight of Darlene's hand on her own. At first, the gesture was so startling she viewed it as though it were a sculpture. Then she could not look at the girl, for Ginger had tears in her eyes.

WHEN EVELYN AND GINGER BEGAN TO LIE, THE WORLD BROKE apart, revealing unearthly, beautiful things. They began with extravagant tales of woe, deformed babies, murdered husbands, terminal illnesses. They constructed Hair-Ray caps for bald men, yarmulkes with thin metal inside so that in the sunlight their heads would get hot and they would think they were growing hair. They bought nun's habits at a costume shop and said they were collecting for the construction of a new church.

She remembered particularly one scam in which she wandered through the cavernous Los Angeles train station with a cardboard sign declaring: *HELP. MUTE. HALF-BLIND.* When strangers came up to her, she wrote on a chalkboard that had chalk attached to it on a string: *HELP ME FIND MY SISTER OUTSIDE.* She handed the stranger, usually an elderly lady, her purse, an open straw bag. She let the stranger guide her out the door and carefully fell forward, tilting the bag so that an envelope inside fell out. Ginger did not pick it up. Then there was Evelyn running inside, yelling, "Violet!"

Evelyn looked in the purse and said, "Where's your money?"

IN THE PURSE, Ginger wrote.

They looked at the kindly woman holding the purse. "Did you take my blind sister's money?" Evelyn yelled; that was Ginger's cue to weep.

"I didn't," the hapless stranger would protest, but there she was, holding the purse, with a blind mute weeping beside her; they could get ten, twenty, thirty dollars out of the stranger. When the sucker left, Evelyn would walk Ginger around the corner and hug her.

"Good, Violet," she said.

"Thank you," said Ginger, feeling the solidness of her sister's arms around her, and she closed her eyes and let herself breathe.

When Ginger woke up from her nap the following afternoon, she did not know where she was. The dark afternoon light streamed through the mint blue curtains. She shivered and sat up. She flung open a drawer, looking for clues. The room felt as though it were moving. She was not in a hotel. Where were they going? She opened the curtains and saw mountains covered in ice. Her mind was a crumpled ball of paper. She stood up quickly, as though to straighten her thoughts. The phone rang.

"How are you feeling? Do you want to go to the dinner tonight?"

Her heartbeat slowed at the naturalness of the question, at the caller's belief that Ginger would continue this conversation. She remembered that they were on a cruise to Alaska. She also remembered that the girl had said something kind to her.

The room was decorated to flatter the passengers into believing they were traveling in opulence. There were plaster Roman columns, painted gold, topped with bouquets of roses. The waiters' jackets were adorned in rhinestones that said: *Alaska '03.* Outside the large glass windows, the water and sky, black and clear, surrounded the ship.

Tonight, Darlene's hair was slicked up into a topknot and shone, a metallic blonde, in the light. Her eyelids gleamed blue, unearthly.

"How are you?" asked Ginger.

"I just want to say . . . I am someone," said Darlene. She looked dazed. "I am going to graduate with a B average in communications." She sat down. "Listen." She closed her eyes. "I left a message on his answering machine. I said, I'll do anything. Let me. I'll change."

"What?" Ginger asked, alarmed.

"I tried to do what you said," she said. "I know how to fool him. I'll keep calling him. I'll be what you said, generous, you're right, I have been selfish—"

"No," said Ginger. "That's not what I meant—"

The girl stared at her with her reptilian eyes. "Then what do I do?" she said, and her voice was hoarse.

Music exploded from a band gathered near the stage. The audience clapped along. "Let's hear where everyone's from, all at once!" the cruise director called. The room rang with hundreds of voices. Los Angeles. Palm Springs. Ottawa. Denver. Orlando. New York. "Welcome aboard!" the cruise director called. "Time to relax. Shake off those fancy duds. We want to make you a deal. We need a pair of pants. Someone take off a pair! We'll give you fifty dollars! Come on, you'll never see these people again in your life!"

Ginger did not know what to tell the girl, and the sorrow in her eyes was unnerving. Instead, Ginger turned her attention to the stage. She used to love crowds, the way the people in them became one roar, one sound. But now, for the first time, all the people appeared vulnerable to her. Passengers drifted onto the stage, performing various tricks: singing "God Bless America," attempting to juggle, dancing the rumba. They wanted to take off their pants in front of each other, or scream out the names of their home cities; they were confused about their place in the world. They had everything in common with her.

Yet everyone on the stage also looked pleased to be up there, happy to be briefly bathed in light. They smiled at the sound of cheering, their faces simple in their hunger for recognition. She did not know what to tell Darlene, and then she envied everyone on the stage. She wanted to be with the others, to have a talent, to simply stand in the clear white light.

Ginger raised her hand. The cruise director called on her, and she made her way to the stage. The lights glared hard and white in her eyes. Clutching her velvet purse, she felt the weight of her money in it. "Passengers," she called. They stood like sad soldiers before their futures.

"My name is Ginger Klein, and I'm going to make you rich. Give me a dollar," she called. "Everyone. A dollar."

They dug into their pockets, and a few brought dollars out. She enjoyed watching them obey her. But what was the next step?

"Catch," she called.

She reached into her purse and pulled out a handful of bills. She threw them into the spangled darkness. There were screams of disbelief, laughter. She dug into her purse and tossed out more. The passengers leapt from their seats and dove for the money. They were unhinged, thrilled, alive. Their screams of joy blossomed inside her. Her purse grew lighter and lighter.

After awhile, the cruise director strode onto the stage and gently moved her off. "Thank you, Ginger Klein!" he shouted. "Best talent of the night, huh?" She paused, wanting to tell them something more, but she did not know what it would be. Applause thundered in her chest; she had, somehow, been successful. She walked slowly down the stairs, looking for Darlene. "Darlene," she said, softly, then louder. "I'm here."

She did not see her. Ginger imagined how the girl would walk, carefully, off the ship by herself at the end of the week. Darlene would join the living pouring toward the shore, clutching her souvenir ivory penguins and Eskimo dolls, going to her future boyfriends and houses and lawns and exercise classes and book clubs and games. "Darlene," she said as she walked down the hallway; she wanted to walk down the ramp with her, shading her own eyes against the dazzling sunlight, gripping Darlene's arm.

SOMETIMES, GINGER COULD HEAR EVELYN LAUGHING IN HER SLEEP, a harsh, broken sound, and she touched her shoulder, trying to feel the joy that her sister could experience most fully in her dreams. During the day, Evelyn talked about ordinary people, the loved and loving, with too much scorn; Ginger knew that her sister wanted her life to be like theirs. She believed that Evelyn wanted to get rid of her.

One evening in the bar, Evelyn was talking to a man who claimed to work in the movie industry. His hands jabbed the air with the hard confidence of the insecure. He gazed at Evelyn as though he could see a precious light inside of her, and Ginger watched Evelyn's shoulders tremble, delighted. She told him offhandedly that she was an orphan with no family. He leaned toward her and took her hands in his.

"I'll take care of you," he said.

Evelyn went home with him that night. The next day, she met Ginger at their room and said, "I am going to live with him. He likes the fact that I have no family." She paused; her face was relieved. "You will have to be a secret."

Evelyn packed her suitcase and was gone, leaving only a lipstick the color of a rose. Ginger waited. Each morning, she put on a new costume, applied Evelyn's lipstick, and murmured the same false pleas to strangers. Ginger made more money without Evelyn. Strangers could see a new emptiness in her eyes that touched them. After two weeks, she tried, briefly, to find her sister. She stood outside the walls of the movie studios, waiting to see the man. Her search paralleled her fantasies of what Evelyn would desire; she waited outside of expensive restaurants, wandered through fancy clubs, but as she rushed past the crowded tables, the patrons' faces bloomed up, monstrous, unknown.

It was three weeks before she saw Evelyn again, at the palisades overlooking the Santa Monica beach. Evelyn walked toward Ginger with a curious lightness in her step. She covered her mouth when she laughed. She flicked her wrist at the end of a sentence, as though trying to toss away her words.

"He loves my hair," Evelyn said. "He loves my laugh. Listen."

The sound made Ginger cold. It was difficult to stand straight; the ground was rising like slow, heavy waves.

"You look well. I have to go," said Evelyn. She backed up, as though fearful that Ginger would grab onto her. Then she stopped and pulled a small red purse from her pocket. "Here," said Evelyn. "It has two hundred dollars."

"No," said Ginger, stepping back.

She felt her sister shove the purse into her hands and press her fingers around it. "Just take it."

Evelyn quickly ran toward the bus stop. Ginger understood that this would be the last time they saw each other. It would be Ginger's own decision to move and not tell her sister where she was going. She sat down for a long time after the bus had pulled off, eyes closed, imagining that the wide blue sky, the gray elephantine palms would be gone when she opened them. When she looked again, the world was still there; Ginger left the purse on the bench and started walking.

THE NEXT MORNING, WHEN SHE WOKE UP, SHE DID NOT REMEMBER how the crowd had buffeted her like an ocean, how she had finally found a man in a maroon uniform who helped her find her room, but her legs were weak, as though she'd walked a great distance, and her mouth was dry from calling out Darlene's name.

She knew what she wanted to do. She wanted to buy a present for Darlene. She wanted to do this simple action: go into a store, select a gift for her, buy it, and give it to her. That was all. She imagined the expression on Darlene's face, her surprise at being given a present; she imagined Darlene's happiness blooming, slowly, in herself. Ginger stood up, wearing the same dress she had the night before, faint with the scent of smoke and alcohol, and walked slowly to the gift shop.

There she stood, surrounded by the store's offerings: the butterfly-sequined blouses, the porcelain statues of grizzly bears and leaping salmon and deer, the authentic replica Eskimo fur hats, the jars of glacier-blue rock candy.

"May I help you?" the girl at the counter asked.

What would Darlene like? She scanned the glass case of jewelry; there were snowflakes and bears and seals, turquoise and silver and garnet and gold; Ginger selected a large opal set in a gold snowflake. Its price was $300.

"Beautiful taste," the salesgirl said.

"Hey," said a voice. It was Darlene. "I've been looking all over for you."

The girl stood before her. Ginger put down the brooch.

"Are you all right?" asked Darlene. "Who's that for?"

Ginger looked at her. "You," she said.

"That will be $315.73," said the salesgirl.

Ginger put her hand into the red velvet purse. There was nothing in it but the silk lining. She shook out her purse. Now she had $1.37.

"I have no money," she said, softly.

"Is it in your room?" the salesgirl asked.

"This is all I have," Ginger said.

She pushed her hand deep into the purse, feeling its emptiness. Her coins fell onto the floor. "You don't have to buy me anything," said Darlene.

The lights were extremely bright, as though someone had turned them on all at once.

"I want to buy it," said Ginger. "Don't you understand? I want to."

She stood, swaying a little, aggravated that Darlene did not recognize what she was trying to do. Darlene squinted at her, and Ginger wondered if she had begun to disappear.

"What are you looking at?" she asked Darlene. She lurched toward her. "What?"

"Hold on," said Darlene, looking at the salesgirl. "I'll be right back." She backed up and began to hurry down the hallway.

"Where is she going?" asked Ginger. She stepped toward the door. She went into the hallway and began to follow her.

An elderly couple floated toward her. The woman wore a white brimmed sunhat, and the man had a camera hanging from a strap around his neck. "Thief," Ginger whispered. She passed the maid clutching armfuls of crumpled sheets. "Thief," she said. The maid turned around. Ginger began to walk onto the deck, the sunlight brilliant and cold on her arms. She staggered through the crowd in their pale sweat suits. "Thief!" she yelled. She believed one side of her was becoming heavy. She heard her voice, flat and loud; she heard the jingle of ice cubes in people's drinks. "My money!" she yelled. Her voice was guttural, unrecognizable to her. "Give me my money!"

The girl was running up to her.

"Thief," Ginger yelled.

The girl blinked. "What?" she asked.

"Thief," said Ginger. She wanted to say the word over and over. Ginger's face was warm; she was exhilarated by the act of accusation. She had forgotten the girl's name. It had simply disappeared. Her knees buckled. The girl grabbed her arm.

"Call a doctor!" the girl yelled. "Quick!"

The ocean was moving by very quickly, and Ginger stared, unblinking, at the bright water until she was unsure whether she was on the deck looking at the water or in the water looking up at the light.

The girl's firm grip made her feel calmer. Ginger placed her own hand on hers. Ginger did not know who this friend was, did not know who had loved her and whom she had loved. She leaned toward the glaring blue world, the water and ice and sky, and she felt a part of it.

"You're not who you say you are," murmured the girl. "I don't believe you. You're not a swindler. You're a nice old lady. It was all a joke, wasn't it . . ."

Ginger breathed more slowly and clutched the girl's arm. She saw everything in that moment: the trees on the shore giving up their leaves to the aqua sky, the ocean shimmering into white cloud, and the passengers' breath becoming rain. She felt the vibrations of the ship's motor in her throat. Through the clear, chill water, the ship moved north.

Anything for Money

Each Monday at eleven o'clock, Lenny Weiss performed his favorite duty as executive producer of his hit game show, *Anything for Money*: he selected the contestants for that week's show. He walked briskly across the stage set, the studio lights so white and glaring as to make the stage resemble the surface of the moon. In his silk navy suit, the man appeared to be a lone figure on the set, for his staff knew not to speak to him or even look at him. He had become the king of syndicated game shows for his skill in finding the people who would do anything for money, people that viewers would both envy and despise.

The assistants were in the holding room with the prospective contestants, telling them the rules: No one was allowed to touch Mr. Weiss. Mr. Weiss required a five-foot perimeter around his person. No one was allowed to call him by his first name. No one was to be drinking Pepsi, as the taste offended Mr. Weiss. Gold jewelry reminded him of his former wife, so anyone wearing such jewelry was advised to take it off.

He stood by the door for a moment before he walked in, imagining how the losers would walk, dazed, to their cars, looking up at the arid sky. They would try to figure out what they had done wrong. They would look at their hands and wonder.

Then he walked in, and they screamed.

He loved to hear them scream. They had tried to dress up, garishly; polyester suits in pale colors, iridescent high heels. The air reeked of greed and strong perfume. Some of the women had their hair done especially for the occasion, and it shimmered oddly, hardened with spray.

"Pick me!"

"We love you, man!"

"We've been watching forever!"

A woman in a rhinestone-studded T-shirt that said *Dallas Cowboys Forever* lunged forward, grabbed his arm, and yelled, "Lenny!"

"Hands OFF Mr. Weiss!" shouted the security guard.

There was always one who was a lesson for the others. The door slammed, and the woman was marched back to her life. They all listened to her heels clicking against the floor, first sharp and declarative, then fading. The others stood, solemnly, in the silence, as though listening to the future sound of their own deaths.

They were all on this earth briefly; for Lenny, that meant he had the burning desire to be the king of syndicated game shows, one of the ten most powerful men in Hollywood. He did not know what the others' lives meant to them, just that they wanted what he had. Money.

Now he needed to choose his contestants. They would be the ones with particularly acute expressions of desire and sadness; they would also have to photograph well under the brilliant lights.

"All right!" He clapped his hands. "You want to be rich? You want other people to kiss your ass? Well, listen. You're going to have to work for it. Everyone!" He knew to change his requests for each new group; he did not want any of them to come prepared from rumors off the street.

"Unbutton your shirts!"

He knew this one was more difficult for the women, but that was not a concern to him. Some of the people stiffened, pawed gingerly at their buttons. Others tore through their buttons and stood before him, shirts loose.

"Take off your shirts!"

He lost a few more with this request. Others removed their shirts as though they had been moving through their lives waiting for such an order. They stood before him, men and women, in bras and bare chests, some pale, some dark, some thin-shouldered, others fat.

"Repeat after me. Say: I am a fool."

He heard the chorus of voices start, softly.

"Louder! Again!"

Their seats had numbers on the bottoms; he knew immediately whom he would call back. He would call Number 25, the woman with the lustrous blonde hair, and Number 6, the man with the compulsive, bright smile. Lenny clapped his hands.

"Thank you. My assistant will contact those who have been chosen." Lenny turned, almost running down the hallway. He walked around for fifteen minutes before he could get back to work.

He had grown up in Chicago in the 1940s, the only child of parents who had married impulsively and then learned that neither understood the other; Lenny dangled, suspended, in the harsh, disappointed sounds of the house. His father died when Lenny was eight. Lenny's mother moved them to Los Angeles and got a job as a secretary at one of the movie studios. The boy was shocked by the desert light, the way it made everything—the lawns, flowers, cars—appear stark and inevitable. His mother was the only person he knew in this world, and at first, when she left him at school, he was wild with fear that she also had disappeared. He pretended he was collecting clouds to make a wall around her, and when the sky was cloudless, he pretended he was sick. Then his mother brought him to the place where she worked. He sat on the floor watching her, and then everything else going on around her, too.

When he graduated high school, he became an errand boy on a soap opera, then a writer. He enjoyed making bad things happen to other people: troubled marriages, sudden illnesses, kidnappings. He married a woman who was impressed by his job and his descriptions of various actresses on the set. They had a child, a girl. Then one day the producers gathered all the employees into a windowless conference room. "There's no more show," they said.

It was the recession of the early 1970s, a bad time for hiring in any field, and he and his wife had little savings. He looked for work for six months without luck, setting his sights lower and lower, but already there was an odor of desperation on him. One night, his daughter was screaming in pain from an ear infection, but he was afraid to take her to a doctor for what it would cost. The child's pain so horrified him that he bolted out of the house.

He did not stop running for several blocks. Strangers walked down the street, their wallets bulging with money he wanted. The money was so close to him, he could almost smell its dusky green scent. His jaw hurt. Suddenly, he had an idea: he could rob a liquor store. He had thought about how to do this when he wrote his soap operas. The simplicity of this idea made him stop in astonishment. He could wear a stocking over his face and stuff a bottle in his jacket pocket as a gun.

There was a liquor store a few blocks away, and he stumbled toward it. Lenny stood outside the liquor store for a long time. He sobbed softly. His tongue tasted like a dry, bitter leaf. The other customers entered the store, noble in their morality and their innocence. He had become this: a man who would do anything for money.

Later, he would tell people that this was the moment he became God—for he had saved himself. *Anything for Money* could be a show in which contestants would do terrible, absurd things to receive vast amounts of money.

The next day, he sat for ten hours in the waiting room of his former employer. When Lenny saw the head of programming, Mr. Tom Lawrence, come out, he hurtled toward him, thrusting out a proposal. "Read this," he told Mr. Lawrence. Lenny did not know why the man decided to listen to him, though he understood, in an honest part of himself, that it was simply a grand moment of luck. Later, he chose to describe this as a sign of his own inherent glory. Mr. Lawrence took the thin sheet of paper, folded it in half, and stuck it in the pocket of his blazer. Lenny watched him walk off. A month later, Mr. Lawrence bought the idea for the show.

Now he was sixty-five, the show's executive producer, and his limousine took him from his studios to his home in the hills above Los Angeles. As a young man, he had never quite believed the success of *Anything for Money*, the way his longing formed itself physically into homes, boats, cars. He used to wake up with his heart pounding as though he were running an immense race. His daughter and wife were mere shadows to him, for he needed to get to the studio with a breathless craving. He was there from eight in the morning until eleven at night.

Thirty years ago, his wife, Lola, left. He blamed his wife's leaving on her excessive demands; many of his colleagues' wives had left them, too. The few times he had seen her since she left, she looked entirely unfamiliar to him. It seemed that he had not been married to her but to a lookalike who resembled her. She had come up to him at a party and said softly, "You never knew anything true about me." When she said this, he felt deeply wounded, felt his honest attempts at goodness had been misunderstood. All his attempts at romance had been clichéd—he bought her diamonds, midnight cruises, silk gowns. "All I wanted," she said, "was a poem written about my eyes." He stood before her like a little boy. Did this mean they had not loved each other?

His memories of his daughter were glazed with exhaustion. Charlene stood, naked in the bathtub, water streaming down her tiny body, a pale angel absolutely convinced of her own glory; he could not believe she had come from him. Sometimes Charlene clung to him with such fierceness, such pure trust, he felt himself crumble inside. He was afraid she would see in his eyes the weakness of a lame dog and laugh at him. She was a toddler running, stiff-legged, across the lawn, then she was six and running, legs outstretched, like a small antelope, in gaudy, colorful clothing; then his wife left and he could not see his daughter running.

CHARLENE BELIEVED THAT HE HAD KICKED THEM OUT OF THE house. That was what Lola had told her. He tried to explain to her that this was not the truth, but she said, bluntly, "Mom said she asked you thirty times to stay at home for my fifth birthday. And you did not." He did not remember any of these requests. He had thought he belonged to a family, but suddenly they accused him of misdeeds and crimes that made him—and them—unknowable.

Charlene called him only to request money, which he always gave her. He once heard her on a talk show denigrating him with a fictional story: "My father was so self-centered he had a special mirror only he could look into. If anyone else did, he'd tell us it would crack." Much audience laughter. Lenny would not hear from her for months, and then he'd get a long letter, dissecting injuries done during her childhood; she had been arguing with him in her mind the whole time. Then, when he called her to discuss the letter, she would hang up on him.

The calls came more frequently immediately after Lola's death. His ex-wife had died in a car accident fifteen years ago; she was gone, and his remnant feelings for her were interrupted—he still had not divined whether they had loved each other or not. Charlene seemed to hope that, as her only living parent, he would have the capacity to read her thoughts. He sensed then how remote she felt from other people. When he could not read her thoughts, she reacted with anger so forceful it was as though he had told her he hated her.

Over the last fifteen years, he heard about her mostly through gossip items in the paper: *Charlene Weiss sub eatery sinks. Charlene Weiss briefly hospitalized for alcohol abuse. Charlene Weiss has fling with Vance Harley, sitcom star. Charlene Weiss has daughter, Aurora Persephone Diamantina Weiss.* A quote from the happy new mom: "I have reached a pinnacle of joy."

She did tell him about Aurora. She had become pregnant from one of her many suitors and decided to have a child on her own. He received an elaborate birth announcement, a silver card with a photo of the baby girl swathed in white robes like a tiny emperor. The inscription below the picture said: *Aurora: A Child Who Will Be Loved.*

For thirty years, he lived alone in his mansion on top of the Santa Monica Mountains; he had told his architect that he wanted to feel he could put his hands on the entire city. He could see all the way to the Pacific Ocean, the expanse of ocean like black glass, all the way to the luminous blocks of downtown, to the cars pouring, twin rivers of red and white lights moving east and west, north and south. His loneliness had buried itself deep within him, and he experienced it as the desire to be in the seat of every car. The architect had set his living room at the edge of a hill, so that when Lenny looked out his twenty-foot-high glass windows, he almost believed he could fall into the trembling party of lights. He stood there many nights, full of longing so deep he could not name it; he was aware only of his quiet desire to thrust himself into the dark air.

THE CALL CAME IN HIS LIMOUSINE FOLLOWING A MEETING WITH the producer of the talk show *Confess!* His maid's voice floated over the speakers.

"Mister Weiss," Rosita said. "Come home."

"Why?" he said to the air.

"A child is here."

"I don't know any child."

"Her name is Aurora."

He stared at the speaker.

"Yes," he said. "I know her."

When they reached his house, Lenny stepped out of his limo. His home was made of pale marble, and clear white wavelets from the swimming pool shimmered on its empty walls. Black palms, bathed in blue light, swayed in the warm wind. The bushes in his gardens had been trimmed to the shapes of elephants, giraffes, bears, and they made a silent, regal procession through the darkness. He stood for a moment, in the quiet he had made, before he went inside.

The girl stood at the top of the stairs. He would not have been aware of her but for the ferocity with which she stood there, as though she had dreamed herself in this position for years. She was gripping the railing, staring at him. Her face was dim, but he could see her fingernails holding the rail—they were an absurdly bright gold. She ran down the stairs so fast he thought she might fall.

"Hello," she said.

His legs felt as insubstantial as water. He looked at Aurora. He believed she had to be about twelve years old. Her face had the hard, polite quality of someone who had been scheming quietly and fervently for a long time. Her auburn hair reached halfway down her back. She had Lola's eyebrows, two arched Us that gave her an alert, surprised expression. She had Charlene's navy blue eyes. They were the color of steel and moved around restlessly, but they had a hard gaze when they settled on something. He knew because they were also his eyes.

"Hello," he said. He offered his hand. She grabbed it. He still wore the Bluetooth headset he usually wore so as not to miss any calls.

"What are you doing here?" he asked.

"I was sent."

"By who?"

"My mother."

She handed him a letter. The letterhead said:

BUENA VISTA REHABILITATION CLINIC
Your secrets are ours.

Dad—
I am here for the next three months.
Take care of Aurora.
She likes chocolate.
I'm so tired.

Charlene's signature resembled a tiny knot.

The letter's tone was so polite he knew that she had been trying to please someone watching her as she wrote it.

"Is this where your mother is?"

She nodded and stepped carefully toward the enormous living room windows. "This was in a magazine," she said.

"*House and Garden*," he said.

She nodded. "It's bigger in real life."

He wanted to stop her. She was standing against the window, pressing her fingers against the glass. He saw her make a breath on the glass, a pale oval, and the intimacy of the action made him want to walk away.

Two large suitcases sat in the foyer. He gestured to them and said, "Carlos can take them up for you."

Aurora rushed up to one and grabbed the handle. "No!" she said. "I want to do this one myself."

The bag was not actually a suitcase, but a large green canvas sack. It bulged, oddly, with unidentifiable objects.

"You can't carry that yourself," he said.

She looked pleased, as if she'd predicted he would say this. "Then you help me."

He could not even remember the last time he'd carried anyone's bag, including his own. "Rosita, call Carlos," said Lenny.

"No," said Aurora. "You."

Rosita brought him a dolly, and he pushed the bag into the elevator. The girl walked beside him, fiercely gripping the bag handle. The elevator rose to the second floor. When they got to the guest room, he stopped.

"You can stay here," he said.

She walked in, dragged the bag into a corner. "Thank you," she said.

"Good night now," he said.

Her eyelids twitched. "I'm not sleepy."

He began to back away. "Hey, look," he said. "I'm sorry. You'll have to entertain yourself. You know." He lifted his hands helplessly. "Sweeps. Nielsens. I don't have time for babysitting. Rosita," he said. "Aurora will be visiting us. Bring her hot chocolate."

Aurora stepped back and stared at the floor. She looked as though she had fallen from the sky.

He felt he should say something more to her, but did not know what.

"Rosita, put some whipped cream on her hot chocolate," he said, and he fled.

LENNY WOKE WITH A SHUDDER IN THE MIDDLE OF THE NIGHT. HE sat, his heart marching, in his bed. Then he got up and went to the kitchen. He sat in the blue midnight and drank a glass of milk.

He heard footsteps—peering through the doorway, he saw Aurora in the foyer. The girl was walking barefoot, in her pajamas, through the enormous room. She made almost no sound and moved through the darkness in a careful, fevered way. She went up to the statues, lamps, couches and touched them tenderly. She walked quickly, from room to room.

He fled back into his room. He was shaken, furious, wondering if he should wake Rosita, call the police. The girl was walking through his home. Now it seemed that anything could happen— the clock could walk off, the curtain could burst into flames. He lay awake for a long time.

HE WOKE UP AT SIX, FAR EARLIER THAN HE BELIEVED THE GIRL would be up. After he made his way down the stairs, he realized that his headset was gone. He had left it on the kitchen table after his midnight glass of milk, and its absence made him feel anxious, excluded from the news of the day. He ran to Rosita and asked her to look for it. He would give himself twenty-five minutes for breakfast. About ten minutes into his food, Aurora walked in. She stood, a little tentatively, in the doorway; her face was carefully blank.

"Hello, Grandfather," she said. She said this title loudly, as though they both should know what it meant.

"Hello."

Her face was heavy with exhaustion. She sat at the other end of the table. Before she did this, she moved a large crystal urn of flowers to the floor.

"What are you doing?" he asked.

"I want to be able to see you when we talk."

He eyed her and ate a forkful of eggs. Rosita placed a croissant before her. Aurora was staring at him, drumming her fingers on the tablecloth.

"I have a question."

"Yes?"

"How does it feel to be syndicated in forty-three countries?"

"Forty-four. Somalia just signed on."

"Forty-four."

"Very good."

"Your first episode of *Anything for Money* had the biggest television audience ever."

"That is true."

"How did you get Ringo Starr to do a guest spot?"

"He asked to come on." He looked up. "Is this an interview?"

"I've read 127 articles about you. In all the major magazines. More on the Internet. On the authorized sites." She went through four slices of bacon. "Is it true that you only stock water in the back of the set so that contestants will get hungry and meaner?"

"No." He lifted the paper in front of his face. "Anything you need, ask Rosita."

"I would like an office."

He lowered the paper. "For what purpose?"

"The production of my feature film."

He folded the paper.

"I am currently in preproduction."

"You are twelve years old," he said.

"I know," she said, as though that were a compliment. "I have read many books on the subject. I am writing a script. If you want to know the title, I can—"

He marched out of the dining room; she followed. He was not used to waiting for another person, and he could sense her trailing behind him, trying to catch up.

He pushed open two doors embossed with a gold pattern identical to the doors of Il Duomo in Florence. The room overlooked the rose gardens.

"Your office," he said.

She seemed surprised that her request had been obeyed so swiftly; then she walked in, hands clasped behind her back like Napoleon inspecting the troops. She went to the windows and looked outside. The morning sun fell in wide bright strips across the lawn, so that the pink- and cream-colored roses gleamed like satin.

"Do you require use of a phone?"

"No," she said.

"A fax machine?"

"No, thank you."

She rose up on half-toe and then down again—later, he realized this was the gesture she used when she had more on her mind that she wanted to talk about, trying to make herself physically taller to give herself stature to ask for what she wanted.

"Your office," he said. "Now. My headset."

"Your what?"

"My headset. I need it." He tried to smile, attempting to appear more relaxed than he felt. "Now."

"I don't know what you're talking about," she said, curtly, so like her mother in fact it confirmed she knew where it was. She sat in the dark vinyl chair and leaned back in it. "Now. Tell me your opinion. I want to describe the sky over a new planet that has been created by the explosion of a supernova. Should it be pink or yellow or blue or a combination?"

"I don't know," he said.

"Pick."

Her stubbornness made it hard for him to think. "Blue," he said, helplessly.

She spun the chair. "Thank you. I have to get to work."

LENNY DRIFTED THROUGH HIS DAY AT WORK, LISTENING TO HIS writers knock around ideas: How about having contestants drink a concoction made by a four-year-old out of items he found in the refrigerator and medicine cabinet? What about telling people they had to walk down the street dressed like a chicken, slapping every third person on the face? That's *Anything for Money*! When he left, the sky was dark and furred with purple clouds. He told the chauffeur not to drive him home immediately. He was glad for the sensation of motion as the car floated over Beverly Hills, West Hollywood, Silver Lake; he did not want to be still.

When he got home, he found the staff assembled in the living room. They were clutching pieces of paper. Rosita was wearing a large pot holder on her head. Carlos was wearing a cape. He saw other employees, whose names he did not remember: a gardener wearing a chiffon scarf around his neck, the pool man. Aurora was standing on a chair in front of them. They were listening to her.

"Rosita!" Aurora commanded. "Your turn!"

"You! You have cursed me!"

"It is what the forces said to do," Carlos said, in an eerie voice.

"Hello," Lenny said.

There was a silence. Rosita took the pot holder from her head. Carlos removed his cape and smiled brightly.

"What is going on?" asked Lenny.

"We're rehearsing," said Aurora.

"For what?"

"My movie." She smiled. "They're all good in their parts. I didn't know they all wanted to be actors!"

He had not known that they had any other aspirations at all. He studied them. They looked away, trying to erase the animation in their faces.

"Thank you all," she said. "We're done."

Carlos picked up Lenny's briefcase and walked, stiffly, up the stairs.

"Rosita! My dinner," Lenny ordered.

"Can I have mine, too?" Aurora asked.

"You haven't had dinner?"

"I wanted to wait."

"Children shouldn't eat at nine o'clock," he said. It occurred to him that he had no idea when a child should eat dinner.

"I always wait for my mom to come home."

"When is that?"

"Six. Nine. Never."

"What do you eat when it's never?"

"Whatever's around. Yogurt. Ritz Crackers. Raisins. Chips."

"Rosita, give her some dinner," he said. He went to his room.

HE ENTERED HIS BEDROOM AND CHANGED INTO HIS SILK SWEAT suit. Then he looked for his favorite comb. It was not in his bathroom or his bedroom; nor could he locate his cologne. Standing in the middle of his bedroom, he wondered what the hell was going on. He went to the balcony and listened; he heard the clatter of a fork and knife; she was eating. He went down the hall to Aurora's room and opened the door. The large green sack was on the floor; he unzipped it. It was full of small brown paper bags. One was marked *MY GRANDFATHER LENNY*; inside was his headset and his comb and cologne. He peered into the other bags. One was marked *MADAME FOURROUT*, and inside was a postcard of Paris, a snapshot of a friendly baker, and a wooden spoon. Another bag said SAM FROM OXFORD, and inside was a snapshot of a college student and a silver pen engraved with the initials SNE. There were men and women of all ages and nationalities, and their toothbrushes, cosmetics, office supplies. The people represented in the bags were from Paris, Milan, Athens, Buenos Aires, everywhere that Charlene and Aurora had lived.

He zipped up the sack and walked out of the room, embarrassed by what he had just done. Embarrassment was an unusual feeling for him—he mostly encountered others experiencing it—and he did not know what to do. His chest felt empty, and he had to sit down, waiting for the feeling to go away. He did not know why she had taken these objects from these people, but he believed he understood in some way as well.

Lenny did not come to the table for another half hour. He was shaken and did not want her to see him. But when he came into the room, she was still there, waiting for him.

She was eating very slowly, scraping the sauce from the poached salmon off the plate. He was not used to anyone waiting for him at the dinner table. He was used to the mobs surging, gray-faced, in the holding room, staffers pacing, tense, outside his office. She was spelling her name in the sauce: *AURORA*.

He strode in quickly and took his seat. She had removed the urn again.

"I was a little hungry," she said.

He could see now that she was enormously tired, that she had spent her life keeping herself awake far longer than she should have.

"So," he said. "Time to get to know each other." His laughter fell into the room. Rosita brought out a tray filled with glistening pieces of sushi. "Where were you and Charlene most recently?"

"Paris. Vienna. Argentina. We had a fine time—"

"What do you do there?"

"I hang around. I'm sociable."

"What does your mother do?"

"She is busy." She shook much more salt on her dinner than was necessary.

"Doing what?"

"Many people want to know her." Her hand gestured grandly in the air. "You know, she started her own line of baby clothes. Le Petit Angel. She was going to work with Christian Dior—"

"Before she got thrown into rehab?"

"No!" she cried out, and her voice curved, suddenly, into a wail. She looked into her lap and pressed her hands against her face. Then she glanced past him and said, quickly, "I want to talk about success. I want to be a success. I have my own theory—"

"What is that?" he asked.

She sat up. "Success is about keeping your eyes open. Being organized. Having a plan. Getting to know people—"

"Success is luck," he said. "Some people are winners. Some are not."

She gazed at him with an expression that straddled, equally, opportunism and love.

"I have created the most successful show on television. One quarter of the world watches my show." His voice was husky, honeyed; he wanted to convince her of something. "The ones who win, they're lucky. They get the question they know how to answer, or they called the office the moment we needed to fill a show."

"What about the unlucky ones?" she asked.

"We need them, too. So people are grateful not to be them."

She was listening.

"We're choosing contestants tomorrow in Las Vegas for a special episode there. To be broadcast opposite the Super Bowl." He punched the air enthusiastically. "Why don't you come see how I do it?"

He could not look directly at the joy in her face; it blazed with a terrible brightness.

HE TOOK HER IN HIS PRIVATE JET, THE JET THAT HE HAD LOCKHEED build for him on a special commission. The earth fell away, the ocean a swath of silver, Southern California suddenly silent and remote; he looked out the window, and he felt a sweet relief blow through him.

He took a break from the planning session and grandly walked her around the plane, making sure the staff was watching. "This is my granddaughter Aurora—I'm telling her how to become a success. Aurora, here is the plane sauna. My staff tells me that anyone of any stature must have one of these on a plane. Over here, the plane game room, this is the biggest pool table in the sky . . ."

They landed in Las Vegas and set up their camp on a full floor in the MGM Grand. On the show, the contestants were going to run naked through a large, slippery pit filled with bills, trying to grab as many as they could. However, they would be allowed to use only their teeth. Some of the bills would be ones, but some would be thousand-dollar bills. Most of the plane trip had been consumed with discussion of whether to use olive oil or Crisco for the pit. The contestants would have to look good naked, be adept at sliding on curved surfaces, and have large mouths. Hundreds of people showed up and were funneled into a large conference room, where they were instructed to wait until Lenny arrived. He told Aurora to sit in the room with the contestants so that she could hear his staff prepare them.

The group looked like they'd been up late for too many nights—their eyes were rimmed violet, their hair desert-burned. They had been around the prospect of instant luck for too long, and they looked worn but grimly entitled.

Lenny walked in. "All right!" he shouted. "You want to do Anything for Money? Show me!" Their eyes were set on him. "You, what's your name?"

"Betty Valentine."

A slight woman came up. She had the blank, watery expression that meant she had been dragged here by a friend; she was in her forties, with short pink-blonde hair.

"What are you worth, Betty Valentine?" He pulled a wad of bills from his pocket. "Five dollars? Ten? A hundred?" He flicked the bill against her nose; she blinked. "A thousand?" He let the bill fall to the floor. Everyone regarded it with interest.

"Two of those are yours. If you can sing 'The Star-Spangled Banner.'"

Betty smiled slightly: this was easy.

"In here."

He snapped his fingers. An assistant rolled over a ten-foot-high wooden box. He opened a door. Inside, a hundred cockroaches were crawling on the walls. Betty's face was still.

"Come on, Betty."

Betty looked around at the others; putting her hands over her face, she slowly stepped inside the box. Her arms were shaking. Cockroaches crawled all over the insides of the box, onto her arms. She covered her face with her hands and began to make a high-pitched sound.

"Sing it!" he said.

Betty coughed. "Ohhh, say . . ." her voice trailed off.

"We're waiting," he said.

"Oh, say." She stopped and ran out of the box.

"Stop!" he said. An aide nimbly scooped the thousand-dollar bill off the floor.

"You call that singing? Are you winners or losers?" Lenny shouted at the group. "What are you worth?" His voice boomed. "Betty couldn't take it, could you?"

There was the sound of someone running behind him; he was appalled that anyone had moved. He whirled around to see Aurora standing up, her hands balled into fists.

"STOP!" Aurora yelled at him, and she ran out of the room.

The room went still; Lenny lunged through the doors. She was walking with stiff steps down the hotel hallway.

"Aurora!" he yelled. "Why did you do that?"

She spun around. Her face was pale. "You were a jerk."

"Hey," he said, lightly, "this is my job."

She began to run away from him.

"Wait," he said. The sight of her running away—from him—made him start, quickly, to follow her. "Aurora. Stop."

He remembered how, as a toddler, Charlene would run around the garden, talking to the flowers. "You are Astasia," she once said. "You are Petunee. You are Clarabell." Her innocence was so pure it was almost grotesque. He remembered how she would run up and kiss him, her mouth wide open, as though she were trying to consume his entire cheek.

"Aurora. Why did your mother send you to me?"

Aurora stopped. She scratched her leg. "I don't know."

"Why?"

"There was nowhere else to go."

He stood, dizzy, watching her run from him; then he told his staff to take over for the afternoon. He walked through the hotel, past the slot machines, where the sounds of people hoping to change their lives were as loud as a thousand bees. He continued through the cocktail lounge, the cigarette smoke a silver fog. He pushed through the hotel exit and stared, trembling, at the pure blue sky. He, too, believed he had nowhere to go.

IT WAS DUSK WHEN HE FINALLY FOUND HER. SHE WAS SITTING ON a bench, staring at a fountain surrounded by arcs of blue light. He approached her slowly. He did not know what he wanted, but he felt just as he had many years before, when he was about to rob the liquor store—as though he wanted to grab hold of the universe and change it. Then what he had wanted was practical. This universe he wanted to change with Aurora was different; it was abstract, constructed of feelings, and he did not know how to live within it.

"Aurora," he said.

"What do you want?"

He stood before the girl, an expensively dressed man, worn down, sweaty, against the dark Las Vegas sky. "I'd like to talk to you," he said.

She shrugged.

He sat down and leaned forward, clasping his hands. "What's the title of your movie?"

"Why?"

He shrugged. He did not know what else to ask.

"*Danger,*" she said, a thrilled edge to her voice. "This is the poster. It'll have a picture of an exploding world. There will be huge clouds of smoke. People from other planets will pick up stranded earthlings in their rockets. The saucers will fly through violet rain . . ."

"*Danger,*" Lenny said, slowly; it seemed a beautiful word. "It is a great idea."

THE NEXT DAY, THE JET TOOK THEM BACK TO THE MANSION. THEY walked the grounds together, and Lenny showed Aurora the whole estate, but mostly he listened to her tell him about her film. The girl spoke quickly, desperately. The plot of *Danger* was unclear but enthusiastic. It involved runaway missiles, a child army, aunts possessed by aliens, and other complex subplots. Lenny's contribution to the conversation was to not interrupt. If he did, the girl became furious. Aurora had thought through many of the marketing elements: the poster, the commercial. She wrote the title of the movie on a piece of poster board, decorated it with pieces of red velvet. She became so passionate during her description of the trailer for *Danger* that she got tears in her eyes.

HE WAS NOT SURE WHAT THEY SHOULD DO TOGETHER. HIS JET TOOK them to Hawaii one weekend where she could swim with dolphins, and to London the next for a lavish tea. He imagined that intimacy would feel like the sensation he had when the jet swung up into the sky, a feeling of airiness, of vastness; but she was not interested in the green sea around Hawaii, the heavy, sweet cream spooned around a scone. Instead, she wanted, strangely, to talk. She wanted to know the smallest, most peculiar details about him. What was his favorite color? What was his favorite vegetable? What kind of haircuts did he have as a child?

One day, she asked him what he was most afraid of in the world.

"You first," he said.

"Spiders," she said.

"Snakes," he said.

She looked dissatisfied. "Something better," she said.

"Earthquakes."

These were lies; he really had no idea.

"Ticking clocks," she said.

"Why?"

"When my mother doesn't come home," she said, "I listen for ticking clocks. I can hear them through walls."

"When does she not come home?"

"I hear them everywhere—in the walls, down the street."

She covered her face with her hands in a small, violent motion and held them there a moment. When she lowered them, her face was composed. "What are you afraid of?" she asked him.

"Nothing," he said.

"You have to say something."

"Let me think," he said, for no one had ever asked him this before.

THAT NIGHT, LENNY COULD NOT SLEEP. HE WENT TO THE KITCHEN at 2:00 AM for a glass of milk; again, he heard the girl's footsteps. He watched her walk lightly through the foyer again. He waited until she had left and then followed her through the silent house. Aurora padded across the cold tile until she reached one of his coat closets. She picked up some of the favorite pieces in his wardrobe—his Armani loafers, his Yves Saint Laurent gloves. She did this quickly, efficiently, plucking up items and dropping them. She picked out two shoes and a glove, and lightly, like a ghost, she ran back to her room.

He did not move. He wanted her to take everything.

HE STILL HAD NOT FIGURED OUT WHAT HE WAS MOST AFRAID OF when, about a month later, she did not come to breakfast. He was surprised by her absence but thought she was just sleeping late. He called from work to check in.

"She has the flu," said Rosita. "She's sleeping. Children get sick."

He found it difficult to concentrate on his work and came home early to see her. She was groggy with fever, but mostly she slept. Her fever was 105. The pediatrician told him to take the girl to the emergency room.

They were borne together on a stale, glaring current of fear. The children's wing of the hospital was like a haunted house: babies screamed as nurses held them down to take blood from their arms, children were wheeled out from operations, tubes rising out of their mouths. The parents walked slowly, like ghouls, beside the gurneys rolling their children out of surgery.

Aurora was with him, and then she was in the pediatric intensive care unit. The flu had developed into myocarditis, an illness of the heart. The doctor brought the residents around to discuss Aurora's condition, for it was so rare it had never happened in the hospital before. They stared at her with smug, glazed eyes. Lenny tried over and over to reach Charlene at the clinic, but finally an administrator got on line and said, primly, "She left. She ran away two days ago with another patient."

"Ran away?" he said. "Why didn't you call me?"

"We were waiting to see if she called us." She paused. "We assume no responsibility once they leave the premises. There were mutterings about South America."

"Find her," he said, "Or I'm suing you for so much money your head will spin."

"What do you propose we do, Mr. Weiss? Send our counselors to South America? She wasn't ready. We can't force her. We'll let you know if she contacts us."

During his life, he had commanded budgets of millions of dollars, negotiated with businessmen on every continent on the globe. Now he had to act as Aurora's guardian, and he stumbled wildly across the hospital linoleum. He tried to make sure Aurora would get good care from the nurses by offering them spots on his show.

"We're having a special episode. Pot of $500,000. You'd have a one-in-three chance." Standing at the large, smoky windows of the waiting area, he gazed at the cars moving down the freeways. Closing his eyes, he tried to will them to go backward, to change the course of this day and the next, but they pressed ahead, silver backs flashing.

WHEN AURORA HAD STABILIZED A WEEK LATER, THE DOCTOR called him into his office. The office was filled with diplomas and drab orange chairs. Lenny perched on the edge of the chair while the doctor read the chart that Aurora's pediatrician had sent him. "She was in Thailand two years ago," he said.

"Her mother took her there."

The doctor read the name of a disease Lenny did not know. "She wasn't treated properly. You shouldn't drag children around on these treks to developing countries. Her heart suffered some damage then. This flu did more harm."

Lenny remembered a postcard Charlene had sent from Bangkok: *Having a super time. Aurora loves curry. River rafting next week.*

He closed his eyes.

"Well, there's no good way to put this," said the doctor. "She needs a new heart."

Lenny could not breathe. A sharp pain went through him, immense and shocking because its source was wholly emotional.

"We'll put her on the transplant list," the doctor said.

"List?"

"She has to wait."

He had not waited on any list for over thirty years. Lenny stood up. His hair was uncombed and his face gray with exhaustion, but he felt the large, powerful weight of his body in his expensive suit. "What's your job here, doctor?"

"I am the head of pediatric cardiology." He was a slight man;

his hair was thin. His eyelashes were feminine and curling. His desk glimmered with crystal paperweights.

Lenny put his hands on the man's desk. "What do you need in your wing?"

"Pardon me?"

"Let me tell you how I see the new wing of the hospital," said Lenny, glancing at the doctor's nametag. "The Alfred A. Johnson wing. Twenty million dollars. A children's playroom. Top equipment. A research lab. Endowed chairs." He listened to the hoarse, meaty sound of his voice. "I am the producer of *Anything for Money*. Look at me."

THE HOSPITAL SENT AURORA HOME. SHE WAS WEAK BUT DID NOT know how ill she was, and Lenny did not tell her. He did not allow himself to think about her physical state. Instead, he indulged in feelings of pride at his wealth and its ability to bend the rules. When he received the letter from the hospital a few days later, he almost wanted to frame it, for it seemed to reflect some magnificence in his soul. The letter said: *Aurora Weiss is number one on the list for transplants of the heart.*

Lenny called the doctor once, twice a day. He awaited the ghoulish harvest reports: a young boy killed in a car accident, a teen stabbed to death in a fight. But none of these hearts had the right antigens that would match Aurora's; they had to wait for the correct heart.

Waiting was what fools did; he decided to take things into his own hands. He stayed up all night, making calls. He spoke into a phone that did automatic translating to doctors in Germany, Sweden, France. His price soared. Thirty million dollars. New wings. Top equipment. Huge salaries. High-tech playrooms. He shouted these offers into the phone at 2:00 AM, floating on the imagined gratitude of others. They would all talk about how Lenny Weiss had saved his granddaughter by calling every doctor in the world.

AURORA CAME INTO THE ROOM ONE NIGHT WHEN LENNY WAS MAK-ing his calls. She stood in her pajamas, staring, as he shouted into the phone.

"What's wrong?" she asked.

He put down the phone.

He told her that her heart was not well and, in more detail, how he was going to help her. "I'm going to find one," he said. "People know me and they want to help—"

She saw through this immediately. "I'm sorry!" she cried out. "Sorry, sorry—"

He saw, at once, how his daughter had behaved as a mother.

"Aurora. I'll save you," he said; the sound of these words comforted him. "I swear it."

But she did not let him touch her—she backed away from him with a dim expression. She was already disappearing and believed this was what people had truly wanted from her all along.

HE SKIPPED WORK. HE DID NOT SLEEP. THE RIGHT HEART WAS NOT appearing. He tried to think about who would give up their heart for millions of dollars. Drug addicts, the terminally ill—but their hearts would be in poor shape. He sat behind the dark glass of his limo, grimly watching girls play soccer, wishing one of them would trip. He imagined his Mercedes plowing into a group of teenage boys running on the sidewalk, killing enough of them to give Aurora more of a chance.

He proposed to his staff a special episode: "Who Will Die For Money." They would audition people willing to give up their hearts for a staggering pot of $5 million. His staff thought it was a PR stunt and called an audition. The holding room filled with an assortment of the homeless, individuals not in the best health, and well-dressed, shifty types who seemed to think there was some way to obtain the money without dying.

They were all busily filling out their names and addresses when he got a call from Rosita.

"A heart has arrived on the doorstep," she said.

He rushed home.

A man identified himself as a cardiac surgeon and a purveyor of black-market hearts. He was from Ukraine. Dr. Stoly Michavcezek sat in Lenny's living room, holding a Styrofoam ice chest on his lap.

"Whose heart was this?" asked Lenny.

"A man. Olympic gymnast. Fell on mat and dead. Few hours. Payment up front."

They transferred the heart, quickly, to Lenny's enormous Sub-Zero freezer; then Lenny brought in a specialist from Cedars-Sinai to look at the heart.

"This isn't a human heart," said the doctor. "This is the heart of a chimp."

When he returned to the studio, the prospective contestants had all been dismissed, and black-suited men from the legal department were waiting in his office.

"Lenny," said one. "This has got to stop."

Aurora worked on her movie obsessively; she spent much of her time in her room. When they had a meal together, he did most of the talking; he lied about his closeness to saving her. "There's a doctor in Mexico," he'd say, "a small hospital. International laws, they're all we have to get around . . ." She ate very little and watched him like a child who had disbelieved adults her whole life.

One night, she burst out of her room and hurried to her seat at the table. "My plot has changed," she said. "Listen. There are seventeen aliens from the planet of Eyahoo. They have legs in the shape of wheels and heads like potatoes. Their planet is very slippery, and they move very fast on their wheels. Often they bump into each other. Their heads are getting sore."

He listened.

"They need a new cousin who can make their planet less slippery. Their cousin is named Yabonda, and she lives on a neighboring planet. She has long legs with huge feet that are very absorbent, like paper towels. They want to learn how to have feet like her. Now. Do you think they should maybe invite her to Eyahoo for dinner or just come and kidnap her?"

She leaned back in her chair, clasped her hands tightly, and watched him.

"What would happen with each?" he asked.

"If they asked her to dinner, she would be transported in a glamorous carriage made of starlight."

"Uh-huh."

"If they kidnapped her, it would hurt." She stretched out her fingers, as though trying to hold everything. "Tell me," she said, sharply.

WHEN AURORA HAD LEARNED ABOUT HER CONDITION, SHE STOPPED stealing. Lenny began leaving things out for her—his cell phone and toothbrush and car keys—in the hope that she would take them, but in the morning, they remained where he had left them. He missed her midnight rambling through the mansion, waking up to see which objects of his she would find precious.

One night, he heard her footsteps padding down the hall.

Lenny jumped out of bed and followed her. This time, Aurora seemed to have no particular direction, but went around the foyer like a floating, circling bird. Then she saw Lenny. They stared at each other in the dusk of the hallway, and the shocked quiet around them made Lenny feel that they were meeting for the first time.

Aurora began to cry. "I don't know what to take."

The girl knelt to the floor and threw up. The child's distress made Lenny feel as though he himself were dissolving.

"Take me," said Lenny.

The girl stared at him.

"I'll go with you," said Lenny.

"Where?"

"Wherever. I'll go too."

"How?"

"I can find a way to do it."

He did not know how to stop these words, did not know if they were lies or the truth—they simply came out of him.

"I don't want to be by myself," said Aurora.

He closed his eyes and said, "I'll be there, too."

When the dawn came, he was sleeping on the floor beside Aurora's bed. He woke up, his promise an inchoate, cold feeling in his body; then he remembered what he had said.

He got up quietly and left the room.

IT WAS JUST SIX IN THE MORNING. LENNY WENT TO HIS GARAGE AND got into his red Ferrari convertible. He shot up the Pacific Coast Highway, feeling the engine's force vibrate through his body. The highway stretched, a ribbon reaching through the blue haze to the rest of the world. He felt poisoned by the girl's presence in himself and wanted to get her out.

By eight o'clock, he had hit Santa Barbara. The main street was filled with a clear golden light, and the people strolling the sidewalks looked so contented and purposeful he wished they were all dead. He thought of the way Aurora stood on half-toe when she wanted something, the sweet, terrible optimism in the girl's walk when she headed down the hallway. He wanted to stop his car and rush out among the strangers and find a woman, proposition her, and have sex with her in an alley. He wanted to strip naked and run into the ocean. He wanted to drive his car into the glass windows of a restaurant and be put in jail. He drove back and forth down the main street for a while, hands trembling on the steering wheel.

He turned the car and roared toward where people knew him best: the studio. At 11:00 AM, he walked through the doors and stood in the shadows, watching. Eight contestants were white-lit, hitting buzzers, shouting out answers to questions, and the producers and crew were scrambling noisily in the dark around the stage.

Lenny stared at the brilliant stage set. On this stage, he had seen parents allow their children to walk them on a leash, like dogs, for five hundred bucks. He had seen teens who agreed to twerk in front of their grandparents for a thousand. He had stood in this brightness, watching others fall dimly around him.

"Lenny," he heard. "Hey, Lenny—"

Now he stood in this corridor, a strange, familiar fear in his mouth. He knew what would be unbearable.

He turned around several times before he saw the exit. Pushing the metal doors, he ran into the parking lot, jumped into his car, and drove home.

When the Ferrari drove up to the mansion, Aurora was sitting on the stairs. The girl was still, as though she had been sitting there for a hundred years. Her blue eyes were fixed on Lenny as he began to walk up the stairs.

"I thought you weren't coming back," said Aurora.

"I had to do an errand," said Lenny.

He sat beside Aurora on the stair.

"I have a new plot idea," she said. "To help Yabonda."

"What do you mean?"

"Her paper towel feet have dried out," she said. "Whenever she lifts her feet, they make a weird crackling sound. Everyone on the planet wants her to go away. They can't stand the noise her feet make. It keeps them all awake. There is mayhem and murder." She looked right at him; her gaze was stern. "She meets Glungluck, a kindly alien who was kicked off her planet because her ears, which resemble long straws, suck up everything around them, and people were losing their purses and keys."

"Go on," he said.

"They make a neighborhood," she said. "They add other sad aliens, Kogo and Zarooom. They build big walls around their neighborhood made of glass roses. The only aliens who can move in are other losers. They all have had bad luck. In their neighborhood, they can talk to each other. They make up songs and have contests. Nobody wins. When the good-luck aliens try to see through the wall of roses, they are jealous and lonely."

He looked at her face. Her forehead was gray and creased, like an old person's.

"I'll produce," he said.

He did not stop looking. He had kept the audition slips of the people who had been willing to give up their hearts for $5 million and was meeting one, Wayne Olden, secretly, for lunch at a Fatburger in Hollywood to check him out. He was planning to take him in for a full medical exam; after that he would hand over the organ donation forms. Lenny had not figured out how he would kill the man, particularly to maintain the integrity of his organs. They were finishing up a hot dog when he received a call.

"I'm not feeling good," said Aurora.

"What's wrong?"

"I don't know."

Lenny jumped up.

"I have to go," he said to the man.

"You're kidding," said the man.

"Here," said Lenny, throwing him a thousand-dollar bill. "That's for lunch."

The man looked disappointed. "I thought I was going to get five million bucks!"

LENNY'S MERCEDES RACED HOME. IT WAS LATE AFTERNOON, THE shadows long and dark across the grass. Aurora was sitting on the lawn by the pool. She had brought out the sack of stolen items and had set out everything that she had taken. There were pens, staplers, shoes, caps, some loose change, postcards, a spoon, a sock, paper clips, some crumpled Kleenex. The brown paper bags that held them were crumpled up, a pile of small paper balls. All of this surrounded her; the late sun made her face look gold.

"What's wrong?" he asked.

"I don't have enough," she said.

He sat down beside her. His throat was stiff, tense. He said, "Tell me about them."

She looked at the many items spread out in front of her. She picked up an aluminum cupcake tin. "Sharon Eastman. Cook in the Ambassador Hotel in Chicago, asked me about my favorite foods and showed me how to make cupcakes with buttercream frosting. She made one for me with a rose on it, as I said I wanted one."

She picked up a coat hanger and said, "This was Greg Mixon's, who was the coat-check man at the Century 100 Restaurant in Miami, where we went every night for dinner for a month, and who let me sit and read in a corner in the coat closet and gave me a new button for my coat and said this coat hanger would hold it . . ."

He listened to her talk and talk, her words coming fast, as though she were in a rush to get everything out. She remembered so much that the others had said, as though she had stored each sentence up when she had been told it. She leaned softly against his shoulder, and he put his arm around her. He was aware of the way his hands fell open by his sides, the way they could hold absolutely nothing.

"Aurora," he said. "Wait."

She stopped. Her face was flushed.

"Give me something."

"What?"

"Give me something of yours. I need it."

"What thing?"

"Anything."

"You want something of mine?" she whispered, surprised.

"Yes. Now."

She shrugged and dug into her pocket. There she had a small piece of red velvet that she had used on her poster for *Danger*. She handed it to him.

"Here," she said.

He took the scrap of velvet, closed his fingers around it.

She sat up very straight and looked right at him. Her gaze was sharp. He froze. His skin was as thin as silk. He wondered what she could see, what the light of her gaze detected. He was aware of the palm trees moving gently in the warm wind; he believed he had stopped breathing.

He waited.

Around them, the night sky pressed down like a lid, the stars faint nicks of light in the darkness.

She sat back down; she didn't say anything. It was a flat, immense silence, and it frightened him. He didn't know what she saw, and he never would. He sat, not knowing what to say.

She picked up a paper clip off the lawn. She cupped it protectively in her hand.

"This was from Jennifer Macon in Washington, D.C.," she said. He listened as she told about the paper clip and the rose barrette and the jar of lip balm. She talked, her voice softly piercing the air. The city lit up, a bright, glimmering plain, below them as the sky drained from orange to blue to black. Together, they sat, looking into the dim green exuberance of the garden.

The Third Child

As the streetlights blinked on, Jane Goldman stepped onto her front porch to listen to the faint sound of screaming float from the other houses on her street. The screaming was the sound of children protesting everything: eating, bathing, sharing toys, going to sleep. As the weather warmed, she stood outside on her porch, smoking a rare cigarette and listening. This was her life now, at forty: she had married a man whom she admired and loved, and after the initial confusion of early marriage—the fact that they betrayed the other simply by being themselves—they fell into the exhausting momentum that was their lives. They had produced a son, now five years old, and a daughter, now eight months, two beings who hurtled into the world, ruby-lipped, peach-skinned, and who now held them hostage as surely as masked gunmen controlled a bank.

Jane was a freelance editor for technical manuals, and her husband, after seeing his business as a high-priced website designer dry up, settled into a job as a consultant. They had moved to a midsized city in South Carolina. It was not their first choice, and they did not know if they would ever feel at home there, but they could afford, finally, a small house as well as a car. They had found their own happiness, weighted by resignation: that they were who they were, that they could never truly know the thoughts of another person, that their love was bruised by the carelessness of their own parents (his mother, her father); that they would wander the world in their dreams with ghostly, intangible lovers, that their children would move from adoration of them to fury, that they and their parents would die in different cities, that they would never accomplish anything that would leave any lasting mark on the world. They had longed for this, from the first lonely moment of their childhoods when they realized they could not marry their fathers or mothers, through the burning romanticism of their teens, to the bustling search of their twenties, and there was the faint regret that this tumult and exhaustion was what they had longed for too, and soon it would be gone.

Jane stood on the porch each night, watching the dusk settle on to their street. And when the screaming had ended, she sat watching the other families move behind the windows, gliding silently in their aquariums of golden light.

ONE MORNING SOON AFTER, JANE SAT CROSS-LEGGED ON THE FLOOR of the bathroom, the baby grappling at her breasts, and watched the line form on the test. She and her husband had not been trying for another child. She pressed her lips to her baby girl's soft head, this one she wanted to love, and she understood, clearly, that she did not feel capable of loving a third child. She had given everything to the others. She kissed the baby's head, grateful for the aura of kindness the baby bestowed upon her, for now there was no illusion, as there had been when she was a young woman, that this being inside of her would not become a child; she held the thick, muscular result in her hands. The baby's tiny fingers made her feel faint. They lived in a part of the country where a third (or fourth or fifth) unexpected child arrived and, with jovial weariness, families "made room" for them. She looked at the red line, and it measured all the moments remaining in her life.

The husband staggered awake after a depressing dream in which a childhood friend had retired early and moved to Tuscany. The kitchen smelled fetid, as though an animal had crawled into a corner and died. The boy, still grief-stricken over his sister's birth, utilizing their guilt over this to demand endless presents, described his longing for a Slinky that another child had brought to school. "I did want it," he wailed in a monotone. "I did. I did. I did. I did." He wanted to wear his Superman shirt with the red cape attached to the shoulders and spent his breakfast leaping out of his seat and trying to shoot his sister with a plastic gun. She, too, already had preferences and screamed until Jane put her into a purple outfit with floppy bunny ears. They wanted to be anything but human. Her husband could not find anything to put on his lunch sandwich and, with a sort of martyred defiance, slapped margarine on bread. "What a man does to save money," he murmured.

"Why don't you just buy your lunch?" she asked.

"Do you know how much that costs?" he said. "Do you know how much I'm saving this family by eating crap on bread every day?"

"Get me a Slinky!" the boy yelled, to everyone. The baby screamed.

"Will everyone please shut up?" she said, and then she flinched, embarrassed.

"Don't say that around the children," he said.

"I can say what I want."

"Don't say *shut up*," the boy said, in a ponderous tone.

"Eat your breakfast," she hissed at him.

"I hate it," he wailed, writhing out of his seat and onto the floor, where he curled up under the table as though preparing for a nuclear bomb. She glanced at her husband; their love had been, like all love at the beginning, a mutual and essential misunderstanding, a belief that each could absorb qualities held by the other, that each could save the other from loneliness, that their future held endless promise, that they would not be separated by death. This version of joy was what they had chosen of their own free will.

The baby, not wanting to be outdone, suddenly struck a pose like a fashion model. "How cute," said the husband; they all hungered for a moment of beauty. The baby laughed, a glittery sound. The boy wept. The future lay before them, limp and endless. The husband got on his hands and knees by the son. "Come now," he said, his voice exquisite with tenderness. "You're a big boy now." He pleaded for maturity for five minutes, and when his voice was about to snap, the boy crawled out and donned a backpack, which made him resemble a miniature college student. He turned around, delighted, so they all applauded.

Their son ran out to their lawn. There was a sweet green freshness in the morning air. It was a Tuesday; she believed she was six weeks along; there was a bad taste in her mouth, of ash. Behind them was their house, a flimsy tribute to the middle class, but one bad car crash, one growing lump, a few missed paychecks would send them packing. They could not afford to have a heart attack, to lose their minds. It was just spring; daffodils burst out of the cold earth. She and her husband stood, bewildered, watching the children in the golden Southern sunlight. She loved them so deeply her skin felt as if it were burning, and she also knew that her love, which she had thought contained boundless wealth, could be handed out to dozens, hundreds, had its finite limits as well.

She called the babysitter, kissed her children goodbye, and went to the clinic. She was afraid that he would have tried to convince her to have the third child. She wept on the way there, for her certainty that she could not have another, for her desire to be good enough for the boy and girl. When she arrived at the clinic, she had stopped weeping. She drove home, sore and cramping, three hours later, down the broad gray lanes bordered by fast-food emporiums, wanting to swerve in and run inside to the high school girls in bright hats behind the counters so that she could hear them say brightly, *May I help you?*

SOMETIMES DURING THE DAY THERE WOULD BE A KNOCK ON THE door, and it would be their eight-year-old neighbor Mary Grace. She was the only person who was ever at the door. She was beloved by their son, and for this reason, Jane let her wander into their house at all times. Mary Grace was fiercely competitive in all areas including height, hour of bedtime, and the quality of bribe her mother had given her in order for her to get a flu shot. She had thin brown hair, and her eyes were hooded with the suspicion that her parents would do anything possible to keep from listening to her.

Mary Grace's parents were silent, mysterious types who were very involved in their Baptist church. Jane and her husband tried to guess why the parents never spoke to them and why they never invited the son to their house. Perhaps Mary Grace's father was having an affair. Or the mother was having an affair. Perhaps they never had sex or had bad sex. Perhaps they did not make each other laugh. Perhaps the mother was sad because she wished she had become a ballet dancer, a doctor, a rock star. Perhaps one drank too much. Perhaps he wanted to live in Australia. Perhaps she hated his taste in clothes. Perhaps one of them had cancer. Perhaps they did not want their floors to get dirty. Would they break up or marinate in their sourness for years? Mary Grace's parents did not set up any sort of social life for her. Jane noticed the wife spending most of her free time snipping their front hedges with gardening implements that were large and vicious. Jane saw the husband on his dutiful evening walks around the block, his eyes cast down, his feet lifting in a peculiar way so he seemed to be tiptoeing across ice. Mary Grace scuttled over to Jane's at least once a day, neatly dressed and clean, but always with the demeanor of someone who was starving.

That day, she was grateful for the girl's knock. Jane had returned from the clinic, opened the door to her home slowly, as though she were an intruder. The children noticed nothing; their absorption in their own crises was complete. They saw only that she was their mother and fell toward her. She was aching and exhausted, but the babysitter couldn't stay. Jane needed a stranger in the kitchen, someone to speak because she could not.

"Let's make a magic potion," Mary Grace announced. She believed touchingly that she could realize her great dreams in their home. The girl rushed into the kitchen. Her hands rummaged through drawers, plucked juice boxes from cupboards. "We need to make a magic potion," she said. "We need olive oil. Lemonade. Baking soda. Seltzer."

"Yes," her son said, gazing at Mary Grace.

Jane brought the items over, and Mary Grace poured them carefully into a glass. Her son was now whispering to her, his face intent, and the girl said, rolling her eyes, "No. It will not make you into a cheetah." Jane looked at Mary Grace.

"He can become a cheetah if he wants," Jane broke in.

"Then I want to become a princess," said Mary Grace.

She brought them some vinegar and mayonnaise and seltzer and watched them stir their concoction. Mary Grace looked up and said, "My mother's doing her fitness video. She wants to get to her high school weight."

"Oh," said Jane.

"She was going to become a fitness instructor, but then she was dating my dad and they knew each other three weeks, and then she dropped everything to have me." She giggled frantically, as though she was not sure what sound to make. Then Mary Grace grasped Jane's forearm. The girl's nails were long and sharp. "Can we add perfume to make princesses?" she asked.

Jane allowed the girl to hold her arm for a moment. "No," she said. She patted Mary Grace's hand carefully. "I'm sure she's very glad she has you," she said, and she reached up to a cabinet for some baking soda. Mary Grace released her hand.

"Then she had my brother like that, *boom,* and then my sister, and she says if she gets back to her high school weight, she'll look seventeen again." Mary Grace took the baking soda, poured it in, and the mixture began to fizz and rise. The children shrieked at the possibilities implied in this, and when the potion puttered out they looked toward Jane. "More!" called her son.

"I want a snack now," Mary Grace said.

Jane opened the refrigerator. She felt more blood slip out of her, sharply took a breath. "Do you want some carrots?" she asked.

"I want ice cream with hot fudge syrup," said the girl. "Please."

In Boston, where Jane used to live, her husband had a successful business constructing corporate websites, but he most enjoyed helping people create elaborate personal shrines that floated in no place on earth. People wanted all sorts of things on them: personal philosophy, photos both personal and professional, diary fragments, links to other people whom they admired but to whom they had no other connection. Her husband understood their desire to communicate their best selves with an unknown, invisible public; a shy person, he had forced himself to become sociable and liked convincing people of all the intimate facts they needed to tell strangers about themselves. When they met, he was exuberant, and she was disdainful of websites; she was the only person he had ever met who did not want one for herself. "Don't you want people to click and find out all about you?" he asked. "Your achievements and innermost thoughts?" He was leaning, one arm against a wall, clutching cheap wine in a plastic glass.

"No," she said.

He sensed she was holding back, and that made her appear to conceal something deeply valuable. She admired his shamelessness, the way he could go up to people at a party and convince them to create monuments to themselves. They had both stumbled out from families in which they felt they did not belong: she, second of four, he, oldest of three. He had a beautiful, careless mother who had left the family for two years when he was seven; this created in him a sharp and fierce practicality, a need to ingratiate himself and to hoard money. She had been belittled by her father and for years had cultivated the aloofness of the shy.

The economy quickly broke apart their life. People and companies were running out of money to create themselves in an invisible space. She had been working as an editor for a small publisher, and that was the first job she lost simply because the company was folding. Their rent was shooting up, they were in their late thirties with a three-year-old, another on the way, and they had nothing saved for retirement. It was time to move on.

HER HUSBAND CAME HOME THAT EVENING IN A CHEERFUL, DETER-mined mood, armed with a new digital camera. He wanted to take pictures of them in the garden and arrange them on a website that would record the children's growth as well as that of the various vegetables and flowers they had recently planted. The routine qual-ity of his new job sometimes filled him with a manic, expansive energy. So many parts of him were unused. The camera had cost $345. "We can do this every few days," he said. "We can tell people about it. They can click from everywhere and see our garden. We can start a trend!" He tried, with difficulty, to arrange the children beside the plot of dirt.

She did not want him to take a picture of her. She did not want to see a picture of her face on this day.

"We need more good pictures of you," he said, irritation flickering across his face.

"I look tired," she said.

"No, you don't," he said. "You need a picture with pearls. Holding a rose. Jackie Kennedy. A socialite surrounded by her darling cherubs." He laughed.

"Oh, right," she said. It was a sweet but clichéd worldview that he reverted to when he felt uprooted, and it comforted him. He had nurtured it when he was alone and neglected as a child and had formed his ideas of happiness, what his family and love should be.

She had been the daughter of nervous parents who cut up apples in her lunch so she would not choke and drove only on the right side of the road, and she had been drawn to his point of view when they were dating. She remembered the first time she saw his childhood house, in a suburban tract in Los Angeles—it was a small house that attempted to resemble a Southern mansion, with columns on the porch and a trim rose-bed in the front. There was something in the stalwart embrace of other people's tastes that made Jane envious— not of the house so much as the purity of longing.

She heard the children shriek, and there was no such simplicity. Your own family was the death of it.

"Come on," he said. "Throw something on. Wash your face."

She looked at him.

"What's wrong?" he asked.

She did not want to injure his perception of himself as a good person. But she knew that now, at night, he clutched his pillow as though he were drowning.

Her family stumbled around the barren garden, hair lit up by the late-afternoon sun. He was clutching his camera, eager to record the physical growth of his children. "Look," she said to him, wanting him to see everything.

THE CHILDREN WERE IN BED, SLEEPING. SHE BROUGHT BLANKETS TO their chins, watched their breath move in and out. Their eyelids twitched with fervent dreams. The sight of her children sleeping always brought up in her a love that was vast and irreproachable. No one could question this love. She remembered the first time she and her husband hired a babysitter and went to dinner, two months after their boy was born. They had walked the streets, ten minutes from their home. They had hoped that when they sat down in a restaurant, they would enjoy the same easy joy of self-absorption. But they realized, slowly, that they would never in their lives forget about him. The rest of the date they spent in a stunned silence understanding, for the first time, how this love would both nourish and entrap them for the rest of their lives.

She sat beside her husband in bed. She was still cramping; she went to the bathroom to urinate, and there was still blood. She was relieved as she felt the blood leave her, pretending that it was just another period, but she did not want to look too closely at the material that came with it. The names they might have used came to her: Charles, Wendy, Diane. But they were names for nothing now, air. There was no kindness she could offer it now, and that made her feel dry, stunted. She went to the children's rooms and kissed them again.

She could not sleep. She was sitting in the darkness when she noticed a light go on in her neighbors' house. Their houses were side by side, about ten feet apart, and the neighbors' blinds were usually closed. Tonight she saw that they were open as though they were trying to enjoy the new warmth. The mother had put up curtains, but they were sheer, and Jane could see right into their room.

She saw Mary Grace's mother sitting on her bed. Their bedroom had been decorated with the lukewarm blandness of a hotel room and was so clean as to deny any human interaction inside it. The mother wore a frilly aqua nightie that made her resemble a large, clumsy girl. She was sitting on the edge of the bed and suddenly pulled the nightie over her head. She was watching the husband, who wore bright boxer shorts and no shirt. The curtain lifted in the warm wind. The husband walked over to the wife, and she lifted her face for a kiss; the husband pulled her breast as though he were milking a cow. The wife's face was blank.

"I know what you forgot! The detergent!" she exclaimed, in a clear voice. The husband drew back. His shoulders slumped as though he were begging. There was quiet, and Jane waited for his answer.

"Sorry," he said. There was a plaintive quality to this word, his inability to come up with any sort of excuse; it seemed to designate everything about their future. The lights went off.

Jane got out of bed and went downstairs. She told herself she needed to take out the garbage, but she just needed to get outside. Opening the door, the night was thick and black and the air was fresh. She threw the bag of trash into the can and stood in front of her house. The cicadas sounded like an enormous machine. The sky was a riot of stars. She glanced around the empty street and began to run.

The neighborhood was beautiful at this hour, flowers and bushes randomly lit by small spotlights, as though each family wanted to illuminate some glorious part of itself. It was ten thirty, and the only discernible human sound was the canned television laughter floating out of windows. The houses looked anchored to these neat green plots of land. How much longer would her neighbors wake up, shower, eat their cereal, argue, dress their children, weep, prepare dinner, sit by the television, make love, sleep? She ran quietly, the sidewalk damp under her naked feet; she smelled the flowers, the jasmine, honeysuckle, magnolia, sweet and ferocious and dark.

She ran one block like this and stopped, breathing hard. Her forehead was sweating. She was a middle-aged woman in her pajamas, running from her house at ten thirty at night. Looking at her house, she saw the small night-light in her son's room cast a lovely blue glow through the window. From here, the room looked enchanted, as if inhabited by fairies. Her breathing slowed, and the night air felt cool in her lungs. When she glanced up at the neighbors' bedroom window, she noticed that their blinds were now shut.

MARY GRACE KNOCKED ON THE DOOR AT THREE THIRTY THE NEXT day. Jane thought she was dressed up early for Halloween, with a short blue accordion-skirt and a T-shirt decorated with a halo made of rhinestones, but it was actually a cheerleader outfit. She was going to a practice for Halo Hoops, the church basketball team. "I have to go to our basketball game at church," she said. "I have ten minutes. That is all." Jane held open the door, and Mary Grace jumped inside and did a twirl.

"Can I marry you, Mary Grace?" her son asked.

"No," said Mary Grace. "I'm older than you." She looked at Jane. "I'm going to be a superstar singer. I'm going to be in the top five. Wanna hear—" She belted out a few words of a pop song. She was stocky, tuneless, and loud. Jane's son was enchanted and requested more. He grabbed Mary Grace's hand, and Jane's heart flinched.

"Can we make cookies?" Mary Grace asked. "Quick?"

They bustled into the kitchen and proceeded to bake. No one came to take the girl to Halo Hoops. The kitchen suddenly smelled like a bakery. Mary Grace stood too close to her. "Do you like my singing?" she pleaded.

"Sure," said Jane.

"Me, too," said the girl. Jane felt Mary Grace's breath on her arm. The girl's breath had the warmth of a dragon or another unnatural beast. The girl's belief in Jane's worth was awful. "You have pretty hair," said Mary Grace, reaching up to Jane and touching a strand. The girl had a startlingly gentle touch. Her hand smelled of sweet dough and chocolate.

"Thanks," said Jane. The boy and the baby stared at Mary Grace. The baby, hanging on Jane's hip, reached out and swatted Mary Grace away. Mary Grace's face tightened, aggrieved.

"Do I have pretty hair?" asked Mary Grace.

The baby yanked Jane's hair. "Ow!" said Jane, grabbing the tiny hand.

"Do I?" asked Mary Grace; it was almost a shout.

Before Jane could answer, her son stepped forward and grabbed Mary Grace's arm. "Do you want to stay for dinner?" he asked.

Mary Grace recoiled from his touch. Jane saw all of the girl's self-hatred light up her eyes: that she had no other friends besides this five-year-old, that her parents did not want her at their table. "No," she snapped, "Ick. Why do you keep asking me!"

Her son dropped his head, wounded. Jane slapped her hand on the table. It made a clear, sharp sound. "Then just go home!" she yelled at Mary Grace.

The children were suddenly alert. Jane was frozen, ashamed. The girl slowly picked up her jacket and, shoulders slumped, eyes cast downward, trudged to the door, a position already so well-worn it had carved itself into her posture. Her son screamed, "Stay!"

and skidded toward her, arms open, but Mary Grace moved to the door and was gone.

THAT NIGHT JANE SAT BESIDE HER HUSBAND AND REALIZED THAT they had known each other for fifteen years. She wanted to tell her husband something new about herself, something she had never told anyone before. She wanted to tell him a secret that would bring them to a new level of closeness. What else could she tell him? Would he be more grateful for a humiliating moment in her life or a transforming one? Did people love others based on the ways they had similarly debased themselves or the proud ways they had lifted themselves up?

"What?" he asked, sensing a disturbance.

"I yelled at the girl," she said. "She was mean to our boy, and I couldn't stand it. I shouldn't have. She turned around and left."

"They already hate us," he said, calmly. Then he returned to his book.

She was now revved up for an argument.

"I'm wasting my life picking up towels," she said. "For every ten towels I pick up, you pick up one. I'm sick of it, and they smell like goats."

Now he looked up. "I pick up towels," he said. "Plenty of them."

"Not as many as me," she said.

He jumped out of bed, standing on the balls of his feet, like a boxer who had been secretly preparing for this barrage, and then grabbed a robe and tossed it over himself. "What do I give up for this family! Look at this leg." He held it out. "If I had any time at all to exercise, then I would be able to get in great shape. I could run a marathon! I could make love ten times a day." The edge in his voice, the raw and bottomless yearning, was so sharply reminiscent of her own father's during her childhood that she felt time as a funnel: she'd been emptied into her old home, the same person but just a different size. He sank down into his chair and began to tap his foot nervously, looking anywhere but at her.

"We would have had a third child," she said. "I stopped it."

He looked at her.

"This week," she said.

She remembered the night that she and her husband had brought their son home from the hospital. They had cupped him in their hands, a person just two days old. When he began to cry, his first human wails rising into their apartment, she and her husband realized that they were supposed to comfort him. It was them. They gazed with longing into his hopeful eyes.

He stared at her. Carefully, he clasped his hands. His eyes were bright; she realized there were tears in them.

"Did you forget about me?" he asked.

His voice was soft, and it sounded as though it came directly out of the black night outside. "We couldn't have done it," she said.

"You didn't want to," he replied, sharply.

"You didn't either," she said. "I know you."

"Do you?" he asked. "Look at me. What am I thinking right now?"

She looked into his dark eyes. When they got married, she wanted to know, to own everything about him.

She leaned toward him and looked closer. She and her husband were sitting beside each other, half-dressed, their windows open. Outside, the leaves on the trees gleamed in the orange streetlights. Jane touched his hand. She thought she heard weak laughter in the neighbors' house, carried through the streets on a warm and fragrant wind.

Mary Grace was back the next afternoon, washing up at their door as inevitably as the tide. There was something ancient about her, the way she smiled warily at Jane, scratching her leg and pretending that yesterday had not happened. She loved them simply because they opened the door.

"Could we make a lemonade stand?" Mary Grace asked. "We could sell lemonade for twenty-five cents."

Jane moved outside. It was a cool day, with drizzly rain. "I don't know," said Jane, looking at the sky. But her son ran out the door, bubbling with joy that the girl was back. "Yes!" he yelled. He and Mary Grace arranged themselves around a card table in the front yard, a pitcher of lemonade and some cups between them. Mary Grace clutched an umbrella. Jane watched their small, dignified backs as they regarded the neighborhood, set in their belief that others would want what they offered.

She did not have many plastic cups. She thought she could ask Mary Grace's mother if she had any cups; she looked up the woman's number in the phone book.

"Hello," said Mary Grace's mother. Her voice sounded high-pitched and young.

"It's Jane Goldman, next door," she said. "Mary Grace's over right now. I just wanted to say hi." There was a silence. "Well, the kids are having a lemonade stand, and well, I wondered if you have any plastic cups—"

She heard a deep intake of breath. "Stop," said Mary Grace's mother.

"Excuse me?" said Jane.

"She knows that she can get sweets from you. She needs to lose ten pounds. I don't want her to look ugly. Do you?"

"No!" said Jane. "Maybe she'd stay at your house if you actually talked to her—"

"I'm a good mother," said Mary Grace's mother. "I keep her clean. She minds her manners." There was the sound of growling. At first Jane thought it was the mother but then realized it was the family dog. "Stay away from her," said Mary Grace's mother, her voice rising, "Stop feeding her—"

Jane banged down the phone. "Dammit!" she yelled. She heard Mary Grace and her son laughing outside, and she knew that it would be the last time the girl would visit their house. It would be his first grief, the loss of a friend; it would tip like a domino against the losses to come. Mary Grace would have her own disappointments with her sour and careless parents, and the families would live side by side until this particular race was over.

Everyone—the children, the parents—were visitors on earth; they were here briefly, and then they would vanish. The children sat, stalwart, behind a plastic pitcher. The clouds broke apart, and sunlight fell upon them. She went and bought a cup for a dollar because she had no change. Others bought lemonade, too, with dollars, and the children still had no change, and within an hour they had ten dollars. The children were gleeful at their unexpected riches. "I will buy billions and billions of toys!" her son screamed. The baby, sitting on a blanket, crowed as she regarded them. The children stood around the table, counting their riches, over and over, counting their riches, over and over.

The Loan Officer's Visit

For the first sixteen years of my life, my father was a vigorous man. Once upon a time, he was almost a blur. But when he became ill, he spent half of the morning lying in bed with the curtains drawn. Then he put on a gray suit, walked gingerly to his Chevy, and sat at his desk at Great Mutual in Beverly Hills listening to people—some wealthy, some not—ask for loans to acquire boats, houses in Hawaii, expensive cars. He listened to the customers' excited and rambling descriptions of the trips they were going to take, the second homes they were going to decorate; he set up meetings with imaginary people at 3:00 PM so he could instead shut the door to his office, lay his cheek on his maroon couch, and close his eyes, trying to conserve the energy he needed to get to the end of the day.

He was never quite sure if he could make it to 6:00 PM; his superiors tried to be flexible, as he was a good closer, but he knew they had their limits, and he did not want to lose his job. He was a stubborn man, and he did manage to sit at his desk until the doors of the bank were locked, even if he was sometimes damp with sweat by the end, as though he had run a marathon.

Once, when I was seventeen, I stopped by his office and waited for a ride home. I sat on the couch in his office, the fabric the peculiar spongy consistency of an alien landscape. I always enjoyed watching the oddities who wanted money from the bank, or more personally, my father. That day, a couple thanked my father for helping them arrange a loan to furnish their necessary chalet in Switzerland. The woman wore spike heels that looked like they could puncture a rubber tire. The man, in a peculiar shiny blazer, nodded too often and gripped his gold pen as though it warmed his hand. My father smiled, asked innocuous questions about their vacation plans, indicated the *x*'s where they were supposed to sign.

—It's right at the edge of the Alps, the woman bragged. She glanced around, as though listening to applause from an invisible crowd. —You just walk out your door and hop on your skis. So simple! Fabulous!

I disliked this couple, not for their money, but for the casual acceptance of their freedom. My father laughed and shook hands with them; he was an excellent loan officer because he knew how to make them believe they deserved whatever they sought.

—Have a good time, he said to her. —Bon voyage.

That night, he drove me home. I was about to graduate high school and move off, oddly, to college in Arizona, a place I had applied to only because it was the one school that had sent me a brochure; this seemed a sign of something fortuitous. It was also the only college that had accepted me.

—Why do you want to go there? he asked. —What's there?

—I don't know, I said. I tried to think of something interesting. —Cactuses. Cacti.

—But what's wrong with here?

I looked through the windshield at Wilshire Boulevard. It was the mid-1980s, a rainy night, and the tall, gray marble buildings of the Wilshire Corridor gleamed in the damp clouds. The cars and their headlights trembling in long, pale streaks on the pavement, the streetlights green and red lozenges in the night.

I didn't answer.

—Look at everything we have here! Beaches! Museums! So why go?

The tenor of his voice made me not want to meet his eyes; it seemed in some way reasonable but not what I wanted to hear. I shifted around in my seat, silent because there was no good reason but that I was seventeen and somehow, here, it had become difficult to breathe.

—They offer good ceramics courses, I tried, lamely. —I would like to learn ceramics.

—Well, what do you want to be? he asked. —Doctor, lawyer, what?

—I don't know, I said. This question felt like a vise around my heart. —What did you think of that couple? The Swiss chalet ones.

—I have no opinion, he said.

—Come on, I said. —I know you do.

—Okay, he said, gripping the wheel. —They were silly. What do they need that chalet for? What do any of them need a second house for? I don't know.

My father lay in a shadowed room, sleeping like an infant, while I grew and grew. I strapped myself into a creaky plane and let it take me to college. Ceramics was full of extremely focused ceramicists, who were intimidating, so instead I tried biology, communications, European history, Korean literature, Portuguese, archaeology, becoming the sort of student who was the bane of guidance counselors.

I graduated, settled on the spectacularly jobless field of conserving Renaissance art, sent my résumés out to museums across the country, acquired jobs, hunched over rare paintings in museum basements, trying to return them to their former glory, lost the jobs when funding ran out, which it always seemed to do. I did not know where I wanted to go and let the paintings, the museums that needed me, pull me where I was needed, and eventually I found a man who wanted to marry me.

Years groaned by. My father was interested in learning what was happening in my life, and we spoke once a week, maybe twice. He woke up, parked as close as he could to the door of his office, walked inside and made loans.

—Describe the view out your window, my father asked me, when I was in Greenpoint.

—Cars parked on the street, I said, at twenty-seven. —Some people leaning against a hood, talking.

—Let me try to picture it, he said. —What kind of cars?

—Mostly American, I said. —Buicks. Explorers. Toyotas. One car has a big dent in the side.

—How big a dent?

—Maybe the size of a big steak.

—Hm. They should get that fixed.

—Well, I said. —How are you doing?

—We have a new bagel store that opened up down the street, he said. —Delicious. You have to come try some.

—What do they taste like?

—Uh. Salty. I prefer the cinnamon raisin.

—That sounds good.

My father and I clung to our phones, imagining.

A FEW TIMES A YEAR, I CAME OUT, AND WE SAT IN THE LIVING ROOM where the furniture never changed, sunlight coming through the orange drapes the same way it did when I was a child, the same translucence that had filled the room when my father had been strong, when he laughed and tossed me into the air as though I were a feather, nothing.

I brought my mother and father an apple from the corner grocer I went to in Brooklyn, a greasy donut wrapped in a blue paper napkin from Seattle, a camellia cut from our front yard in Richmond. Then, after a few days, I left, gripping the flimsy metal arms of the airplane seat, always waiting for the plane to pause, shudder in the air, and then start plummeting.

OVER THE YEARS, MY FATHER IMPROVED A BIT. HE WAS ABLE TO work more hours, and on good days, he and my mother went out to dinner and a movie. Then they found they could drive a few hours out of town to sit by a swimming pool and spend the night. My father discovered he could sometimes walk two blocks, but that was it.

He described his successes with a kind of self-deprecating wonder as though at any moment his improvements could vanish. When he told me that they had gone on a two-day trip, and that he had come back and gone to work with just one day of rest, I said, "That's wonderful." And when I hung up the phone, I got in the car, drove to Burger King, ordered two hamburgers and a large fries, and ate them right then. I hadn't known that I was hungry at all.

I started asking my parents to visit. I asked them to visit me in Tucson at eighteen, Seattle at twenty-four, Brooklyn at twenty-seven, Richmond at thirty-five. No. No. No.

—Why not? I asked.

—It's too far. I'm afraid I can't do it.

—Oh.

I had to ask the next question; I was too greedy.

—Do you want to try?

Long silence.

—Not now.

—When?

—Maybe someday, he said.

Ten years went by. Fifteen. Twenty. Twenty-five.

WE SAT, LOOKING OUT OUR SEPARATE WINDOWS.

THEN, ONE DAY, WHEN I WAS FORTY-THREE, MY FATHER SAID, SUDDENLY,
—Now.

—Now what? I asked; I had stopped hoping.

—We're going to try to come see you, my father said. —We're
getting on the plane. We'll try. Next week.

THE YEARNING FOR MY PARENTS TO COME SEE ME, TO BE ABLE TO
board a plane and come to me in a different city, another place, had
illuminated my life, a constant light burning in the distance. Now,
at forty-three years old, there was no knowing how to turn it off.
It seemed important somehow that the house was clean. I mopped
our floors, I washed the bathtub, bought some roses and set them
in a glass vase. I looked at the family whom I had, through no fault
of my own, assembled. They sprawled out on a couch, in the living room. They were living. They chewed gum. They had met my
parents before, I had packed them in a plane to show them off, but
they were happy here, in their natural habitat. We lived in one of
the suburbs near Richmond off I-95, one of those developments in
which newish brick houses, ringing a cul-de-sac, are designed to
look old.

I was at the airport two hours early. I waited. I stood with the
other waiting people, trying to ignore the Homeland Security crew
strolling a few feet nearby, checking bags, confiscating shampoo

bottles. The security crew was looking for anger when really the dangerous emotion was love.

—Flight 237 has just landed from Long Beach, the disembodied voice said flatly.

Flight 237.

I pretended to be casual, sipping a Diet Coke; there was a soft, distant march in my throat.

Then my mother and father appeared. Slowly. Them. They were themselves. They came through the tunnel. They came through the sour gray airport light, dressed casually, in pastel polo shirts and velour sweatpants, resembling ordinary tourists. My father raised his thin arms in triumph. He was pale, and there were sweat stains on his shirt. But he had made it. He was standing here.

My mother reached out to touch my face.

—You don't have to cry, she said.

My parents got into my car, and I drove them to their hotel, a bulky, cement Holiday Inn that resembled a dam. In the carport, there was a sparkling river coursing around a stand of longleaf pine that looked like a small, organized forest. Maroon-uniformed valets lurked around the pine trees.

—I'll check you in, I said. —You go wait in the lobby.

I watched them settle into some plush beige armchairs, and then I went to the front desk.

The lobby held the wonderfully false, cheerful odor of maple syrup, even though a coffee shop was nowhere to be seen. The concierge was done up in gold braid, as though he were part of an army for a cause that none of us were supposed to know. Two people. Mr. and Mrs. Kaufman. Welcome. Room 234. Queen bed. We have continental breakfast 6:00 to 10:00 AM.

How beautiful those words were, complimentary breakfast, queen bed!

Then I strolled—casually—over to the armchairs to hand my parents their room keys. My mind was already making plans. I imagined all of us here, for holidays, in Hawaii. By the time I got to the chairs, I had us all flying, driving around the country, the world.

But no one was sitting in the chairs.

Where had they gone? Was this the wrong set of chairs? In the other beige armchairs were a pair of excited hikers. I rushed around the lobby. Was this all a joke? Had I imagined their stroll in the airport? Had I driven no one to the hotel?

Turning, I smashed into a bellboy.

—Ma'am?

—Did you see a couple? Sitting in those chairs? They were there a second ago . . .

The bellboy stared at me.

—What did they look like?

—I don't know. Short. Gray-haired. Navy blue coat.

—How about them?

He pointed to a man and woman standing by the window. They were chatting happily, gazing out at a view of the parking lot. The man was wearing the same coat as my father. I ran over.

—My god! Don't run off like that! I didn't know where you had gone, I said.

—We're just looking out the window, my father said. He put his hand on my shoulder. —What do you see? he asked.

I looked outside; the light through the window was harsh, metallic. There were a couple hawks floating over the parking lot.

—There are some birds, I said.

—Can you believe we're seeing the same thing? he exclaimed.

He turned around. The light behind him was bright white. I

blinked and could not see for a moment; when I could, I thought my father looked peculiar. Suddenly, he appeared to be forty years old. His arms were slim but muscular in the navy coat. He was pert, stalwart as a captain of a ship, his eyes bright and devoid of any defeat. I had almost forgotten how that expression looked on his face. His skin was glowing, and his beard appeared to be dark brown. His teeth were absurdly white.

—What's wrong? he asked, innocent.

—You look different, I said, stepping back.

My mother turned to me; I gasped. In the hard, aching sunlight, she, too, appeared to have plummeted through the years; her hair was lush, dark, around her shoulders, and her face seemed slim as a deer's.

—I wish you'd cleaned the car, said my mother, smoothing her hair.

—It was clean, I said, a little insulted.

—Not enough, she said. —There was a cup.

—What cup? I asked.

—On the floor. Harold, what are you doing? Let's check out our room.

My father was standing by the window, practicing his golf swing. His arms gripped an imaginary club, they reached back, and *whisk!*

I walked with them to the elevator. I touched my arms, my face. Perhaps I had lost my grip on reality, but maybe it felt good to lose my grip. Maybe there was some comfort in having no grip; maybe that was even the answer. Gazing into the mirrored, gold-veined glass of the elevator, I could see that I was still myself, in my forties and worn and sinking south. I was afraid of scrutinizing them too closely; I liked the idea of them as these other beings. My mother tilted my father's face toward hers and kissed him at length. Thankfully, the elevator door opened.

—Time to get out! I called.

We entered their room. Silence.

—Bad room, said my father.

—Ugh, awful, said my mother.

—What's the problem? I asked, puzzled.

—Look!

I looked. It was a perfectly decent hotel room. There were mints perched on the swirly gold comforters. There was even a Jacuzzi tub in the middle of the room.

—Lucky you, I said. —You have a Jacuzzi.

—No, but we could trip over it! I can't see well at night.

—Call downstairs, Laura. Get it changed now—

My mother was already on the phone. Now, in the sour orange light of the bedroom, they were aged, familiar again. Their shoulders stooped slightly, my father shuffling across the room, his beard faded.

I WENT TO THE CAR, CHECKED MYSELF IN THE MIRROR, SAW NOTH-ing good, tossed the offending cup out of the backseat. After awhile, my parents descended. Now they were in room 126, with no problematic Jacuzzi. They walked, arm in arm, to my car.

—Now I want to show you our home, I said.

I drove for fifteen minutes. What a grand, peculiar sensation, driving my parents. In the various cities where I'd lived, as I cracked thirty and thirty-five and then forty years of age, I had harbored secret hopes of them being my children, of toting them around like this, offering snacks. Now I asked them if anyone would like a peanut butter cracker. This was not the sort of snack to which they were accustomed. However, they accepted them. I pulled up to our house to the sound of crackers being munched.

—Home! I said.

The children ran out of the house, as they had been instructed to do. Burst out of the front door, I said, run like your life depends on it. I had studied our neighbors on national holidays, the way in which they welcomed visiting relatives. They always ran out. Now my children ran out, and they were not acting, I could tell.

My parents clutched their grandchildren. Hello. Hello. You've grown so much. Hello.

They walked through the door of our house. Here was my husband, wearing a clean shirt, his hair neatly parted; he stood up, holding out his hand.

I brought them drinks in our finest crystal glasses. My parents sat in our living room. My mother rubbed her hand along the arm of the blue couch.

—That's the first couch I ever bought, I told them. —I got it in Seattle ten years ago. It was where Jeff and I first sat and talked and thought that perhaps we were interested in each other. We lugged it all the way across the country because it seemed lucky.

How strange the furniture looked, sitting here; it looked like it had been plopped here, without any concern for design or utility. In its randomness, there was, somehow, a sense of shame.

Perched on the couch, my mother brushed her hair. And now the hazy pinkish light of dusk was playing tricks on me. My mother was sluffing off years again! She wasn't the dark-haired, glossy being from the hotel, but now she looked to be around fifty, a little heavy around the hips, her hair graying with more force. I peered through the room's dim light.

—How are you doing this? Getting younger? I asked, alarmed.

—Well, thank you, my mother said. —I am using a new moisture cream.

She was scaring me. There was my father, walking around the room, also clocking in at about fifty, his eyes aglow, his stride buoyant, almost a swagger. He had never walked like this at fifty.

I sat down and rubbed my forehead.

—What do you want to do now? my father asked.

I had not thought this far ahead. Here were my parents, sitting on our old lucky couch, and, I thought, veering crazily from decade to decade, while the children ran around the living room and my husband lounged on a chair. It was too much, really.

—I'm making everyone dinner! I said.

The refrigerator was stuffed with foods I had made in preparation. I wanted to make up for thirty years of not having cooked for them. They wandered in.

—What are we having? my father asked.

—Beef Wellington, leek and pumpkin soup, raspberry granita for dessert.

—Is it low-sodium? my father asked.

—Uh, no, I said.

—Oh, he said. —Well, so what! Let's just celebrate.

They sat patiently and watched as I heated, stirred, poured, etc. The children set the table. The window flushed with the artificial heat. I wanted them to like what I had prepared for them. They waited patiently for their first course. I set the table with the sterling silverware we had received for our wedding. I understood, just then, that I had never set a table with it because no event had seemed important enough.

AFTER ABOUT AN HOUR, THEY WERE READY TO GO BACK TO THE hotel. I drove, hands trembling, afraid to leave them there for the night. They seemed reluctant for me to depart, too. My mother had a sudden, anxious craving for potato chips. My father wanted dental floss. They flipped through the hotel directory, wondering where to get these items. I went to the gift shop downstairs and purchased the chips and dental floss, and then they wanted to shoo me out. They were ready to enjoy their hotel room. I hugged them, feeling their slim shoulders under my hands, and left.

I wondered what age they would wake up in the morning. Sixty? Thirty? One hundred? Did they remember what it was to be forty, fifty? Their faces at that age were a blur to me. What did they look like before I was born?

My car passed the restaurants, businesses, movie theaters of our city. The developments carved out of pine forests, the office buildings, shadowed in the darkness, seemed like they could, at any moment, be stomped by a giant. Our home, bathed in little spot-lights, clung to its patch of lawn.

Was this all a joke? What was it?

Hurtling into the house, I found my husband calmly reading a copy of *Consumer Reports*.

—What are you reading about? I asked.

—There are good deals on lawn mowers, he said.

He sat on the couch, innocent and precious, eating some Cheez-Its, but I was now curdling with dissatisfaction and wanted to pick a fight. In his zeal to find a decent lawn mower, he had forgotten to check the dryer, which had wet clothes in it. Now the clothes smelled like wet dogs.

—I asked you to do this small thing! I burst out.

—No, you didn't, he said. —Why do I have to be the one to check the dryer?

—Why not you?

—You're being self-centered.

—No, you.

We sunk into one of those silent, glum familial nights in which every glass we rinsed seemed about to break, every lampshade unfortunate, our breath too loud and alien. We climbed into bed and I felt my husband's leg, a fine, muscular leg, a leg I knew very well, wrapped around mine, then rubbing against mine, and despite ourselves, our obstinate rightness, of course, all that followed.

This was all I had hoped for, all I thought I would be denied.

Afterward, I lay in bed and wondered how long any of us had to live.

THE NEXT MORNING, I SLID DOWN THE CHUTE OF OUR NORMAL activities—dropping the children off at school, washing the breakfast dishes. I took the day off from work and went to check in on my parents. My breath paused as their hotel room door opened. There they were, in their bright tourist garb, ready for their tour.

—Show us around, my father said.

I drove them around to the important sights in town. This was the museum where I was employed. This was the hospital where the children were born. This was the soccer field where our daughter won an award for best goalie. Here was the elementary school track where our son was first in a race in third grade. Here was the house of Benny Rosenthal, who had the birthday party everyone talked about for weeks, the party to which both children got an invitation. Here was the bar where my husband and I went the first night both our children were off on sleepovers. I went through sites of hope and triumph. Then I wanted to keep going. Here was the Olive Garden where my husband and I ate numerous garlic knots and had a stupid fight over the amount of time each was able to get to the gym. Here was the spot where our son, racing to keep up with Tony Orillo, tripped over a tree root and broke his leg. Here was the spot when that devil girl, Marie Swanson, said to our daughter, "Don't wear that headband. You copied me." Here was the corner where I learned the news that the Iraq war had started, the gas station where I got the call that my best friend had died in Tallahassee, the street where I realized that my hip was forever screwed, the field in which we lost our cat. Here was the place where I got the phone call in which you said you were going to visit me.

When we got through that, I just showed them foliage I liked. Here was an important bush. In the winter, it was dotted with pink camellias like knotted satin bows. Here was a sewage drain where orange leaves got clogged but looked pretty in the fall. Here was a stretch of pine trees that had not been knocked down for a housing development.

I kept driving and driving. I had pretty much covered the city, the joys, the defeats, the memorable foliage, and I wondered what was next.

—I think that's enough, my father said.

—What do you mean, that's enough? I asked.

—I've had it. We should go home.

—What do you mean, you've had it? Are you bored?

—What else are we supposed to see?

I didn't know how to answer that. Everything. I wanted them to see everything they had missed, the events, the recitals, the graduations, all. If they could turn back decades, why couldn't any of us? But they were not asking to turn back decades. They had probably digested the meal I had made for them, perhaps the last one I would make for them on this soil.

—I want you to want to see more, I said, softly.

I could not help this; I just said it. There was a lot I wanted to say. My father coughed, annoyed.

—I can't, my father said.

I looked back, and they were themselves again; my father, white hair wispy on his head, beige patches on his forehead, my mother, shoulders stooped, steel hair curled in a perm. They were old, and I was too, frankly, and I was ashamed because I had wanted this—just to see something different.

I drove the car, my palms damp, tight on the wheel. I wanted to apologize, for something—the crooked stubbornness of my existence—but I didn't.

—Take us back to the hotel, my father said. I drove them back to their hotel, taking the long way, and walked them up to their room. They would be here for about fourteen more hours.

—What else can I do? I asked; I felt like I was begging. —Do you want coffee, mints, magazines, what?

Now they were getting older before my eyes. I thought I could see the translucent white hair of eighty, the slow wither of ninety. I closed my eyes.

—Stop, I said, in a panic. I stepped forward and gripped his shoulder; I could feel the bone.

—Stop what? my father said. —What's wrong? I have to lie down now. Let go.

He reached forward and carefully peeled my hand from his shoulder.

I began, ridiculously, to cry.

—What's wrong? my mother said. —It's nothing new. He's resting. You know how it is.

—Yes, I said. —But.

—But what? Honey.

They stood, staring at me, somewhat bewildered. I pretended I was sneezing and started to edge my way out.

—Just pick us up at 9:00 AM for the airport, my father said. —Bye.

AT NINE, THEY WERE READY, WAITING WITH THEIR SUITCASES OUT-side the hotel, and I picked them up and drove them, slowly, to the airport. I tried to dawdle, go down unnecessary streets, engage them in conversation, but they were already melting from the visit, talking about the movies on the plane and how my father could best nap on the coach seats.

—Just drop us off, my mother said. —So we can go.

I dropped them off by the curb and spent twenty minutes try-ing to find a place to park. After I found a spot, I hurtled through the airport, looking for them. It felt important to say goodbye, this last minute they would be in this place where I lived. The flatly polite announcer shouted out gate changes. I was the obnoxious linebacker of the airport, knocking past suitcases, tripping over rolling baggage, bumping shoulders with the other passengers. My parents were standing in the security line, clutching their shoes.

—Here you are! I said, breathing hard.

—What are you doing here? my father asked.

—I just wanted—I don't know. To make sure you were okay.

—We're okay.

In their trim navy uniforms, the Homeland Security guys glared at me.

—Goodbye, honey, my mother said.

—Well, thank you for everything, my father said.

There was remoteness to their voices; they were moving on. We put our arms around each other, and I could feel their hands gripping my sweater. I stepped back, lifted my sweater off my shoulders, and handed it to them.

—Can you hold this a sec? I asked.

My mother took the sweater. My father grasped a sleeve. I looked at them, standing, holding my sweater. How small they looked, and, simultaneously, looming. Why had I moved away? Why had they not tried to come to see me earlier? Why had my father become ill? Why had I not been good enough to stay, and why had they not found a way to come? How long would we have, on earth, together?

My parents and I stood by the security gate in a sort of polite standoff. Around us was the anxious, determined roar of the airport, the passengers standing on escalators, their faces composed into travel faces, distant and with a sort of grandeur. To my surprise, my parents were assuming this expression too, and suddenly I could recognize it; it was a form of hopefulness.

The Homeland Security crew flanked the entrance to the metal detector.

—Come on through, one announced.

—We have to get going, my mother said. —My feet are getting cold.

They stood, barefoot, each clutching a boarding pass. And my sweater.

—Spit on it, I said.

—What! Your nice sweater? my mother said.

—I have to wash it anyway. Just do it, please.

They looked at each other, bewildered. Who was this weird child they had spawned? Then my mother, slowly, daintily, spit into my sweater. She passed it to my father, who leaned forward and spit, too.

—Okay, I said, somehow relieved. —Thank you.

We kissed again, lips touching cheeks, softly; then we released each other, and they walked through the metal detector, heading toward their gate.

The sweater smelled like them, their peculiar salt, their sweet fragrance. I did not know how long the sweater would smell like them, how long I would remember the way they gingerly walked inside the airport terminal, how long it would take me to drive home, holding onto the wheel, turning through street after street, how long it would take me to go visit them again, how long it would be before they died, and then how long I would own this sweater, how long I would recognize it as a sweater, how long my children would keep it after I was gone. I held onto the steering wheel, and I wondered how long before the tracks from the tires would disappear and it would be as though none of this, none of it, had ever really happened.

Refund

They had no contract. It would be a simple transaction. A sublet in Tribeca for the month of September. Two bedrooms and a terrace: $3,000.

They were almost forty years old, children of responsible middle-class parents, and they had created this mess out of their own desires. Josh and Clarissa had lived for twelve years in a dingy brick high-rise in the Manhattan neighborhood of Tribeca. They had been lonely, met, married, worked at their painting for years, presented their work to a world that was indifferent, floundered in debt, defaulted on student loans, began to lie to their parents about their financial status, and lived in a state of constant fear. They decided once to do miniature medieval paintings that no one would care about but themselves, for the art was just for themselves, anyway, or taking the other tack, decided to do something so deplorable it would have to sell for a truckload of money. They decided to go into pet por- traiture, which could fund their real art, and bought ads in local papers—whereupon they found that pet portraiture was a crowded field, and one in which the local masters were competitive and vengeful. In high school, she had wanted to have a painting in the Met. Now she was trying to figure out how to borrow paints from her artist friends and cleverly not give them back.

They lay in bed at five thirty in the morning, listening to their three-year-old son, Sammy, hurtling toward the first sunbeam with the call: "Hello. Ready now. Hello." The wistful, hopeful cry made their blood go cold. One of them stumbled toward the relentless dawn, inevitably tripping over the trucks that Sammy had lined up in hopeful parades, convinced that there was somewhere wonderful to go.

THEIR SUBSIDIZED LOW-RENT APARTMENT WAS LOCATED IN A SEV-enties high-rise where they had braved the abandoned, crumbling warehouses and hefty rats for a rent so cheap they could not afford to live anywhere else. But then the neighborhood changed. They were on the strip of land known as Tribeca, their building a few blocks south of Canal, six blocks north of the World Trade Center, and now there were lofts selling for $20 million, new restaurants with glossy, slim customers posed as though in liquor ads, movie star neighbors moving in such rarified circles they were never actually seen. The building owners were given government subsidies, which meant the tenants' rents were low, but the owner had said that he would buy out of the program the next year, and thus turn their low-rent apartments into million-dollar condos and effectively send the one thousand tenants out onto the street. Walking into their own building, they heard shrill arguments about the misbehavior of companion animals, feuds about laundry hoisted prematurely out of the dryer. The residents were on edge because they were doomed; Josh and Clarissa now skulked through their neighborhood with the cowed posture of trespassers.

SOON IT WOULD BE TIME TO SEND THEIR SON TO A PRESCHOOL. IN
the park sandbox, mothers talked about Rainbows, the most
expensive preschool in the area. Those who had been turned down
or could not afford the school spoke of it with a strangled passion.
One mother claimed she had stormed out when the director had
asked to see her income tax statement during an interview. But
another mother, whose son was a student there, leaned toward
Clarissa one day after admiring Sammy's exuberant personality
and said, "That's the only place where they truly treat the children
like human beings."

This statement had propelled Clarissa through the doors of
Rainbows to observe a class. The director, dressed in flowing, silk
robes and with large, lidded eyes that made her resemble a wood-
lands creature from a fairy tale, walked Clarissa through the airy
rooms. The director said that the children particularly enjoyed
"Medieval Studies," which apparently meant that the children
dressed up as kings and queens. Clarissa watched the children of
successful lawyers, doctors, executives, and various moguls stack
blocks, roll trucks, and cry. One child had tried to hand her a block.
When she smiled at him, a teacher gave her a laminated list of rules
for class observation. Number 5 was: *Do not engage with a child who
tries to talk to you. It interferes with their work.* She was ashamed that
she had smiled at the child, and that shame convinced her that the
school was the only place for Sammy to go.

"Ten thousand dollars," said Josh, "so that he can scribble?
No. No. No." She mailed in the application anyway—and when she
received the acceptance, she felt it was a sign of some greater good
fortune. Their son gazed at them with his beautiful, pure brown eyes,
his future gleaming, unsullied, new.

"At least visit the other schools," pleaded Josh, and she tried. At
one, she peered through a square window in a door to see a crowd

of children screaming to be let out. One child punched in a security code, a red light flashed, the door opened, and he shot out, to the roaring approval of the others. That was it. They had enough room on their Visa for the first tuition installment; they loaded it on.

Then Josh heard about a job for the two of them teaching art at a small university in Virginia, three weeks paid in September, accommodations for all of them in a hotel. They could hurl the money toward Sammy's tuition. Their apartment would be empty for a month. It occurred to them they could sublet their apartment and pay off part of their substantial debt load. "Let's charge a fortune," said Josh.

Josh's college friend, Gary, an investment banker, delivered the tenant to them. "I think you can get three thousand," he said. Their rent was $550 a month. Josh wrote the ad: *Fabulous Tribeca apartment. Two bedrooms, terrace. Three thousand for September.* Gary sent his friends a mass email, and the call came the next day.

"My name is Kim. Gary gave me your name. He says you have apartment to let. I live in Montreal, and I am looking for accommodations in the city for September."

"Right," Clarissa said. "Thanks for calling. Well, we're by the Hudson, beautiful views, wood floors . . . uh . . . we have a dishwasher." She paused. "Down the block," she said carefully, "is Nobu."

"No-*bu*," said Kim solemnly. There was silence. "I've known Gary for three years," Kim said. "We met in the south of France with his friends Janna from Paris and Juan from Brazil . . . we were in town for the day with the Beaujolais festival. We became friends. Now we follow the Michelin Guide all over Europe together. We have a race to see who has the most frequent flyer miles . . . I have 67,000, but he has more." She paused. "I want to go to Nobu. I want to go with my friend Darla. She is my best friend. I want to walk to all the restaurants there!"

"Now, it's not fancy," Clarissa said, alarmed.

"I want to walk to Montrachet!"

Kim wanted to send the money immediately; she magically wired $3,000 into their checking account, and that was that.

It was September 1. Kim held the keys to their apartment. They checked their ATM as they headed out of town. The three thousand dollars registered on their account. Josh whistled when he saw it. They drove toward a month's employment, a couple in front, a child in the car seat, across the bridges, out of the city. She and Josh held hands. Clarissa turned once to look back at the city, the skyline rising, glittering, frozen and grand in the clear autumn light.

SHE HAD DROPPED JOSH OFF TO LOOK AT TELEVISIONS AT BEST BUY when she heard the news on the car radio. Her body startled. Howard Stern's show came on, and the tone of the hosts was terrifying: lost and humorless. "We know who did it," said a caller, "and we need to go kill them."

Her hands were trembling, so it was difficult to grip the wheel. She raced back to the store, where the staff and customers stood, statues, rapt, in front of the television screens.

She stood with the group in the electronics section, in front of dozens of screens. They saw the Towers on fire. A giant tower buckled on the screen in front of them, frail as a sandcastle. Grown men around her yelled, No! in shocked, womanly voices. Sammy was immediately attracted to the picture. "Booming sound," said their son. She let him watch. "Booming!" he yelled.

THE FACT THAT THEY LIVED BY THE TRADE CENTER MADE THEM objects of concern. "I'm so sorry,'" said strangers. They stood, awkward, marked with an awful, bewildering luck. "Where would you have been?" asked someone eagerly, as though they had been potential victims and they craved an intimacy with the disaster. "We would have been one block away," Clarissa said. Her arms became cold. This admission felt strangely like bragging. It occurred to her that others thought they could have been dead. She remembered that they had signed Sammy up to attend the preschool on Tuesday/Thursday mornings. Around nine o'clock they would have been steps away, bringing Sammy to his first day of school at Rainbows.

The chair of the art department told them to take the day off, and they spent it in the hotel. It was stale and hot, full of a thousand strangers' breaths. She was not supposed to be here and did not know what to do with herself, grubby, ashamed, alive. The TV droned casualty estimates into the room. The curtains were drawn, and the room was dark. They tried all day to get Sammy to nap. He popped out of his room, awake, excited by their fear. "Hello!" he called gaily. "Hello."

Somehow, the day ended. They drove down the dark streets. Almost no one was on the road, and it seemed that everyone had fled to their homes. They passed the stores that resembled giant concrete cubes, Walmart and Target and Old Navy, the buildings strangely devoid of windows, like bunkers. Sammy screamed with exhaustion until he fell asleep. A student had said to them: providence had brought them here. "You have been blessed," the student said in a respectful tone, before inviting them to church. Clarissa declined, though she kept thinking about this. She asked Josh, "Do you think we were blessed?"

"No," he said. "We're not special. Don't feel special. It could be us next time. It could be us any minute."

She looked out the window. This was not the answer she wanted. "Why do you say that?" she said. "How do you wake up in the morning? How are you going to walk Sammy down the street?"

He reached for her hand. His fingers felt strange, rubbery; she clung to them, bewildered by the raw facts of fingers, hair.

"HELLO," SAID THE VOICE, AGGRIEVED, THREE DAYS LATER. "HELLO, Clarissa. It's me."

"Hello?" asked Clarissa. "Who is this?"

"I was on my way there. I wanted to go to the observation deck. I went the wrong way on the subway, or I would be dead. I got out, and there were all these people running. Then I saw the second plane. I started running, and then I couldn't get the windows closed because I've never seen windows like yours—"

"I'm sorry," Clarissa whispered. "I'm sorry—"

"They said there's a bomb under the George Washington Bridge!" Kim shouted. "I can't get the ferry to New Jersey, it's closed. Is there a heliport in Manhattan? I'll pay anything to get to a heliport. Can you tell me?"

"I don't know," said Clarissa, "I don't know where one is—"

There was a pause. "I'm leaving town," said Kim. "I can't stay here. And I want a refund. I want it all back."

ONE DAY BEFORE THEY LEFT VIRGINIA TO RETURN TO NEW YORK, Clarissa received an email: *IN REGARDS TO REFUND:*

> *I have not heard from you in regards to the status of my refund. Perhaps you are too busy to think of me now. All the hotels are giving refunds. Also free rooms in the future, suite upgrades. My pet peeves are injustice and dishonesty. I know when I am being treated fairly. You did not tell me certain facts about the apartment, which was, I am sorry to say, filthy. Black goo all over the refrigerator. I had to wear plastic gloves to keep my hands clean.*

Darla and I planned our vacation for a long time. We are best friends. We were going to buy the same clothes, go to the newest restaurants. People would admire us and say who are those glamour girls. Her hair is red and more beautiful, but I will admit I have nicer legs, we wanted to start a commotion.

I expect to receive payment of U.S. $3,000 within a week.

WHEN THEY GOT OUT OF THEIR CAB AT CANAL STREET, THE BOR-der between civilian New York and the war zone, they unloaded their luggage by the rows of blue police barricades. "Let's see your ID," said the state trooper, standing trim and noble in his brown uniform, surrounded by pans of homemade cookies. "Do you live here, or do you have reservations?"

They looked at him.

"The restaurants gave us lists of people who have reservations," he said, pulling out a piece of paper. They offered their driver's licenses, and the officer agreed: this was where they lived.

He offered to give them a ride to their building. The car floated by the gray, scrolled buildings, the streets deserted, simply a stage set, built quickly, then abandoned. The sky had become a pale, sickly orange and gray. There were too many police cars posted at corners; sirens pierced the warm air. There were American flags everywhere, as though everyone was desperate to have the same thought. People hurried down the streets, carrying groceries, pushing strollers; some were wearing surgical masks.

Kim had left in great haste, sheets piled in the living room, a pale lipstick in the bathroom sink. Clarissa picked up the lipstick and touched the tip; the color was a frosted pink. Sammy ran ahead of them. She thought that they should make some grand entrance, that they should say something profound to each other, but she merely listened to the sound of their presence ring through the apartment.

THERE WAS THE SMELL, UNLIKE ANYTHING SHE HAD SMELLED before. Burning concrete and computers and office carpets and jets and steel girders and people. There was nothing natural about the smell; it tasted bitter and metal in her mouth and blew through their neighborhood at variable times; the mornings began sweet and deceptive, yet the afternoons became heavy with it. She began to get a sore throat, and her tongue became numb. The girls at the American Lung Association table gave her a white paper mask and told her that there was nothing to worry about, but to keep her windows closed and stay inside. She walked against the small stream of people wearing paper masks. The streets were dark and shiny, the sanitation trucks spraying down the street to keep the dust from lifting into the air. A man walked by in a suit and a gas mask. Did he know something that they did not? Where did he get the gas mask?

She went out to the market the first morning after they returned. She pushed Sammy in his stroller downtown, heading straight toward the empty sky. In the market, she picked out cereal, detergent, apples to the pop soundtrack in the supermarket, the cheerful music that usually made her feel as though she were part of some drama greater than herself. Now it floated around her, impossible, but the supermarket did not shut it off.

When she ran into neighbors, anyone—Modesto, the maintenance man in the building, the counter man at the bodega, mothers from the playground—she moved toward them, the fact of their existence, her fingers like talons. It did not matter that she did not know their names. How are you, they asked each other, and it seemed like they were saying I love you.

"How are you?" Modesto asked.

"Where were you?" she asked.

"How is your apartment?"

"I'm glad to see you."

The meetings were hushed and tender, and then, with further discussion, she found that the neighbors had become deformed by a part of their personalities. The mothers who had been angry now were enormous, stiff-shouldered with anger; the mothers who were fearful were feathery, barely rooted to the ground. "Why do they close the park for asbestos," said one angrily, "when before it was just full of piss and shit?"

She stood with Josh, that first week, looking out their closed window at the lines of dump trucks taking the rubble to the barge. They sat, sweaty, greasy, in their living room, listening to the crash of the crumbled buildings as they fell into the steel barge. The swerve of the cranes sounded like huge, screaming cats, and when the heavy debris crashed into the barge, the sound was so loud they could feel it in their jaws.

They drifted quickly from their damp new gratitude for their lives to the fact that they had to live them. One week after their return, they sat beside the pile of bills that had accumulated. They sat before the pile as though before a dozen accusations: then Josh got up and went to the closet and brought out suits that she had not seen since he was in his twenties. She was startled when she saw him, the same slim figure, but now with gray hair. Suddenly, she realized that she had stopped looking closely at herself in the mirror. She dragged out some of the dresses she had worn fifteen years ago: stretchy Lycra dresses that clung to her skin. Now she looked like a sausage exploding from its casing. She had been hostage to the absurd notion that by acting young, she would not age. The part-time jobs, the haphazard routine, had kept them mired in a state of hope, which now made it difficult to get off the odd welfare state that was the adjunct, freelance, part-time job.

"We were fools," he said.

Clarissa looked at herself in the mirror. She tried to hold her stomach in.

"We have to get real jobs. We should have had them fifteen years ago."

"What about your art?" she asked. "We can cut back. We can eat beans more." He stared at her. "We can get another gallery, you're doing great work—"

She hated the tinny, rotting optimism in her voice. It had pushed them forward blindly, roughly, toward an imagined place where they would be seen for who they really were. She had wanted to walk through museums to see her work displayed on the walls. That sort of presence would, she had thought, cure her sorrow for her own death. But of course, it did not.

"We were idiots," he said.

They looked out the window at the smoke rising. His eyelashes were dark and beautiful. She remembered how when she married him, she hoped that their children would have those eyelashes, hoped that this loveliness would be protection against loneliness or cruelty. All of her previous thoughts seemed the musings of a fool. She rubbed her face, which was damp with sweat. Her mind seemed to have stopped. There was a short pause outside; the crane operators stopped for a moment of silence whenever they found part of a body. She looked out and saw one of the workers holding his hat. She opened a window. The bitter, metallic smell entered the apartment.

"Kim wants all her money back," she said.

He lifted his hands in bewilderment.

Dear Kim:

We are so sorry for your terrible experience. We are so glad you were not harmed. This is indeed a terrible time for the world. You did stay in our apartment for ten nights, *and I have calculated this stay, at current hotel rates, at $150 a night. We are also deducting a fee for cleaning the apartment, as you did leave a window open, letting some contaminated dust inside. This leaves you with a refund of $1,000. The first installment, in $20, will arrive in a week. Peace be with you.*

She took a deep breath and pressed "Send."

SHE TOOK SAMMY TO HIS FIRST DAY OF SCHOOL. SHE WALKED down the street, past the taped fliers. The local day spa was offering free massages for firemen and policemen. A neighborhood restaurant offered a $25 Prix Fixe, Macaroni and Roast Beef, Eat American. Donations to Ladder 8 for Missing Firemen accepted. Dozens of Xeroxed faces of the missing clung to lampposts, wrapped with tape; they stared into the street. Loving husband and father. Our dear daughter. Worked on the Eighty-seventh Floor. Worked at Windows on the World. Please call. She walked by them slowly, and she could not breathe. The missing people were on every corner. They were smiling and happy in the photos, and many were younger than her.

The preschool was a block north of the wooden police barricades that separated regular life from the crumbled heap of buildings, the endless black smoke. Her stroller rattled past them and through the doors of the preschool. The school staff floated around, greeting everyone with an unnerving intimacy, by their first names. Sammy darted into his classroom, and she stood with a cloud of mothers. They had walked to school under the smoky, foul skies, wearing leather coats in blue and orange. It seemed a paltry, mean decision, deciding what to wear, waking up and hearing the broken buildings falling into the boats. They had decided to dress up. Their hair was frosted golden and brown, and they were beautiful, and when they left, they cupped hands over their mouths.

"Have you gone out to dinner yet?" she heard one mother ask another. "You wouldn't believe the good deals down here, plus you can get reservations. Prix fixe at Chanterelle, thirty-five bucks, incredible, plus you have money for a good bottle of wine."

"The Independence has a special, Eat American," said another. "The waitstaff is fast and gracious. They have the most exquisite apple pie."

Clarissa closed her eyes and rubbed her face, wondering if she should admire these mothers' resilience or be appalled.

"We were refugees at the Plaza," she heard another mother say. "They had a special for everyone living below Canal. We had to go. Our place was covered in dust. We started throwing up, and I knew we had to get out. It cost a ton to get it cleaned. Should we stay or go? Can someone just tell me?" She whirled around, looking.

The teacher came by. "The children are doing well," she said. "Do you want to say bye before you go?"

Now Clarissa swerved through the room like a drunken person. Your child was not in the world, and then he was, suddenly, part of it. She crouched and breathed his clean, heartbreaking smell. "I'm going bye," she said.

Her child ignored her. Slowly, she stood up.

In the office off the main hallway, the in-house psychologist was holding a drop-in support session in which parents could talk about their feelings about sending their children to preschool three blocks from the site. Clarissa stood with the group clustered around the psychologist. One mother said, "My child screamed the whole way here, saying she was scared and didn't want to go, and I dropped her off, but then, well, I wonder, is she right to be scared?"

"Why is she right?" asked the psychologist.

"Well, because," called Clarissa, from the back.

"You have to believe it is safe," said the psychologist. "You tell them a kid's job is to go to school, and a parent's job is to keep you safe."

"But what if we don't know if it's safe?" Clarissa asked.

"Where is it safe?" the psychologist said. "Here? Brooklyn? Vermont? Milwaukee?"

The parents leaned toward her, awaiting an answer.

"You have to tell them a little lie," the psychologist said.

LATER THAT DAY, SHE RECEIVED AN EMAIL WITH THE SUBJECT: *STUNNED:*

I don't know how you decided on this number as a refund. It is very unfair. Who are you to decide how much money to refund me? You were lucky; I was the one who suffered. I was on my way there!

You did not tell me about the low water pressure or the scribbled crayon on the walls. Those facts would have made me not rent the apartment, and then I would NOT have been there. I thought you were my friend. Some friend. Do you even know what a friend is? Darla, my best friend, is kind to everyone, especially kittens. She once went to the animal shelter and brought her old Gucci towels to make the kittens more comfortable. I could see the attendants eyeing them! She told them to make sure the kittens took their towels with them to their new homes.

You left oily hairs in your hairbrush. I have your hairbrush. I have your Maybelline mascara. It is a horrid color. Who would put Maybelline on her eyelashes? Who would look good in navy blue? Are you trying to be younger than your age? You do not look so youthful in the snapshots on

*the refrigerator. You dress as though you think you are. You
should not wear jeans when you are in your late thirties. I
don't care if it is a bohemian sort of thing, it is just sad.*

*I am requesting $3,000 plus $1,000 for every nightmare
I have had since the attack, which currently totals twenty-
four. You owe me U.S. $27,000, payable now.*

JOSH FOUND A JOB AS AN ILLUSTRATOR AT AN ADVERTISING FIRM,
and each morning he sprinted down their hallway toward the office
that gave him a new life. Sammy would not say goodbye without giving his father one of his toys to keep during the day. "Take one toy,"
Sammy said, thrusting a tiny plastic dinosaur or little truck into the
pocket of his father's suit. One morning, Sammy could not decide
which toy he wanted his father to have to remember him, and when
Josh finally had to leave, Sammy began to wail. He began to race after
his father, and Clarissa had to grab him. "Daddy will be back later,"
she said in a strained, cooing voice. "We'll see him later . . ."

He looked at her as though she were a fool.

One morning she tried to distract him by walking up to SoHo
to see which artists had shows up. She peered at one gallery, where
a member of the staff had expressed interest in her work, but had
then vanished in an abrupt, unexplained departure. Another young
woman, perhaps ten feet tall, wearing the monochrome dark outfits
all the gallery staff wore, came over. Sammy was butting his head
against the glass door like a small bull.

"I'm sorry, but he can't come in," she said.

Her face was perfectly blank, which Clarissa wanted to see as a
personality deficiency, but which was instead an adaptive expression
to New York and the desperate artists who banged on this gallery's
door. Sammy lurched forward. The girl blocked the door. "Sorry,"
she said, sounding strained. "Ma'am—"

Clarissa grabbed Sammy. She bumped into an American flag that was hanging from the door.

"God bless America," said the girl, quickly.

"Come on," Clarissa said to Sammy. "I'll get you a ball."

She bought him a small red ball, and they passed the local park where they had spent much of their time before the attack. It had been beautiful, children playing under large green trees, honeyed patches of sunlight. Now the plants in the garden had been flattened after people raced, terrified, over them. The park had been closed briefly to clean up asbestos contamination. Sammy hurled his new ball into the park and darted in, chortling with joy. His ball was rolling to a garbage bin that said, NO PLAYING ON OR AROUND THIS CONTAINER. On the trees were flyers: EPA IS LYING. TOXIC DUST EVERYWHERE. UNITE!

"No!" she yelled. "No more ball."

She grabbed him by the waist and lifted him. He scratched her, leaving two red lines on her arms. He kicked. She struggled to find a way to hold him so that he would not hurt her, but he was wild. His scream vibrated through his Elmo shirt. She did not know how to protect him from the world. When he was older, he would not remember the Towers. She envied his ignorance, longed for it.

"Hey!" someone called. It was a kindly park janitor. "I got your ball for you," she said.

"It was by that bin, you're not supposed to touch it," said Clarissa.

The janitor looked at her. "You can just wipe it off," she said. She took a Kleenex from her pocket and wiped the ball. Clarissa wondered what sort of person would live with their child in a toxic zone, beside police barricades encircling targets of violence. She shuddered, for that sort of person was herself.

"That's just where they keep the rat poison," said the janitor, cheerfully.

"The rat poison," said Clarissa, numbly. She had never thought the term *rat poison* would sound nostalgic, but she was strangely calmed.

DEAR CLARISSA:

You have forgotten about me. I have not forgotten about you. You were lucky. You were out of town. I had to endure your apartment. I can still feel the dirt on my skin. I cannot believe that you keep a child in that filthy apartment. You cannot control him from drawing on the walls. Furthermore, his drawings do not even show any artistic merit.

This is a pathetic way for someone who is thirty-eight to live. I figured it out. I have ten more years of life over you. Ha ha! This is how I wanted to spend it: wake up, go to the top of the building, look out and take pictures with my new camera, come down, go to lunch at Nobu, walk around SoHo, buy something for my husband, go look at the shoes at Prada, have tea at the Plaza, jet off to Zermatt, stop in London. I want it all. I have the good taste to appreciate what is worthy in life.

My refund is U.S. $29,000, payable now.

DEAR KIM:

Don't try to pass the buck to me. You lived. You were lucky. Do you know what we were doing when you were here trying all the restaurants? Working. We are always working. We never rest. Do you know how many jobs I've had in the last year, trying to make some money and make time for my art? Fifteen. Do you know how close I came to getting a review in the Times? The guy came and loved my work. The word he used (and I heard him) was "groundbreaking." Then

along came this woman who videoed her own vagina and
played the video to the soundtrack of The Sound of Music.
There was room for just one review, and she got it. It was a
good one.

I am considering the refund and the appropriate amount
considering the fact that we should all rise above ourselves
during this terrible time. Peace be with you.

EACH MORNING, WHEN SHE WALKED SAMMY INTO RAINBOWS, SHE
first felt an exquisite rush of relief. Sammy jumped out of the stroller
to a cream-colored room scented like oranges, inconceivably sweet.
"Hello, Sammy," the teachers said, as though he were a visiting digni-
tary. "Sammy's here. Hello, Sammy, hello."

They allowed him into this beautiful room and waved at her,
expecting her to walk out to continue her own life. She looked at the
street, and she did not know where she could go. The hallway was
mostly empty. She sat and watched the children play.

The mother who had been a refugee at the Plaza was heading
a committee to raise money for tuition lost when parents withdrew
their children. She was taking a poll in the hallway regarding how
much to charge for the tickets to a benefit. "I'm thinking something spectacular. Monte Carlo night. Dinner, casino, a silent auc-
tion. Do you think people would pay fifty, one hundred, or two
hundred per ticket?"

"I would pay one thousand," Clarissa said.

The woman looked right at her. It was as though Clarissa had
told her something wonderful about herself. "Yes," she said, softly.

DEAR CLARISSA:

It is not my concern that you never rest. You cannot get
the money from me. It was your choice to pursue this "job"

of artist. Why would I owe you anything? You were not hon-
est with me. Honesty is the best policy. When Darla left her
husband, she told him that she could not stand his skinny
legs. That was just something she felt he should know. We all
have our limits. The knowledge might have helped him in his
later dating life. You should have told me about the water
pressure, scribbled crayon, hallway odor, broken TV, use-
less air conditioner. Why didn't you? I expect U.S. $31,000,
payable now.

THERE WERE NO MORE EMAILS. AT NIGHT, CLARISSA LAY BESIDE
Josh, awake, listening to the wild screaming of the cranes.

On October 30, she sat down and wrote a check for $263.75.
There was no reason for this amount except that it was what they
had left in their bank account that month. She did not know what
to write on the note, so she scribbled, quickly, *Here is your refund.*
God Bless.

HALLOWEEN WOULD BE SAMMY'S LAST DAY AT THE SCHOOL. THE
bad tuition check for $2,000 had been sent a week before, and she
wanted to stop showing up before they could ask her about it. Sammy
dressed as a lion. All the children were in costume. A few mothers
were loitering in the lobby, captivated by the sight of their children
pretending to be something else. Sammy's class was populated with
two miniature Annies, a Superman, a ballerina, three princesses,
some indeterminate sparkly beings, a dog, and Sammy, a lion. The
teacher read them a Halloween story, speaking to them as though
she believed they would live forever. The children listened as though
they believed this, too. Clarissa pressed her hands to the glass window that separated the parents from their children; she wanted to
fall into the classroom and join them.

After school, she wanted to buy Sammy a special treat. She brought him a blue helium balloon at a party store. He marched down the street, grinning; she lumbered after him, this tiny being with a golden mane and tail. Suddenly, Sammy stopped and handed her the balloon. "Let it fly away," he said.

"I'm not getting you another," she said.

"Let if fly away!" he shouted. "Let it!"

She took the balloon and released it. The wind pushed it, roughly, into the air. Her son laughed, an impossibly bright, flute-like sound. Other people stopped and watched the balloon jab into the air. They laughed at Sammy's amusement, as though captivated by some tender memory of themselves. Then the balloon was gone.

"Where is it?" he asked.

"I don't know," she said.

Her child looked at her.

"Get it," he said.

A WEEK LATER, SHE PICKED UP THE PHONE. "TWO HUNDRED AND sixty-three? How did you come up with this number? You owe me $54,200, why don't you give me money?"

"Why do you keep bothering us?" Clarissa asked.

"You were lucky," said Kim. "You weren't where you were supposed to be."

"You weren't either," said Clarissa. "You went the wrong way—"

"Maybe it wasn't the wrong way. Maybe the Towers were the mistake. Why would I have wanted to go there, anyway? Maybe I was supposed to meet someone there, and they never showed up. What do you think of that?"

Clarissa felt cold. "Were you supposed to meet someone there?"

"Would I get my $54,200?"

"Were you meeting someone there?" asked Clarissa. "Were you?"

"She is named Darla," said Kim.

"Why didn't you say this?" asked Clarissa.

"Will you pay me money?"

Clarissa's throat felt hot.

"I was talking to her on my cell phone," said Kim. "She was on the elevator to the observation deck." She paused. "She wanted to go to the Empire State Building, but I thought at the Towers we would get a better view."

What did one owe for being alive? What was the right way to breathe, to taste a strawberry, to love?

"Kim," said Clarissa, "I—"

"Do you know how long I'm going to charge you?" Kim said, her voice rising.

Clarissa closed her eyes.

"Do you know?" said Kim.

This Cat

Let me say at the beginning: it was not the cat's fault. We were at the PetSmart adoption carnival to buy a pet; we had that look of determined acquisition. A cloud of cat rescue people came upon us, presenting their candidates. They started with their hopeless cases. The blind cats. The ones that had tested positive for feline leukemia. The one missing an ear from a fight. The children looked upset. They just wanted a nice cat.

Nice? We have nice. This one is nice but it has six toes. And cat herpes. But that just means it has a runny eye. Give it vitamins.

—That one, said the children.

The cat was skilled at being adorable, stretching and yawning with a tiny squeak. That did it; the children were sold. They were ten and six; by this time, they had stored up enough love to offer it to another being. They mauled him, patting him, making guttural sounds of affection. He was, thank god, tolerant. He stretched again, made that yawn, and I was suddenly, unexpectedly tearful.

—We'll take him, I said.

He was small enough to fit into the crook of my arm, like a football. I had, in fact, asked for him, though I blamed it on the children, who liked the fact there was someone here more powerless than they. They pressed their faces into his black fur, which was so soft it felt as though you were melting into him. We could not come up with an agreed-upon name. Furry. Fluffy. Midnight. Alan. Fred. Licorice. None seemed quite right. We decided that we would name him later. Now he was just The Cat.

In the morning, they went off to school in a big rush, after they had treated us, the parents, like dirt. They were beautiful and holy and problematic. Do you want cereal? No. Can you brush your teeth? No. Can you make your bed? No. The boy rushed upstairs, in a sly, efficient way, to root out the Nintendo where we had hidden it. The girl ate her cereal with slow, elegant mouthfuls, as though we were her servants and school for her would start at 10:00 AM instead of eight. Why did we keep bothering them, and why did we have to rout them into this glaring, strange thing, a day?

When they were finally out of the house, I took the cat into my arms. I felt purring under his thin ribs. His stomach was as soft as a balloon filled with water. He looked at me with tenderness, me, his savior. There was a familiar fullness in my breasts, a sense of heaviness, dropping, a sensation I had not felt in six years. The cat was looking at me with a pert, intelligent expression. It knew. The fullness got worse.

I wasn't sure what to do about it; I lifted my shirt and squeezed the right breast. A droplet came out of my nipple. I imagined the cat opening its tiny mouth and latching on. His little paws would bat gently against my arms. It seemed a pure impulse, not strange at all. It seemed perfectly natural.

I WAS A LITTLE BIT PROUD OF THE DROPLET, AS THOUGH IT REVEALED my great prowess as a mother. It had been six years since I nursed an infant, but I could still do this, even if I was closing in on forty-five. Frankly, at this point, I was a little desperate for things to be proud of. But perhaps I was getting younger in some miraculous way. I passed this information on to my gynecologist the following week. She grew pale.

—What? she asked.

—There was a drop.

—Was it bloody?

—No.

—Was it discolored?

—No.

—We have to get this checked out.

She scribbled something on a sheet.

—Go to Havensworth Radiology tomorrow, she said. —We'll figure it out.

The appearance of the droplet, my apparently perverse desire to nurse the cat, led to a battery of painful tests. I went to Havensworth Radiology center, a giant building full of various X-ray machines. People gathered in the various sections. Knees. Lungs. Breasts. No one looked happy to be in Breasts. The waiting area for the Breast region was decorated in muted greens and blues, clearly designed by someone whose assignment was: create an environment so that patients forget they could lose their breasts or die. The technicians' voices were too calm. Come here, dear. Put your breast on this ledge. We will squish it so it resembles a flattened donut and take a picture. Let me leave the room while the machine floods you with radioactive waves. Thank you. Let's take another. The room flashed its poisonous light.

DRIVING HOME, I NOTICED POLICE CARS EVERYWHERE. I WAS NOW aware of them, floating in their calm and menacing way, down the street. I saw the bulky cars, their metal bodies, the officers inside in their buggy sunglasses. There were no apparent crimes in the city, but they were following me. They were. I gripped the wheel, feeling guilty. I was not young anymore, yet I had many desires, one of which was my yearning to nurse the cat. What did this mean, besides the fact that the gynecologist wanted to diagnose it? The police cruised by, circling.

I got home and resumed normal activities. The cat pretended he had no part in this. He trotted around, arrogant and tiny. I followed him. I waited for the phone. I wanted to hear some good news. But no. There was a call from the school principal, who wanted to talk about our son.

—Something good? I asked, hopeful. —Is he doing well in math? Silence.

—Then what?

—There have been accusations, he said.

—Of what?

—Thievery.

Was this a word?

—Come in tomorrow.

I hung up the phone. The cat coughed and leapt upstairs, two stairs at a time.

THE NEXT STOP WAS THE BREAST SURGEON. THOSE WERE TWO WORDS I did not want to hear in the same breath. She decorated her office with a poster that said, horrifyingly: *Courage.* I did not want to have courage. Who needed it? I wanted Shallowness. Materialism. Sloth. I did not want to be dignified. The surgeon sauntered in. She was young, wearing a ponytail, and looked glossy and trim, as though she had just come from aerobics.

—A droplet? she said. —Can you show me?

I squeezed. There was another. Now I did not look at it so fondly.

—We just got a kitten, I said.

—What type? she asked.

—A very cute one.

—I see.

—Do you have children? I asked, wanting to bond in that way.

—No.

She was kneading my breast as though she were a baker.

—Do you have a pet? I asked.

—I have an iguana, she said.

What kind of emotion can *that* elicit? I thought. An iguana seemed a cold, silent thing.

—I made mistakes raising them, I said.

—Oh, she said.

—I ignored them when they wanted things. I didn't set limits. They hit each other, sometimes with objects. Now there are calls from the principal.

She had an expression on her face. It could have been admiration, or it could have been concern.

—Does your iguana do any tricks? I asked, trying to be cordial.

—We need a biopsy, she said.

NOW THERE WAS FEAR. IT WAS A COLD, SOUR FEAR, INVADING MY skin. I could not get it out. I opened the car windows, which did not help. That fucking cat. What had it wrought? Why this, now? When I got home, I picked it up, gripped its small, thin body. I was afraid to hold him for too long. What would happen next? Where would this embarrassment stop?

The cat was following me, I told my husband, that night.

I did not tell him about the droplets. It would be a stupid secret between the medical personnel and me. The news would not go over well, anyway; he was busy at work. Perhaps he was having an affair. It would make him more understandable if he were having an affair. It would clarify everything. As it was, there was a general gray haze of distraction. He wanted to get away from us. He was in a hurry, to get out of the house, to go to the gym, to flee. He wanted, at midlife, hey, at early life, as we all do, to be somewhere else.

—He's hungry, he said. —Just give him more kibble.

We fell into each other with a kind of relief, that we could find each other through the blind, sweaty maze that made up our days— we were startling, an oasis. The children slept in the other room, moral and forceful as parents; they could not discover us. I locked the door and put a chair against it, for good measure. We had invited them into the world with this act, and now we wanted to keep them out. His hands felt my breasts; he detected nothing; with the deepest gratitude, we held each other down.

I did not tell him the news about the call until we were finished.

—The principal called, I said. —There was thieving.

—Thieving? Of what?

—He didn't say.

I wanted to just lie there beside him, pretending we had only this to deal with. I rubbed his arm; it was hard as an apple; it looked no different than it had when we met fifteen years before, but its ability for combat would soon reach its limits.

—It's nothing, my husband said, reaching and lifting a piece of hair from my forehead with an unwarranted tenderness.

—Don't worry about it, he said. —It's nothing.

THE GRIM WALK INTO THE PRINCIPAL'S OFFICE. I SMILED AT OTHER parents in the hallway, as though we had been invited here for another sort of conference. Invited. We all wanted to be invited to hear a beautiful future. We wanted the school principal to know more than we did. He would tell us that our child had been identified as supremely gifted and would be shot through a funnel to glorious success. Your child is particularly admired by his/her classmates. Your child . . . but no. We were here for the other conference. The bright fluorescent bars in the ceiling spat and buzzed. My husband's hand was a knot in mine.

We said hello to the principal. He was worn out as a piece of flannel. Our son sat in a chair, not wearing his cleanest shirt. Was that his fault or mine? Hi, our son said, his eyes travelling the ceiling; he pretended not to know who we were.

—Well, said the principal. —I am sorry to say that your son has been thieving. Here's a list. A donut, a pen, $2.25. And the crowning glory, the teacher's diamond bracelet. Wanda Jenkins found it in his desk.

I wondered if the principal could run the school effectively because he used this word: *thieving.*

—Could this Wanda have slipped it into his desk by accident? I asked.

—No. She saw it in there. Other kids did, too.

The principal clasped his hands as though he were trying to hold himself from some other frenzied movement. We all did; we were the epitome of politeness.

—So. Do you understand the seriousness of this?

Our son was frozen. His head barely moved. He was this other thing now, a defendant, and he took to it like a character in a movie. We all sat there, perched on our chairs in this moment of history. We were barely real.

—What do you say? asked the principal.

—I didn't do it, said our son.

—But you did, said the principal. —We have proof.

—What did you want? I asked our son.

He assumed a blank expression, as though he did not understand this question.

—I don't know, he said.

This was not the right answer, for the principal said, —He has to go home.

—You mean we have to take him home? Now?

—For two days.

—But we have to work—

—Sorry. You have to figure that out.

—We'll replace everything, said my husband. —Even the donut.

THE DRIVE HOME WAS NOT FUN. SILENCE EXCEPT FOR OUR OCCAsional outbursts. Why? And why the donut? Don't we feed you enough?

We got home and sent our son to his room. It was a dumb solution, but what else could we do? He ambled there, shoulders drooping. He was so obedient I was somewhat touched. My husband and I stood, startled to find ourselves here at midday with our boy in the house.

—You call in sick at work, I asked my husband.

—No. You.

He did not know that he was being insensitive.

—I want Mom, our son called.

—Me? Why me?

—I just do.

I called into work. I lied, said I had a sore throat. If only. My supervisor sounded envious. A sore throat. Why did I get to stay home?

—You can get sick next, I told her, and then I felt guilty for saying this.

The cat kept following me. He was in a merry mood, as though he sensed an opportunity; intent on displaying his cuteness, jumping up and twisting in the air as he batted at a moth. I went into our son's room, closed the door, and sat down next to him.

—What happened? I asked him. —What did you want?

—I don't know.

—Did you want to be important?

—What?

He scratched his neck.

—Did you feel ignored? Bullied?

—No.

I could still see the imprint of the infant face in his current one, a perplexing shadow.

—Then why did you do it? I asked.

—I just wanted it. The donut had sprinkles on top.

He smiled, oddly joyful.

—Mom. Guess what. I can do a Heimlich.

He leaned forward and hugged me so hard I was breathless. I wrapped my arms around him and did not want him to let go. He smelled a little rank, like wet sand. It was the smell of future adulthood.

—Honey, I asked. —Why are you so happy?

—I like sitting here with you.

THE BIOPSY. THE SAME CALM BLUE COLORS IN THE WAITING ROOM. It was as though all the doctors had consulted the same color therapist. The magazines were carefully selected to contain no news of any sort. Interior decorating and cooking appeared to be the only subjects in the world. Other people waiting here wore glazed expressions or were chatting happily, pretending they were at a bus stop.

I was escorted to the patient room, also blue. I was sitting there when the breast surgeon walked in.

—Ready? she asked.

—For what?

She prepared her needle. The nurse gently put her hand on my arm.

—How is your iguana? I asked. I wanted her to tell me something wise.

—He did the sweetest thing, she said.

There was the needle, and there was pain; I was sweating.

—Easy, said the breast surgeon. She was drawing out something.

—You're doing great! said the nurse. She puffed out her cheeks. She said, —Take a deep breath.

—What did the iguana do? I asked, between breaths.

—Oh. His name is Blinkie. Because he never does. So. I was putting some lettuce in his cage, and he was chewing it, and he looked up at me and, I think, smiled.

The breast surgeon was suddenly eager to share.

—It was just a reflex, she said. I've studied medicine. I know that. But, you know, there was something, I don't know. Giving. You know?

—I know, I said.

—It just can't help it, she said. —You know?

—Yes, I said.

She applied a bandage to my breast.

—I'll tell you the results tomorrow, she said. —Early afternoon. I'll call you.

It was like a date, the way she said it. But so much less joyous.

—I'll be waiting, I said.

I CAME HOME WITH MY SECRET BRUISED BREAST AND LET MYSELF sink into the muck of self-pity. What the hell was going on? Why me? Why not my friend, my boss, my neighbor? Not me. The cat was following me. He coughed a couple times, a tiny, almost satirical sound, and when I held him, he stopped coughing. His heart beat, small, miraculous, against my palm.

The next morning, I was waiting. I was waiting when I poured the children their cereal, I was waiting when I kissed my husband goodbye, I was waiting when I watched the children run from the car to their classrooms, I was waiting when I sat down with my coffee at work, I was waiting when I came home to pick up my lunch, which I had forgotten. I was not present for anything at all.

I walked into the kitchen and saw the cat lying in the corner; from far away, I thought that he was sleeping.

However, the cat was not sleeping. He was dead.

I knew this fact in one second. My heart went cold with the shock at the presence of a dead thing. There was no blood, no vomit, nothing; he was merely curled in the corner, suddenly as lifeless as a teapot or fork. The cat. I thought it was a prank, but it was not a prank; he was, in fact, dead, dead, dead. I saw him and knew everything.

I was weeping before I touched him. He did not feel like himself; there was that horrible, stark hardness. I called the people at PetSmart.

—How old was he? asked the unlucky sales associate who picked up the phone.

—Maybe three months. I got him at the adoption carnival.

—Are you going to want a refund? he asked, tentatively.

—No! I just want to know what happened.

—You never know about the adoption carnival, said the sales associate. —Some of those cats have fatal diseases, you know, and they don't show up until you've paid your eighty bucks.

—How did this happen? I asked.

—You gave him food, right? asked the sales associate.

—Yes!

—Was there any poison in the house?

—No!

I was crying. I heard the sales associate start to panic.

—He coughed a few times, I said.

—We can get you another cat, said the sales associate, quickly.

—Uh. We also sell coffins.

I made him listen to me cry a little longer.

—Ma'am, said the associate, now sounding a little irritated, — You know, you can get another cat.

—I want this one, I said. —Don't you understand? This cat.

I WRAPPED THE CAT IN AN OLD DORA TOWEL THAT THE CHILDREN now found appalling. Then I moved him to the backyard and sat with him until the children got home. I sat in the yard, beside him, this small lump in the Dora towel, for it somehow was important to sit beside him. I was close enough to the house so that I could hear the phone.

There was that fullness again, now sad and useless.

THE CHILDREN CAME HOME FROM SCHOOL, BICKERING. WHAT A luxury their arguments were! She stepped on my foot! He ripped my drawing! The arguments were endless, borne out of the mere boredom of existence. I gave them popsicles and waited for them to ask.

—Where's the kitty? our daughter asked.

—Something bad happened, I said.

They looked at me with their small, perfect faces, always ready for some news. I did not want to say it, to ruin everything.

—The cat, I said. —He's dead.

I watched their faces, curious what they would do. They did not have a facial expression ready to deal with this. Their mouths were open, slack with disbelief. Death always seemed like a joke. They ran around the yard, looking for the cat. They called all of the names that we tried.

—I'm sorry, I said.

I showed them the shroud, from far away.

—That's not him.

—It is. Trust me.

—No it's not.

They wanted, like little scientists, pure and irrefutable proof. Before I could stop them, they ran over, and our daughter lifted the towel a little and jumped back. A shriek. I ran toward them and brought them to the patio, away from the cat, which was now not the cat they had known. I held them as they sat, absorbing this.

They asked, —What happened? over and over, as though this question had the power to reverse time. It was a stalwart, beautiful question that did nothing.

WE SAT IN THE GLARING SUN; THE AIR PRESSED DOWN ON US LIKE lead. It was my job to carve a route out of this, though maybe not out, maybe that was not possible, but around. Around this.

—Maybe we could make him a memorial, I suggested.

This cheered them up! A memorial! They loved the idea. Let's do it! We would pay tribute to the dear unnamed cat. We dug a hole in the backyard, dirt flying. They were flushed and chatty and helpful. The children suddenly believed in an Egyptian theory of the afterlife and wanted to throw in anything the cat would find helpful in an alternative existence: the ball he chased; a handful of kibble; an old sweater; a spoonful of tuna; a poem.

—I'm getting him a blanket! So he won't get cold!

—I'm getting him some cat litter!

They rushed back and forth from the yard to the house, collecting items. The yard was green and shadowed and lush. I could almost taste all of this; I wanted to taste the pale, thin light filtering through the leaves and the blue sky above me and the children's golden arms. In the house, far away, the phone rang. The children grabbed flowers from bushes and arranged them artfully around the cat's grave. They began to pick up handfuls of dirt and throw them into the hole. Their palms were gray and chalky. The children didn't understand any of it and they did, completely. The phone rang again.

The children finished their memorial. They turned to me, hands empty and open. Now they didn't know what to do. They ran to me, their faces aglow with sorrow and triumph at what they had made.

—Mom, they said.

—Yes?

—Now what?

Now what. The phone stopped ringing. It was quiet for a few minutes. I sat on the grass. They did, too. I sat with them, listening to the soft sweetness of our breath. We gazed at the pure, dark trees, and we had but this, this one moment, and the next.

—Listen, I said.

—To what?

—The air.

We listened to the air, to the gorgeous, peculiar sound of nothing. We could hear anything in it; that was our revenge. We could sit there, each moment, and listen.

Inside, the phone began to ring again.

—Mom. Did you hear that? my son asked.

He looked at me, waiting. I did. I was held by the moment; I knew it would lift me to the next one and the next. I let it lift me to my feet. Then I went inside to pick up the phone.

A Chick from
My Dream Life

I loved helping my sister Betsy hide her bad hand. In the morning, she'd be standing on the side of the bathtub, looking at her body in the bathroom mirror. "Make it fashionable," she'd say. I'd flip through my tube tops, finding one the same color as her swimsuit. Betsy examined her tan lines or put on Sea Coral lipstick because she thought that was right for the beach. She ignored me when I pulled her bad hand—the one with no fingers—toward me and put a tube top over it. She liked tube tops because they hid her hand completely and made her look like she was carrying something bright. "Maybe tape it shut," I said. "Or paper clip it. And bunch it at your wrist. There." Betsy would hold the tube top up and examine it. "Cool," she said. I smiled, the expert.

My parents were the ones who started helping Betsy hide her bad hand. After my mother hemmed the bottom of Betsy's coats, she would sew the extra material to one sleeve. Betsy always had sleeves that were too long for her. I thought all her coats looked like they were coming alive and taking over her body. My mother took forever with those sleeves. I hated watching her with Betsy. Because of her hand, Betsy possessed my parents in a way that I did not. Sometimes when I played with Betsy, I pulled my coat sleeves down over my hands; but the sight of me with gigantic hands always seemed to annoy my mother. "You don't want to look like a waif," she said, and she rolled my coat sleeves all the way to the elbow.

Helping Betsy with her bad hand was the only thing I could do right that summer. Betsy was only eleven, a year younger than me, but she had become pretty. The sun went into her skin, and she held it easily, her hair, knees, glowing. Everyone knew her walk at our junior high school, a slow, watery step, her hair lifting and slapping her shoulders. Betsy understood something that I didn't, and as her older sister, it was my job to stop this.

That was the summer when my father moved from his bed to the couch every morning and when my mother tried to figure out what was wrong with him. It was 1973. Sometimes he was the one who waited in the gas lines, sometimes it was my mother. In the car he read books about success. They had words like *Win* and *Conquer* and *Pinnacle* in the titles. He and my mother ran a tutoring business for high school students, and students had maybe gotten smarter, somehow, and now nobody seemed to need much help.

The books made my father tired. After he read them, my father came home and lay down on the couch. He watched the news reports. Before he felt tired, I used to sit with him on that couch and watch Sherylline Rivers talk disasters: My father would say two things to me, either "Listen, Sally," or "This is sick." "Listen, Sally," included anything in the Middle East and teenagers who were more successful than I was. "This is sick" included everything else. I wanted to sit on that couch until my father organized the world for me.

Now he didn't want us in the den, so we sat where the carpet turned from rust to brown and watched him. It was Betsy's idea to toss balls of paper with messages at our sleeping father. She wanted to see how far she could throw a ball of paper if it was placed on her bad hand. She said that if the messages hit him, maybe he would feel better. We scribbled notes we thought might work: *The Greatest Father in the Universe!*, *Smile!*, *Hugs and Kisses!*, *We Luv You!* I crumpled up *Smile!* and put it carefully on her bad hand.

She reached her arm back and served *Smile!*, full force, into the den. The ball bonked our father on the forehead.

He opened his eyes. We waited for him to thank us.

I knew our father was different when he woke up after our message hit him. He didn't instruct us about the world, something he would usually do. He threw back the blanket and sat up.

"Enough, girls," he said. "Out."

Hearing our father talk that way sent Betsy all the way across the yard. She put her towel as far from the den as she could. She said she was going to make a project of thoroughly reading all of her *Seventeens*.

I couldn't decide where to sit. I didn't know what we had done wrong. Sometimes I sat with her across the yard. Sometimes I sat on the edge of the den, like an anchor.

Our mother began to walk through the house. She walked hard through each room, as though into a wind. She was different, too. When she looked at us, she wasn't in her face; she was somewhere with our father.

When my mother yelled at my father to get up or see a doctor, I ran to Betsy, who was involved in her *Seventeens*.

"What do we do!" I yelled at her.

She turned the page on a quiz on kissable lip gloss. "How should I know?" she asked.

I started to walk away until we heard our mother's voice rise again, louder than I had ever heard it.

Betsy jumped up. She began to run, arms flapping. I ran, too. She turned on the sprinklers. "Doe," she sang. "A deer. A female deer. Ray, a drop of golden sun . . ."

"Me, a name I call myself . . ." We ran. We ran over the water; we ran as though we had practiced. I followed her around the yard, over the magazines, cover girls all wavy under the water.

We ran as far from the house as we could. We sang so loud our voices blurred. The house shimmered through the water. It almost looked beautiful.

BEFORE MY FATHER GOT TIRED, HE TOOK US DRIVING. HE WANTED to take us somewhere we had never seen. Sometimes he reached over the seat to us, his arm waved in front of our faces, and Betsy and I would decide what to put in his hand. "Guess what this is," we'd say, giving him anything—a shoe, a comic book.

I hated the game the moment Betsy put her bad hand into his. My father would rub her bad hand gently, as though he were trying to erase something, and then his fingers would close completely over her. "It's . . . a banana," my father would say. "A croissant." Betsy would fall into the seat, giggling. "Wrong," she'd say. "It's a boomerang tip." Sometimes I would also put my hand into his. He would lightly lace his fingers into mine. "This is—um," he would say, thinking. I waited for him to tell me something special I could be.

I had to be good at something. I was the older sister. That's what I could do. My favorite older sister job with Betsy was when I was in charge of her bad hand. Before we played, she put her hand into my lap. I had so many ideas. We pushed it into Play-Doh to see the dents it made. We molded chocolate chip cookie dough around it to make a cookie that was full of air.

When Betsy was six, we were sitting in the yard, and I was holding her bad hand, wondering what would happen if we put on a sprinkler, when she took it away and put it in her lap.

"Why is it different on me?"

"What? What's different?"

"Tell me."

I repeated what our father had told me. You're the same as me, you just can't take piano lessons.

She began to bang her bad hand on the grass.

"Give me a thumb," she said to me.

"What?" I asked.

"Come on," she said. She put her bad hand into my lap.

I had no idea what to do.

I took her into our bedroom, and we looked through our closet. My Potato Head. Clue. Nothing seemed right. Our fifty-two-color marker set.

"Sit," I said. I held her bad hand in mine, and I began to draw. Bumps of aqua, olive green, burgundy. I wanted to find the color combination that would make her fingers sprout.

When I was finished, Betsy had five colorful fingers drawn on her bad hand. We had a good day. I carried her around the yard; we sang. I lifted her up, she giggled, her bad hand raised like a beautiful flower.

When she woke up the next morning, the colors had run. Her hand looked like it had been beaten up. "What did you do!" I shrieked. I was afraid I had deformed Betsy in a new, horrible way; now she would also be purple. But as soon as we had cleaned her off, Betsy turned around and put it in my lap.

"Do it again," she said.

Betsy's hand wasn't exactly a hand. Her arm just ended in a point, like a tail end of whipped cream. I thought it looked like

Betsy's arm just didn't want to stop when it entered the world. I thought her arm sensed something wonderful in the world and was shooting right out to meet it. Like Betsy. She seemed always to have some new way to leave me behind. A few days after we had been sitting at the gate, she stood up and said, "I'm going to the beach."

That was an older sister's idea. She went ahead and stole it.

Betsy headed out the next day. I couldn't believe it. I sat in the backyard and waited; I was afraid of the world. I opened the gate and started walking, walked until I hit the busy street. At the intersection, I stopped, feeling the car wind on my arms. I stood there, hoping, lifted my arms. But I was grounded without Betsy. There was nothing to do but turn around and go home.

The next day, I let her pull me with her. We took the blue bus to Santa Monica. We dropped off the bus and looked. The sand rolled, bluish-white, to the flat silver of the Pacific Ocean. Betsy pushed out toward the water so fast I thought she'd belly-down the air, skid toward the sparkling blue.

I was slower. The fear started from nothing sometimes. I felt it rise through my body. Betsy looked fine, flapping out the towel; all I could think of was our father pulling at me, trying to bring me back home. "The ocean's polluted, Sherylline Rivers said," I told her.

"It is not," said Betsy.

I started unfolding the bus schedule. Betsy chewed her hair, watching me. "Wait," she said.

She grabbed my arm and started walking. She led me past a few lifeguard stations and up a hill. From the top of the hill, I saw a group of boys standing and pissing into a ditch.

"How incredibly gross," I said.

The boys were standing in a zigzag row along the ditch, which was shallow but dark with something I didn't want to think about.

We were far enough away to lose the smell, but we could see the thin yellow lines go down into the ditch. We had put our towels on the top of the hill and had watched the boys walk up to the ditch. They had unzipped themselves quickly and stood, hips forward, all aiming for the same place.

Betsy pointed at her discovery. "The one on the right could be named Tim," she said. "Beside him might be Gus, and across could be Harvey." I was impressed; that was more information than I knew about any boy.

"Lie down," said Betsy, and we did; she said we could hold them on the lengths of our arms. She said if we could get all the boys in our arms, they would be ours. We lay facedown, fingertips touching, but we couldn't quite do it; there were a couple of boys that kept getting away from us.

I breathed slowly, my chest pressing into the sand. I decided that I needed these boys to turn all at once and call: *Sally*. I imagined their voices filling me until I rose above them all. But the boys just stood, holding themselves, looking into the air. "John's cute. Will's a grosso. I don't know about Ed," said Betsy. Her good hand was in mine, hot and sticky. I could feel the air in my palm, and she pushed toward them, let go.

WE MADE IT TO THE HILL BY TEN EVERY DAY; WE COULD SPEND FOR-ever watching the boys. They came by twos or threes to the ditch and left quickly; after a few days, we knew them all. "There's the cute guy we saw yesterday, the one who thinks he's James Dean," Betsy might say. "Okay. He's . . . I think he's . . . okay. He's going. God, what did he drink this morning?"

That was the fun part.

"Grape Kool-Aid," I said. "A gallon."

"Minute Maid, instant," said Betsy.

James Dean yanked his shorts shut. He was replaced by Fonz Wannabe.

"Lemonade," I said. We watched, open-mouthed, as he went and went and went.

The hill was the one place in the world where I began to feel light. My father was far away, in the den with the curtains shut, but we were at the top of this hill. For a few hours a day, I felt like the manager of everything. The sun burned my arms gold. The sand was warm under my stomach. Sometimes I imagined a random cloud floating by and landing on my perfect hand. We sat for hours, waiting to see who would walk up next. Betsy and I made up things the boys would say if they liked us.

"You are a total foxy babe," said Betsy.

"You are one hunk o'woman," I tried.

"You are a chick from my dream life," she said.

Betsy and I rolled close to each other. For a second we owned the boys. We owned the rumpled shadows on the sand; we owned the water, a scatter of diamonds; we owned the sun. We owned all of it.

She leaned forward and quickly kissed me on the lips.

"Ow," I said, though it didn't hurt.

She kissed me again. She didn't bump my nose that time either.

"Ow," I said, again.

Betsy rolled away. I loved her.

"Ow," she said.

UP ON THE HILL, BETSY AND I NEVER TALKED ABOUT OUR FATHER. WE did that only on the long block between our house and the bus stop; then, we discussed our various theories about what was wrong with him.

One day I told her I thought he wasn't doing anything because he was part of a contest. "Like how much TV you can watch," I said. "He's going to win a trip to Hawaii for four."

"No," said Betsy. "But maybe he's getting ready to go on *Anything for Money*."

"He's going to win the *car*," I shrieked.

We hugged each other and jumped up and down. We were proud of our father. But the idea did not seem right when we got closer to the house. Our father was not going to Hawaii.

I moved closer to Betsy. "There's a bug on your shoulder!" I shrieked.

"There is not," she said.

"Yes!" I shrieked. I swatted an invisible bug off her back and left my hand there. She didn't move.

We also had different theories about what would make our father feel better. That day, I decided the answer was French braids. Betsy pulled her *Seventeen* from her tote bag, and we sat on the curb, braiding each other's hair. We marched up to the house, arm in arm, giggling. We looked like new people. He was going to love us. I began to knock, but Betsy grabbed me, hard.

"He's not going to like them," said Betsy.

"Yes, he will," I said.

"No," she squeaked. "He's not going to know who we are."

I didn't know why I believed her, but it seemed better than believing myself. We destroyed our French braids in a little thunderstorm of work, quickly and viciously. We stood by the front door, quietly. Betsy put her hand on my back.

"There's a bug on you," she said.

WHEN BETSY WAS EIGHT, I TRIED TO SUCK HER FINGERS OUT. WE SAT, backs pressed against old games of Clue and Candy Land in our bedroom closet, legs tucked so our knees hit our chins. First I kissed her bad hand. I was delicate as a suitor: a circle of kisses around her wrist. "Eat it," she said. Her bad hand was spongy and a little salty.

My mouth rode it as though it were corn on the cob. I thought of fingers. I bent down and tried to wish them out of her, making us, finally, the same.

"What?" she asked, excited.

I wiped her on the carpet and inspected: nothing.

"What?" asked Betsy. She was three years from becoming pretty. She put her bad hand in my lap.

"Please," she said to me.

IT HAPPENED BY THE SNACK STAND. BETSY WAS PLUCKING STRAWS out of the container while I held our drinks. A row of boys leaned against a wall that said in loopy, black writing, *NO FAT CHICKS*.

Betsy was struggling with the straw container. One of the boys, with a cute cotton candy pouf of brown hair, walked right up to her. He slapped a hand on the metal container. A few straws rumbled down. He plucked them out, very gently; then he held them out to Betsy as though they were a bouquet.

Betsy looked at the straws and, slowly, at the boy. He was just standing there, being a boy, but that was too much for me. I stared down at the sand. Betsy took the straw from him. And then she ran to me.

"What!"

"He said his name was Barry and he hung out at Station 5," she said.

"Oh my God," I said.

We ran across the sand, the ice in our drinks jingling.

"What does that mean?"

"He likes you," I said.

She shrieked. "Do you think he's cute?"

"No."

"Are you sure?"

"Yes."

"Oh," she said. She stabbed her straw into her drink top. The boy was still there, watching. It took too long for him to disappear.

BETSY AND I BOTH CRAWLED INTO MY BED AT NIGHT. SHE LIKED TO run her bad hand along my arms. Starting at my wrist, she slid it up to my elbow; then she stopped and slid back down again. We wrapped our legs around each other, Betsy smoothing me over and over, and often fell asleep like that, my mouth wet against her hair.

Sometimes, when we held each other, she would try to figure things out. "Daddy chopped them off when I was born," she whispered. "He came into the hospital and chopped them off with a knife." Or, "Mommy shoved them back in when I was a baby. Probably when I was crying too hard." Her imaginary good hand was destroyed by can openers or car washes; it was savaged by parents or music teachers; but it was never ruined by me. I waited for her to say it—"You, Sally, slammed it in a car door"— but, instead, she just looked at me, waiting for my answer.

"That is totally whacked," was what I usually told her.

"Really?" she asked me. "You think so, Sally?"

AFTER BETSY HAD BEEN PICKED AT THE SNACK STAND, I DECIDED there had to be a change in our boy-watching. "The one who could be Jake looks too much like Donny Osmond," I said. "The one who could be Hugh has weird lips." Now all I could see were the mistakes in the boys. Pat's tubby stomach. Brian's spindly legs.

Betsy seemed loosened from her body, able to fly out and away whenever the chance came. "The one who might be Fred is a total hunkola," she said. "The one who could be Jeff has cool hair."

I told her she was blind. Or just sick. I was the older sister. I knew these things. She shrugged. Since the day of the boy by the snack stand, she was spending a lot of time looking in mirrors. I think she was wondering why she had been picked.

The day she went down, we were debating the one who could be Earl. "The most disgusting thing on the planet," I said. "I mean, if I were born looking like that, I wouldn't ever leave the house . . ."

"Oh, come on. He's not *that* bad," she said.

"Not *that* bad," I said. "Are you crazy? Are you in love with him?"

Betsy stood up.

"Bye," she said.

She turned and sailed down to the ditch. I leaned over the edge of the hill, as though I could reel her back, but she was already there, she was already walking. The boys saw her, and a few comments came, like the first zippy pieces of popcorn that explode inside a pan:

"Hey."

"You have a name?"

"Nice day, sweetie?"

"Wanna come hold it for me?"

"Bitch," I said, quietly, into the sand. She stopped. I hoped she'd run then, make a break for the parking lot, but she didn't; she was brave. She zeroed in on one boy who had finished and was standing away from the others. He was thin-armed, freckled, pressing a boogie board close to his chest. Betsy walked right over and stood beside him. She kept the tube top wrapped right around her bad hand. You couldn't see it, couldn't see that there was anything different about her. She was just a really pretty girl who was trying to make this boy like her. The boy kept his eyes on the sand, and she kept talking. Then she leaned forward and touched his arm with her bad hand.

I thought he'd know it in a second, feel the bump through her tube top and run. I thought that would teach her, and all those boys would come running to me. But she had him. My sister made him like her. The boy toed the sand, smiling. And even though he wasn't a very cute boy, even though he was probably named something like Earl, I had never wanted so much to be her.

I flopped onto my back and closed my eyes so she wouldn't know that I had been watching. When I opened them, she was there.

"You know what?" she said.

"What."

"I think he liked it."

"What?"

And she held up her bad hand.

"*That?*"

Betsy smiled.

"I think he did," she said.

THAT NIGHT, WHEN OUR FATHER FELL ASLEEP IN FRONT OF THE TV, we slipped in low, flat, to sit beside him. Once we made it, once we were finally beside our father, I wasn't sure what I was supposed to do. Betsy sat, staring into the bright white of the TV; then she unwrapped her tube top and took out her bad hand. It glowed in the light of the TV set. I thought it looked as though it entered the world more purely, simply, than a complete hand would. Betsy pulled my father's feet onto her lap; then she began to rub her bad hand back and forth along them. "Idiot," I hissed. "What are you doing?" I thought this was it. She was going to be Queen of the Hill; now she would cure our father in some sick mutant way.

"Fine. Fine," I hissed. "Wake him up. Just kill him, while you're at it." But nothing happened. Betsy stopped.

"Bitch," she whispered. "I'm not doing anything." Neither of us moved from our father. We looked at him for a long time.

As soon as we got to the hill the next day, she announced, "I'm going to kiss a boy for an hour, and I'm going to tell him my name is Sally."

She ran down the hill; I followed. She put me against a truck. I started to go back to my towel but stopped: I had to see what she was going to do with my name. Betsy steered clear of the boy she had picked the last time and found one I thought was cute. Clutching the boy with her good hand, she led him over to the truck. She stopped about ten feet from me, turned him around so he couldn't see me. All I could see of the boy was his pinkish back. She stepped close to him, fiddling her good hand in his hair. I stood against the truck, pretending to look at the seagulls circling. Then Betsy, my sister, reached up and kissed him.

I could almost feel it inside me when she did that; I could almost taste that boy. But I wasn't kissing him. It wasn't me. I was just there, in the shadows, trapped against a truck.

I wanted to say things. *Tramp. Slut o' the Universe. Crazed Maniac of the World. Major Bitch.* Of course, I didn't. There was nothing to do but stand quietly and watch my sister pull love out of someone else.

I left the beach early and headed for Sav-On. It was where our family went when we needed to fix things. I went down the Cosmetics aisle and thought of my mother. I thought hard about her, trying to make her stop yelling. I went down Toilet Seats and thought of Betsy. I tried to keep her from taking over the world. I went down Lawn Chairs, and I thought of my father. I tried to make him well.

I found it by Gardening. A small bottle filled with bright blue fluid. Fern Encourager. In small print: *Bring your thirsty ferns to life.*

I did something I had never done before: I put Fern Encourager in my pocket and went for the door. I walked out past the girls ringing the cash machines, stepping right into the parking lot. I didn't stop walking for five blocks. In front of me the sidewalk rose up, shining.

I SHOWED IT TO HER IN THE BATHROOM THAT NIGHT.

She rolled up her bikini top, flashing her brown nipples, her tiny breasts. Then she ducked, knocking the bottle out of my hand.

"Are you insane?" she said to me.

I watched her move into the mirror as though she were in love with it.

"I can make you sprout fingers," I said.

"Sally, you're such a geek," she said.

I swallowed. I stood so hard on the floor I hoped it would begin to tilt and spill Betsy, my family, somewhere.

"I can," I told her.

I WENT OUTSIDE AND SAT WITH MY FATHER.

"Do you have cancer?"

He shook his head. "No."

I felt something, full as a balloon, shrink inside of me. "Do you have heart failure?"

"No," he said.

"Well, then, what?" I said.

He held out his arms. I stood inside them. They did not surround me the way I wanted.

"I get tired after I read these books," he said. "I get tired after I walk one block." His voice swelled, as though he were in an argument. He rolled over. "Forget it, Sally. Go play with your sister."

I didn't know what to think. My father had just stopped.

My father closed his eyes. He looked like he could just sink into the lawn chair and disappear. It wouldn't take long for me to follow. I wouldn't even have to try. I tried to tell one of the boys at the beach to come get me. The one who could be Craig, pushing open the gate and walking right to me, leaning over, knowing how to kiss.

That was the first time in ages that I sat right beside my father.

THAT NIGHT I WOKE UP, BLINKING INTO THE DARK. I MOVED DOWN the long hallway to the kitchen. I stood in the doorway and scanned the utensils. The can opener wasn't sharp enough. I didn't know how to put together the Cuisinart. So I took the biggest steak knife, silver and heavy. And I put it against my left hand.

That knife was stubborn. I held it hard, stood there breathing; I thought of all the love I would possibly get. But the knife wouldn't go down. It wouldn't move.

I lifted the knife off my skin. I put it in the very last trash can in the garage. I dumped garbage over it—old TV dinners, soda bottles, banana peels—until I was sure no one would know it was there. In bed, my hands went slowly all over my body. My body, still ridiculously complete.

THE NEXT DAY, I TOLD BETSY I WASN'T GOING WITH HER TO THE hill anymore.

"It's boring," I said.

She was stepping into that day's swimsuit; she stopped.

"How?"

"It just is," I said.

Betsy slapped her arms at her sides. "Fine," she said. "Be that way." She whirled around. "What color do I wear?"

"I don't care."

"Pink," she said. "I totally need pink." She began to hurl shirts and towels. "Fonz Wannabe looks like a fish when he kisses," she said. "It's really gross. You have to see."

"No," I said.

She zoomed out of the bedroom. I listened. She was running. She was also throwing: magazines, big pillows, chairs.

"Sally," she yelled.

She was in the kitchen.

"You stole my pink one," she said.

"I wouldn't want it," I said.

"Bitch," she said. "You know you do."

She grabbed a spatula lying on a counter. "You know you do," she yelled, and she went for me with the spatula. I leaped on Betsy. She whacked the spatula everywhere: into my chest, under my armpit, between my legs. I hit her all over; I didn't want to miss a spot.

She shoved me off and ran to the den. I couldn't believe it; she ran inside.

"Daddy!" Betsy yelled.

She began to jump all over the den. I did, too. We bounced up and off chairs, the card table. I pretended our father wasn't sleeping. He wasn't even there.

Our father opened his eyes. "Girls, out," he said.

Betsy hoisted herself on top of the entertainment console. On the big square TV under her feet, a contestant touched a new Buick. Betsy was the tallest thing in the room.

Again, she had picked the center of the universe. She had found the best place to be. I wriggled toward Betsy, getting ready to push her off.

Our father was faster. He lifted her off the TV. Betsy started kicking. He was holding her, in the air, kicking. It was the first father thing I saw him do the whole summer. It was the first thing he did that made him look strong.

He gently set Betsy on the floor. I loved him, then, instantly, ridiculously. Now he would talk to us again; now he would tell us what to do.

But our father didn't say anything. He didn't even smile. He stepped away from us as though he thought we were ugly.

"Just go out," he said. "Go."

I let out a big breath. I wondered how our father felt, watching me and Betsy leave for the beach every day. I couldn't imagine what it was like, staying in this dark room when outside the sun warmed our shoulders, our arms.

Our father was alone in the den again, and I had no idea how to save him.

Betsy shot out of the room. I followed. When we made it to the bathroom, she began to cry.

She leaned into me, her whole face salty. I wanted to help her stop. I frantically scanned the bathroom. Blow-dryers, lip gloss, a loofah sponge. The bottle of Fern Encourager was beside my toothbrush. I grabbed it and held it out to her.

"Oh, please," she said.

I poured out some blue on a paper towel and touched her bad hand with it. I knew the Fern Encourager wouldn't work. I knew she didn't think it would, either. But it was all I could think of then, in the bathroom.

"Idiot," she said, softly.

WE DIDN'T TAKE THE BUS THIS TIME; WE RAN THE WHOLE WAY. BETSY dashed up the hill first, sand flying from her feet like white sparks. When we got to the top, we turned to the sun, and I lifted her arm.

She twisted away from me, embarrassed, but I held her arm there, hard. "Higher," I said. "On your toes."

The boys at the ditch turned toward us, but they were too far away, I think, to see anything but that she had kissed some of them by the parking lot.

"Hey," a couple of them began to call. "Hey."

Betsy was frozen in her salute, and the boys began running, across the sand, toward us. I stood behind her and held her arm so it was closer to the sun.

"Try," I said. "Push."

Betsy closed her eyes. It seemed like she was trying to fling her whole self into that hand. I wrapped my arms around her skinny waist and lifted her, kicking, to the sky.

"Push."

The boys coming up the hill saw me holding Betsy and slowed down. I squeezed my sister, tighter, tighter. I waited for something beautiful to come out of her; I waited for anything at all. Then Betsy started to cough, and we fell, separate, on the sand.

Betsy was still. I took her hand out of the sand. She kept her face down as I shook the sand off. She must have known there was no difference. And, of course, there wasn't. Because when her hand was out, I could see that it was the same. It was still my sister's bad hand.

The boys began to rush the hill. And they began calling her by the name she had given them. "Sally." "Sally."

When she heard they were still coming, Betsy sat up, yanked her bad hand back.

"Oh, great," she said. "Give me something."

"What?"

"Don't be stupid. Your shirt."

She snapped up my shirt with her good hand, and then I was on the top of that hill in my bikini top, the wind touching my shoulders. Betsy wrapped my shirt around her bad hand in about half a second, whip-fast after years of practice. The boys were coming for us. They were coming. Betsy pulled me. "Let's go," she said. She took my hand with her good one. Her good hand fit into mine perfectly. It had never fit so well.

"Come on," she said. And we walked off the beach, all the boys calling, "Sally," "Sally," the whole beach ringing with my name.

Candidate

Diane Bernstein paid the babysitter, the third one to quit this month, extremely polite when doing so, blaming it on other issues—sorority functions, heavy schoolwork—as though the boy had not unnerved her at all. When Diane walked through the door, Liza, the baby girl, fell into her mother's arms, weeping so hard she began to choke. The boy, Tommy, was curled up in his bed, rocking himself, for he had scratched the babysitter in a fury ("I wanted to play the radio," she said, "and he just went insane"), and the young woman had shut him in his room. Why hadn't Diane found a better babysitter? It was not a question she allowed herself anymore. She had long stopped worrying about forgiveness, of herself or others. When the therapist had told her, again, that it was not her fault, she laughed. Everything was her fault; everything was everyone's fault. "Even if it was his fault," she said, meaning her husband, to the therapist, "What would it matter? He's gone."

Diane had to figure out whom to comfort first: two-year-old Liza, who clung to her, frantic with love, unwilling to peel herself from her mother after their long day apart, or Tommy, a knot of frustration in his bed. "They're cute kids," the babysitter called back, apologetically, pulling her long sleeves over the scratches the boy had given her; clutching her thirty dollars, she got into her Jeep and drove off.

Diane had spent the day working in the remedial writing lab of a private university in the Southeast. She hunched in a dimly lit cubicle with the undergraduates, glossy, overfed children who drove SUVs that were gifts from their parents and who could never correctly use a comma. Their essays were supposed to address the upcoming 2004 presidential election and involved passionate, ungrammatical declarations stating why the Republicans should win. *Lazy people should not get my tax mony,* they wrote, *I don't want any gay agenda on my family. Marriage is between a man and a woman.* That day, Diane sat with a young woman dressed like a prostitute, her pink spandex halter top stretched across her breasts. Her hair was styled, confusingly, in two pigtail braids, like an eight-year-old's. The girl smelled of the beach, of coconut and salt. She had written a diatribe about how the United States should not only invade Iraq but Saudi Arabia, Egypt, Russia, and Japan, as revenge for Pearl Harbor. It was an extremely long and angry run-on sentence.

"Do you worry about how other countries might respond to this?" asked Diane.

The girl glared at her. "The terrorists want to kill me," she said.

The girl's previous paper had recorded her frustrations about her parents' divorce, the insensitivities of her superiors at Walmart, the cheap gifts her boyfriend had given her. It had been a more interesting paper, though it still lacked any punctuation.

"The terrorists would come to Briar Wood College?" Diane asked, before she could stop herself.

The girl's eyes narrowed. Then, as though concerned about her grade, she smiled and said, sweetly, "You're just from the North," which was true, though "the North" seemed to imply anywhere slanting north or west; Diane had moved here from Seattle.

Diane closed her eyes; the school where she worked had raised tuition too many times, and faculty had been cautioned not to discuss the upcoming election with the mostly conservative students. They lurched about campus, students and teachers, pretending to ignore each other's pins and T-shirts. She had done what she could: covered her car in bumper stickers and stuck signs in her lawn that were later torn down.

Sometimes, Diane thought it best to unplug the phone. Then she would not have to decide whether or not to answer it. The father, who was now residing in Florida, was not supposed to call at this hour; he was supposed to speak to the children only in the morning, for his voice upset them when it was time for dinner and bed. She carried the girl up to the boy's room and sat on his bed. Liza put her head on Diane's leg and closed her eyes, quiet; her breathing became calm. The boy did not like to be touched, but was generally soothed by coloring in squares in black and yellow. She gave him crayons and paper and he sat up, filling each box with extraordinary love.

Diane listened to the silence in the room and envied the girl's belief that she had been rescued. It was an acute misunderstanding between parents and children, one that sometimes comforted her but also felt like a joke.

SOMEONE KNOCKED AT THE DOOR. DIANE JUMPED UP, HOLDING Liza, and she and Tommy ran for the door. There she found a man in a crisp white shirt and navy pants. His outstretched hand sliced the air in two.

"Hi there," he said. "Woody Wilson here. Running for state legislature. I want to represent you."

Before he said his name, he was just an ordinary stranger, standing there, slim, brown-haired—a salesman of encyclopedias or cleaning equipment—with the belligerent, trudging optimism of someone who went door to door. After he declared his name, she hated him. This shift in feeling was so abrupt she felt she had been slapped. His face seemed to glow the way a famous person's did; perhaps it was an accident that he was walking around on earth. He lived most fully on the newspaper ads and billboards all over town. *Woody Wilson, Republican for North Carolina State Senate.*

"And what's your name?"

"Diane," said the boy.

"Man," the girl said, looking up at Woody Wilson.

It was late afternoon. The house smelled like a rotten melon. The afternoon was weighted toward night. The golden light already held an undertone of darkness. Diane had read what he stood for, and she hated all of it. It would be so simple, so luxurious, to slam the door on him! But she did not. His eyes were clear and blue as a baby's.

"Diane, can I have just a moment of your time?" he asked. He kept smiling, but his face was red from the heat. "I can see that you're a family person." He stepped back and began to arrange the plastic vehicles scattered across her front porch. He put Big Wheels behind sedans. "I have a family, too. How old are your kids? I have two, eight years old and five." He laughed, brokenly; it almost sounded like weeping. "I've come to ask for your vote, Diane," he said. "And—" he lifted a manila envelope marked *CONTRIBUTIONS*— "perhaps a donation to my cause. I am for family. We are what make America great." He swept his arm toward her in a grand, appropriating gesture; she stepped back from him. "What does your family need? If you want more money in your wallet, I have the answers. If you want better schools, I can answer that, too."

She tightened her arm around Liza's waist. She knew that her political beliefs were opposite to his. "And how are you going to make the schools better?" she asked.

He heard the blade in her voice; his smile brightened. The pale, clapboard houses behind him seemed to be melting in the heat. "Good question, Diane," he said, speaking quickly. "We want to bring faith back to our schools. Every child should be allowed to pray. No cost to the taxpayer." His words sounded a little breathless.

"Pray to what?" she asked.

He blinked. "I'd say Jesus," he said. She was silent. "But it's a free country," he said. He sounded hesitant on that one, she thought. He tapped a rolled-up leaflet against his hand.

"I believe in the separation of church and state," she said, crisply.

He nodded vigorously, as though by making this movement they would be in agreement. The optimism in the gesture was ridiculous, almost moving. But then he handed her a leaflet. "Some folks may say it's hard to know whether to choose me or my opponent, Judy Hollis. So I wanted you to know this."

Did you know that JUDY HOLLIS is a lesbian?
That she is bringing her gay agenda to Raleigh?
Vote for WOODY. FAMILY VALUES.

Diane set Liza down on the floor and slowly stood to face him.

"Diane, our campaign is getting the word out," he said. "Judy is bad news for our state."

"Because she's gay?" she asked.

"Yes," he said. "We don't want them coming here. I stand for values, Diane, family values. You know what I mean—"

"No, I don't," she said. "I don't want to hear this bullshit. Stop."

Woody blinked but did not move. The boy glared at Woody Wilson as though he were an animal the boy wanted to eat. He regarded most men who were tall with brown hair this way—it was the simplest way they could describe their father. The boy lay on the floor and rolled from side to side. Why did they work, the ways he tried to comfort himself? He rolled and screeched and turned; they were strategies that adults found amusing at two but now made them look away. The girl gazed at him. The girl's love for the boy poured out of her; she could not help herself. She stretched herself on top of him. She screeched and tried to lick his lips. "Stop!" the boy roared, trying to push her off. She clutched his foot as he tried to crawl away from her. Diane plucked the girl off the boy and set her on the couch, where the girl began to scream.

"Please," Woody Wilson said. "Let me say—" His face went white. Then he toppled forward onto her living room floor.

THE GIRL LET OUT A PIERCING SHRIEK OF DELIGHT, AS THOUGH THE man was entertaining them. The boy jumped back, his hands pressing his ears. "Stop!" he bellowed. He rolled into a ball on the floor.

Woody was lying facedown across Diane's hardwood floor. His envelope marked *CONTRIBUTIONS* fell open, and a couple dollars emptied out. He seemed as incongruous as a whale washed up on a beach; she looked down at him, afraid. Diane lightly tapped his shoulder, and then rolled him over. His shoulder was soft as an avocado. He had recently eaten a mint, and his breath was medicinal; she was embarrassed to know this about him.

"What'd he do?" yelled the boy.

She jumped up and grabbed the phone off a side table. Woody's eyes opened, and he was staring at them.

"I'm calling a doctor," she said.

"Don't call anyone. I don't want them to know." His presence on billboards made the mundane facts of humanity strange and troubling. His forehead was pink, with creases in it like clay. There was golden hair on the backs of his hands. He touched his eyebrow; a dark bruise was forming. She was afraid of him, which translated into a great and useless pity. She rarely pitied anyone but herself now, so that superiority was somewhat enjoyable.

She left the front door open. Moths flew in. Woody Wilson put a hand on his forehead. "Ow," he said. He took a deep breath. "Exhaustion. That's what the doctor said. Nothing wrong at all. He said if it happens, sit down for a few minutes, take some breaths, and keep going. I have to keep going."

"Okay," she said, reluctantly. She felt afraid of being blamed.

"I don't know what happened," he said. "But when I feel strongly about something, sometimes I see black. I feel my heart churning. Perhaps the Lord is telling me something. Ow," he said, softly.

What did he mean, the Lord told him things? She sat in her cubicle every day, convincing her students: Evidence. A clear and organized argument. Sometimes, she heard herself ranting about evidence, concrete examples, and she felt herself sweating, pathetically, with her own zealotry. He rubbed the bruise on his forehead. She went to the kitchen and brought him an ice pack. He sat up and pressed it to his face.

"Why are you running for office?" she asked.

"He told me to do this. It is the grace of God. Woody Wilson. I will stand for values. Speak out. The town needs to know your name."

Through the open front door the clouds were knitting together in a searing, bright sky. She could see the houses on their lawns, each life parceled out into its plot of land, the determined, clipped order of flowers and shrubbery. There were two registered Democrats on her street that she knew of and five Republicans. They went in and out of their houses, shaving their lawns, picking up their newspapers, remarking on the weather. They would all walk into their voting booths, educated and uneducated, intelligent and dumb, and their votes would be worth the same. They sat, diligently filling in bubbles on paper, and, she thought, because of the voters' impulsive, careless yearnings, wars started, debts soared, the land grew barren, and their great-grandchildren would starve.

The bump on Woody's head was growing larger and larger. The phone began to ring. Her husband was most lonely around dinnertime. He did not love them but did not know who else to call.

"I'm sorry," said Woody Wilson. His right foot tapped on the floor like a rabbit's. "A minute, and I'll be on my way." He paused. "Does it look very bad?" he asked.

"I don't know," she said. "Maybe you should keep the ice on it."

The phone rang ten times and then stopped.

"Thank you very much, Diane," he said. He carefully scooped the dollars on the floor back into his envelope and closed it.

They sat in silence for a moment. He smiled, so his injuries seemed slight.

"Okay," she said. "While you're here, I have a question." She folded her arms, then unfolded them, then folded them again. "Why do you hate so many people? I just want to know—"

"I do not hate them," he said. "Listen. I am trying to help them from leading lives of so much pain—"

"Why do you assume that people who are not like you are in pain?" she asked.

"I know a lot about pain," he said. "My mama died when I was eight. My father had to work three jobs. He was always tired. He was so tired we had to forage for dinner ourselves. I got a job working a paper route when I was six. I worked hard. I was angry, I did not know what to do with it, but I said, God, take this anger, and He did.

I worked my way up, the good days and the bad. Hard work and faith, that's what got me to college, law school, to where I am today."

He recited his litany of pain solemnly, like a prayer. Everyone was competitive in terms of their pain. Did it matter more that Woody's mother had died when he was young or that Diane's husband had left the family? Was a troubled, problematic child worse than infertility? What about the fact that Diane's hours working as a remedial composition instructor had been cut in half, the sudden eczema that spread across her skin, how did that weigh compared to diagnosis with cancer, losing your family in a war, fearing that you might not make love to another person again?

"You were lucky that you succeeded," she said. "Some people don't."

"It was not luck," he said, sternly. "It was faith. Let me tell you something. A few months ago, before I decided to run for office, I was waking up one morning, and I swore I saw a pit bull rush toward the bed. It wanted to eat me. It had a huge, pink mouth. It had been waiting for me for years. It was probably a dream, but it looked real. I said, 'Jesus,' and it disappeared."

The boy noticed Woody's bag of buttons and stickers. He began, methodically, to take them out and count them. The phone rang again.

"Don't you need to answer that?" Woody asked.

How did anyone know the right way to live? Diane's husband, at forty-five, had begun to feel pains in his chest. The pains were nothing, the doctor said, but anxiety, but her husband felt, abruptly, the slow, inevitable closing of his own life. He had awakened one night, damp and trembling, after dreaming that his children had him by the throat. In the dream he had peeled their hands off and risen up, free, into the sky. She had these feelings, too, for she had her own disappointments—it had not been her dream to berate undergraduates to turn in gratuitously late papers, for one thing—but she was going along with what was given them, and when she tucked the children in, she had not thought there was anything else to do. But suddenly her husband believed that their family was killing them. He was almost gleeful in this, a solution. He was a large, healthy man, but after this dream, he began visiting doctors, checking not only his heart, but also his lungs, his kidneys, his skin. He said that something was dirty in his blood. No doctors found anything. He searched the Internet for remote adventures; he logged onto sites that described trips into mountains, forests, deserts barely developed by human hands. He said he wanted to go somewhere clean. His home office—he was a free-lance reporter for a variety of computer magazines—was papered with posters of Tibet, mountains white, iridescent with snow.

This business intensified shortly after the doctor had explained to Diane and her husband that testing had placed their son on the autism spectrum. The boy, he said, loved rules so intensely it could be difficult for him to get married or live with someone. He might be tormented in public school, so make sure to explain his issues to his teachers. He could receive therapy to help him understand when another person was happy or sad. On the bright side, the boy would be excellent at math.

After they had heard this, her husband asked her to drive the car home. She stared at the shiny, broad backs of the cars in front of them. His silence made her aggressively talkative.

"I don't know if he was the best guy," she said. "We could see someone else."

He sat, hunched, arms wrapped around himself as though he were freezing.

"Don't you have anything to say?" she asked sharply, in the tone she sometimes used, despite herself, with the children.

He glanced at the dashboard. "We're low on gas," he said.

THE PHONE STOPPED RINGING. SHE COUNTED; THIS TIME IT TOOK twenty rings. Woody lowered the ice pack. "Someone wants to talk to you," he said.

"No," she said. "Actually, he doesn't."

The boy looked up. "There are fifty-eight Woody Wilson buttons in your bag," he said.

"Really?" said Woody. "There are, I think, 108 signs all over town. Yard signs, billboards. I drove around counting them. My wife, Daisy, helped me put up the signs. She did a good job. It was a good day for her." He pressed the ice pack to his head and closed his eyes. "I am her rock," he said. "I am her anchor in troubled water."

The hope in his face, his desire to be seen in this role, made her look away.

"You are your husband's rock," he said, eagerly. "I can see it." He picked up the ice pack again. "My wife used to work in real estate," he said. "Did I tell you? She sold a house three blocks away." He paused. "She was very happy," he said. "We had wine and steaks at the Port House." He was staring at his shoe with the frozen gaze of someone banishing other thoughts from his head. Then he looked at her. "What kind of work does your husband do?"

"I don't really know right now," she said.

She did not know yet how to answer this. Should she say he was dead? "He left three months ago," she said. Telling Woody was practice. She hated other people's pity; their sympathy, she felt, was a way of flattering themselves. She tried to laugh, a hollow, cheerless sound—why? She did not want him to be afraid of her. She was certainly afraid of herself. "That was him on the phone."

"I'm sorry," he said. "I call His name when I cannot take another step." He looked at her as though she would understand this. "Do you ever feel that, Diane? Who do you call when you cannot take another step?" Woody Wilson lowered the ice pack from his forehead and touched the dent in the blue pack. He bit his lip, concerned.

She needed to change the subject. "So your wife sells real estate," she said lightly.

"She did until a year ago," he said.

He set the ice pack beside him and stared at it. When he looked up, he stared through her, as though another person were simply a clear window to a better view. "She won't get out of bed. She stays there with the curtains shut. She says the light hurts her hair," he said.

She looked at Woody Wilson, the blazing whiteness of his shirt, the way his hair was parted very neatly in the middle. She imagined him standing in front of the mirror that morning while his wife lay silent in the dim bedroom, drawing his comb tenderly through his hair. "I'm sorry," she said. "It sounds hard."

"Hard," he said, and he laughed, a sad laugh. "Life is hard. But you know, marriage is a sacred union."

"Fine," she said, thinking that this was what she resented most of all, the lack of specifics, the cheerful vagueness. "But you know, I think that each person has to give something."

"I give her my devotion," he said, sitting up, excited, ready for a debate. "She does the best she can. I wake up in the morning, and sometimes I look at her face, and I just want to know what she is thinking. I tell her she needs to go to church. God will help her." His face was naked, a boy's face, the pale, terrible lids of a child. "I want people to see that I'm trying. I want people to say that Woody Wilson is a good man."

A FEW WEEKS BEFORE HER HUSBAND LEFT, DIANE HAD HEARD HIM crying at odd moments: when he was in the bathroom shaving, when he was in the garage bringing in the trash. His crying was soft, private, not meant for her or the children, and each time she came upon it, she felt both wounded and enraged. He only wept away from her, and she knew this meant she was not supposed to comfort him. One night, during this time, she had woken up and made his lunch. In the dark kitchen, she had put a peanut butter sandwich, an apple, a strong cheese, and a cookie in a brown bag and left it on the counter. The next day, he took the bag to work, and when he came home that night, he said, "I took your lunch today. Sorry."

She was then ashamed of her gesture. "I know you did," she said, and they were both more familiar in this, the feeling of deprivation, their quiet, growing anger toward something they could not quite describe. The next morning, that same lunch was on the counter; he had made it for her. She had wept and had begun to eat it slowly; after a few bites, she stopped. He would be leaving soon; they both knew this.

The phone was ringing again. Woody clapped his hands over his ears. The boy suddenly stood up and went into the kitchen. The girl wandered off to join him. There was the scream, "Stop!" by the girl followed by the boy yelling, "Give it!" and then the sound of a body falling in the kitchen. Diane ran into the room. She heard the candidate stepping behind her.

The boy had the girl pressed to the floor with his body. She was coughing. He was trying to unpeel her tiny closed fist. "Give it!" he growled.

"I want it!" screamed the girl.

"Get off her!" Diane ordered the boy. She grabbed his thin shoulders and tried to shake him off, but the boy would not move. "Now!"

Diane imagined how Woody Wilson saw them, the disheveled middle-aged woman in the putrid kitchen, wrestling with the enraged son who was stronger than she was. *Legislate against this*, she thought. The girl opened her mouth to bite the boy's hand.

Woody grasped the boy's hands. "Let go of your sister," said Woody quietly.

"She stole it!" screamed the boy.

Woody held a hand out, as though to calm the air. "Now wait, everybody," he said. "Wait." He reached into his pocket to pull out a Woody Wilson sticker. "I'll trade you." He handed the girl his sticker: *Vote for me.* The girl grabbed it. She was already possessed of a startling rage, as though she foresaw the difficulties her life would bring her. When the girl stared at someone, as she did at her brother, Diane saw how she would someday regard a lover, the assumption that the other would feed some endless hunger inside of her. She gazed at Diane with the same expression, and Diane whispered to her, ashamed before its vastness.

Woody pressed the boy's sticker back into his outstretched hand. The boy turned away from him and hunched over his sticker. It had the green, smiling face of Shrek on it.

"Where'd you get this?" Woody asked the boy.

"At school. They called my name in the cafeteria," the boy said. "I heard my name. They said it like this: Tom. Mee. Bern. Steen. They chose me. They said I could go home. The lady gave me this when I walked out. She said hold this and go right to the car. I held it the whole way."

Diane remembered this from the day before, the first time she had picked up her son by car at school. The car riders waited for their parents in the cafeteria, while the parents, in cars at the traffic circle, told their names to the pickup coordinators, who called their names on the walkie-talkie. "Tommy Bernstein," Diane had said to the coordinator. She imagined her son's name floating over the loudspeaker in the cafeteria, where the children were sitting on long steel benches. She pictured all the children, Tommy and Raisha and Juan and Christopher and Sandra and the others, hunched over the tables, waiting to be summoned back to their lives. How many times in their lives would they sit like this, waiting to be called—for work, for love, for good fortune or bad, for luck or despair? What joys or sorrows would each of them be chosen for? She wished she could see how her son hurried down the dingy, dim brown public school corridors, how he walked to the doors that burst open to the afternoon light.

She was relieved when she saw him coming to her car; it was as if he had just been born. "What happened?" she asked. He had told her the same thing: "They said my name like this"—her son cupped his hands together and spoke into them—"Tom. Mee. Bern. Steen." He said these words with awe, as though they had been spoken by the voice of God. She watched his face in the rearview mirror, blank but suffused with a new brightness, and she wanted to touch his beautiful young face and feel what hope was in it, but she simply drove on.

Now Woody leaned toward the boy. "Tom. Mee. Bern. Steen. You did a good job," he said.

The boy nodded at Woody's correct pronunciation. "Yes," he said.

"Your parents will be proud," Woody continued.

"My father calls in the morning," Tommy said. "I hear him, but I don't see his face."

"He must miss you," said Woody.

Stop, she thought. *Don't pity him.* Woody rolled up his shirt-sleeves. He bent so he was looking into the boy's face. "Tommy," said Woody. "I know how you feel. When I was a boy, I woke up, and the house was quiet. No one called me. Tommy, I didn't have a mother. My father was at work long before I got up." He ran his hand through his thinning hair. "I dressed and got myself to the bus stop. I rode the school bus. I waited for it to pick me up. Sometimes I said my name, too. *Woody Wilson*. I said it over and over. *WoodyWilson. WoodyWilson.* I said it so many times it sounded like the name of some other person."

His voice had become quieter as he spoke to Tommy. The boy gazed at him, strangely lulled. She felt the little girl grab her leg, and Diane touched her hair. How had her life come to this, hoarding minutes of kindness doled to them by strangers who knocked on her door? She wondered if this would be the future texture of their lives, this hoarding, and she wished Woody Wilson would leave but also appreciated the fact that someone was with them in the room. She looked away from his pale, thin hair, his shirt rolled halfway up his solid, pink arms. She was afraid that her son would ask him to stay.

But the boy suddenly turned his back to Woody, squatting over his stickers with a fierce expression. "Tommy?" Woody asked. "Are you all right?"

"I don't care," the boy said sharply. "Guess what? I don't care."

She did not know what would comfort him; she barely knew what would comfort herself.

"Well," said Woody. "Hey." His voice broke a little, and he laughed, a hearty, rehearsed laugh. "Well, you never know what will work with kids, what will help them. Never hurts to try, right, Diane? Got to keep trying?"

He wanted to be reassured, and so did she, and for what? They were soft, graying, halfway to their deaths. They both knew that each person's love for another resided within oneself, miraculous and blind and strange; they both knew that everyone would die alone.

"Okay," she said carefully, and shrugged.

"Thank you," he said.

The tinny sound of "The Star-Spangled Banner" burst into the room. It was Woody Wilson's cell phone. Woody's face assumed a stern expression as he held it to his ear. "Yes. Still on Greenfield. Yep." He turned it off. "Well," he said. "Time to go."

He picked up his briefcase. "Thank you for your hospitality, Diane," he said brightly. The politician's voice burst out of him; he seemed almost surprised to hear it. He smiled as he had on the billboard, holding out his hand. "Goodbye," he said.

"Goodbye," she said, shaking his hand, the firm, remote grip of a stranger. His palm was soft and startled her; she let go and stepped away.

He gripped the envelope marked CONTRIBUTIONS and smiled shyly. "I suppose you wouldn't care to contribute to my cause?" he said.

"I don't think I can," she said.

He nodded, as though he had expected this. He stood on her porch and slipped his envelope under his arm. The bump on his head was dark and monstrous.

"What should I tell people?" he asked. "How did this happen?"

"I don't know," she said. "Tell them you tripped."

"Yes," he said, brightening, delighted by the idea of simplicity. "I just tripped."

Silence bore down on them; there was nothing more to say. Woody Wilson hurried up the sidewalk to the next house. His lips were moving; she believed that he was murmuring his name. Stepping out into the pink air, she looked at the names of all the candidates stuck in the green lawns. They sat, arranged in rows under the sky. Woody Wilson reached the next house. He rubbed his palms against his jacket, took a flyer from his briefcase, and, slowly, he lifted his hand to knock on the door.

The Sea Turtle Hospital

The lockdown at Arthur Elementary was the second at the school this week. It began while we were doing our class presentation: the Amazon Council of Beings. The secretary's flat voice announced it just as Keisha Jones was introducing herself as a harpy eagle. The Council of Beings capped off the kindergarten's Amazon rainforest unit and involved twenty-two five-year-olds sitting in a circle wearing paper-plate masks they had made of their assigned endangered animals, with Mrs. Reeves, the senior teacher, on a bongo drum. Keisha Jones announced she was a harpy eagle, and we all said, in unison, "You are one of us!" and Keisha was describing what foods she ate and before we could tell her, also in unison, "We hear your needs," and watch Mrs. Reeves majestically bang the bongo, the secretary said, statically, over the intercom, "Lockdown. School is currently in lockdown." The golden lion, tamarin, manatee, and jaguar were mad because they hadn't announced yet what they were; Mrs. Reeves told me to lock the door and draw the blinds while she got the safer job of herding the kids into the reading nook. This pissed me off because she clearly didn't mind if I took a bullet before she did. It was as though she voiced what I was thinking: the assistant should go first.

The school shut down, locking windows and doors, supposedly allowing no one in or out, when there were reports of violence in the neighborhood. The first lockdown of the week happened after a tenth grader at the nearby junior high stood up during algebra class, brought out a hammer, and started whacking his classmates. A month ago, the owner of a convenience store two blocks away had been killed during a regular transaction, and I passed the memorial of supermarket torches of roses and carnations set out by the mart every morning. I had seen the man the day before, a bald figure with a shiny, toffee face, who had moved here from Beirut. He had been sweeping the sidewalk then, and I remember brushing against his arm as I passed him, the way his upper arm was soft like a balloon. I read about his family in the newspaper for a couple days, the fund to send his award-winning clarinetist daughter to summer camp, and then I had to stop reading. I put a rose wrapped in a plastic paper on the memorial site. The next day, I walked down a different block.

I didn't know what was going on today. I had worked here for a year and a half, and the lockdown protocol still messed me up, the click of the lock, the brisk, absurd drawing of the blinds, as though the thin plastic provided any protection from anything. I was not in a mood to be locked anywhere now, not since my boyfriend Hal left about four months ago. The kindergartners were supposed to go into lockdown position, sitting, crouched, knees to chest, in their uniforms, the blue pants and crisp white collared shirts. I was secretly glad that they ignored this. The girls clustered to make their own hair salon. The children didn't want to stop introducing themselves; the Bengal tiger, orangutan, and poison dart frog wanted their turns even if, or perhaps especially if, a gunman burst into the room. Tyree rose slightly out of the group and announced, "I am a tapir," and we all chimed, "You are one of us!"

Who was going insane this time? Was it a husband and wife? Was it a fed-up parent? Was it someone so lonely her body felt like it might split? Was it someone who had been stomped on so many times he had forgotten how to feel anything good? I stepped away from the nook and lifted one of the flimsy plastic blinds, peering at the empty playground; it was blanched, white from the sun, the metal slides starry with heat.

The school had been generally tense the last week, too, as the third, fourth, and fifth graders got ready for the End of Grade Tests, or EOGs. The flyers in the hallways started twenty days ago. *Twenty days to the EOGS!* Then *Nineteen days*, and so forth. It had the subtlety of a hurricane watch. Did they really think any of us would forget? The administration wanted Arthur to again be a "School of Distinction," getting more government money if their test scores kept going up, and teachers gave the students the practice tests every day for three weeks; some demented fifth-grade parents kept showing up at school with the intent expressions of hunters. They were in search of scores. They followed them with the discrimination of statisticians, knowing the slight advantages a 95 gave over a 94; they stared at them as though they could predict the future of the world. Miss Eileen Hill, the guidance counselor and expert in student evaluations, was the one the parents sought out this time of year; she believed in numbers, percentiles, which all parents—suburban, inner-city, white, black—ate up. A score in the top 5 percent got you into Gifted. A score in the top 10 percent got you into an Honors track in sixth grade. The parents were greedy for every point, every question, every tiny glimmer of hope.

My cell phone buzzed. Tyree's mother texted me twenty minutes into the lockdown. *R U OK?* I hoped, in a sanguine moment, that she was asking about me. That made her one of the good parents. The good parents were the ones who complimented my blouse, who touched my shoulder and asked, how are you? We were all there "for the children," black, white, and brown, poor and rich, the ones who lived in the district and the ones who clamored for the waiting list. We were the public magnet school with the best test scores in the city—top five in the state. Mostly the parents wanted compliments about their children; no, the correct word was *craved*. They craved reassurance that their kids wouldn't end up in the same sorry messes they were in, and this was true across the board, upper-middle class to lower.

"Who is it?" Peter Olsen whispered.

"I don't know," whispered Savannah.

"Do you think he has a hammer?" whispered Peter.

There was the sound of walking in the hallway, a skittering kind of walk, someone not running but falling across the hall. Mrs. Reeves looked up. She walked to the nook and gripped the sides of one of the bookshelves.

"Give me a hand," she said.

She pushed one end, and I pushed the other, and we positioned a bookshelf so it was blocking the children. I looked at her.

"Class!" said Mrs. Reeves, clapping her hands in a rhythm that the children were supposed to imitate. They did, in a straggly way. The cramped nook, the bookshelf wall made them chatty. It was a bit hard to see them through the tower of chairs. Mrs. Reeves paced to the door and back and said, "It is time to sort macaroni." She said this with a honeyed, calm authority, as though, of course, this was the only activity permitted at this moment in time. "Each of you move forty pieces of macaroni from this bowl into this one." She set a few plastic bowls inside the reading nook. "Get exactly forty in each bowl. Go."

WHICH CHILD WOULD I SAVE FIRST? I TRIED TO IMAGINE HOW MANY
my body would cover. Five? Mrs. Reeves, taller than me, maybe
eight? That left twelve of them to fend for themselves. Mo Sampson,
the biter, maybe on one of his vampire-ish days, he could go. The
girls . . . I couldn't sort through the girls. Keisha, the best reader, and
who seemed, for an unknown reason, to see something good in me,
could be saved first.

They sorted the macaroni. Mrs. Reeves sang "If I had a
Hammer," which was, I thought, a poor choice. Travis bit his fingernails until one began to bleed. I sat down in the nook with them.
"You all turned in your permission slips for our field trip to the sea
turtle hospital tomorrow, right?" I asked them, trying to normalize,
distract, which was a teacher's first strategy, in all situations; I told
them all I knew about turtles. They leaned forward, the air thick
with the salty sourness of their breath. They wanted to know how
the injured turtles were rehabilitated, and if your hands smelled bad
after you petted them. Keisha climbed into my lap. I tried not to
encourage sitting on laps or they would all Velcro themselves to me,
but since Hal left, and I was now alone in this town where we had
moved together, I was so lonely I felt it, a cold pain, when I breathed.
Keisha leaned back against me, and I let her.

Fifteen minutes went by. Twenty. I stood up, started organizing the chairs around the nook again. Outside, Tyree's mother
was unraveling.

LUV U WE'LL GET ICE CREM

TIE UR SHOES

U CAN WATCH TV TONITE

I LUV U

I texted back *TYREE IS FINE*, which led to a flurry of more
texts: *MAKE SURE HE PEES HE HOLDS IT IN HUG HIM CAN U
JUST GET HIM OUT OF THERE*

Mrs. Reeves looked up.

There, somewhere in the school, was a faint lifting sound, which I realized were screams. Then there was the gunshot somewhere in the school, one, two, sounding just like and unlike a gunshot, a firecracker. I thought my skin was starting to crumble. Mrs. Reeves dropped a package of macaroni, and the pasta skittered across the floor. She looked around the room, picked up the rainbow shag carpet, dragged the large square of it over to the nook, and flapped it over the children. They coughed; the underside smelled like rubber that had fermented in some disheartening way.

"It's a tent!"

"Smells like shit!"

With the class under the tent, we couldn't tell who had made this second statement, and usually it would have led to a few minutes sitting in the "office," aka timeout zone, but right now it seemed that anyone could say anything.

Mrs. Reeves stood, holding the carpet at a slant over the kindergarteners; I went to the door. I peered through the window; there were police in vests and helmets running down the hallway—headed past the first-. Second-. Third-. Fourth-grade classrooms, running. Then right. The fifth grade. The administration. Cafeteria.

Another gunshot.

There was no place we could go.

The children were silent; they huddled under the rainbow rug. People in situations like this sometimes say they stop thinking. That was not true for me. I was thinking of everything: the way Hal had looked at me as he walked out the door, the freckle on his shoulder that I watched when we slept, Darryl's expression when he sounded out his name on the page, the sweetness of the cinnamon roll I had for breakfast.

Then there was a knock at the door. "Police," said a loud voice on the other side. "Checking the classrooms. You are okay to open up."

I looked at Mrs. Reeves, and, slowly, she nodded. I went to the door and unlocked it; it took a minute because my hands were shaking. A policeman came in, a black gun in his hand. The children sat up on their knees, openmouthed. It now felt like we were in a play. "We have a suspect. One victim, injured."

We stood there, frozen, unknowing.

His face blank in a practiced way. Oddly handsome for a policeman. Maybe he was an actor. The children peering out under the horrible-smelling rainbow rug. There had been gunshots in our school somewhere. We did not know how to act. The phone buzzed again. He nodded.

"Clear. We can get you out. Everyone, line up."

We moved the bookshelf and the children, who went, without us asking, to the ordinary actions of their dismissal—putting on their outdoor shoes, hoisting their backpacks onto their shoulders. The policeman watched them line up and said, "This is how we're going to do it. Put your hands on the person in front of you. Then close your eyes."

A couple children laughed. A couple cried.

"How am I gonna see anything?" asked Darryl.

"You won't," said the policeman.

"But I want to," said Darryl.

"This is the procedure," said the policeman. "Hands on shoulders, everyone, now."

The children were in two lines, and they grabbed each other's shoulders. They now looked as though they were at a party and about to do a group dance.

"Okay. We're going. Shut your eyes."

I watched them squinch their eyes shut, or loosely flutter their eyelashes; they gripped the shoulders of the person in front of them and started to walk. We were in the hallway. There were the pictures of things that began with the letter R; there were the collages made of pine cones from the playground; there were other students marching out the same way, eyes closed. My eyes were not closed. Neither were most of the others'; there was the sound of an adult crying, which instantly meant no one's eyes were shut; there were some footprints made of blood; there were the fourth-grade's pastel drawings of their recent trip to the zoo; there were the children, hands on shoulders, most of them with their eyes open, looking at each other, stunned, I think, by the strange quality of the orderliness, the fact their drawings were still on the walls. The footprints. Whose were they? We had to keep walking. We were walking out and out and then through the doors and we were outside.

The air was unspeakably sweet with the scent of jasmine. Today, in addition to the yellow buses parked in front of the school, there were two ambulances and a news truck and police cars and more parents than I had ever seen. It was as though they had fled their workplaces, in their crisp business suits and their green nurses' scrubs and their bright polyester uniforms from Chick-fil-A and McDonald's and Hardee's, and when they saw us come out, a roar came up, kind of a cheer and a shriek, everyone's names called out at once. It was as though everyone was being named, for the first time, right then, in the parking lot. There was no order to the parents' grabbing for their children—they surged forward, ignoring the rules of the pickup line, and no one stopped them, which seemed almost weirder than the shooting itself. A sheriff's car whizzed past the school so fast it left a burned-rubber smell in the air.

The buses roared up, lumbering yellow dinosaurs, and the children jumped onto them, and the ambulance zoomed away, and after the endless wait in the classroom, the strange walk with the eyes no one closed, the footprints, in fifteen minutes everyone seemed to have gone home. A couple teachers were talking to a news crew.

There was another small group that had gathered to cry. Some were being met by husbands, wives, assorted loved ones. I stood in the front, and I realized that no one had come for me.

I REMAINED THERE WITH DOLORES JEFFERSON, THIRD-GRADE teacher, who was the repository of all current events. She was heading to her second job; peering into a tiny mirror, she was patting her copper-dyed hair, which was organized into a kind of small obelisk; she was making sure it was all in place. When she saw me, she lowered the mirror.

"You okay?" she asked.

"I guess," I said. "You?"

"You know who was shot?" she said. "Mrs. Hill."

My blood lurched. Mrs. Hill.

"Holy shit. Is she okay?"

Mrs. Jefferson looked at me. "Alive. ICU. Hit her in the back."

Mrs. Hill, with her stacks of tests, parents trailing after her, wanting tips, the way she smiled at them with a bemused expression and said, "This is what they need to do."

"Is she okay?"

Mrs. Jefferson shrugged.

"Who did it?"

"Trevor Johnson's dad."

"Oh," I said. I'd seen him striding down the hallways a couple times this week, waiting by her office; he was a realtor, a top-20 producer for his company, as the newspaper ads said, his face winking out of the pages, but he could not stand still as he waited for Mrs. Hill—he roamed around the hallway, staring at the fourth grade's artwork.

"He came here for her?"

"Trevor's math score didn't go up."

"What the hell," I said, "What the . . ."

According to the school handbook, teachers were not sup-posed to swear, but she did not correct me. "We started a get-well card," she said, "Angela's taking contributions for flowers." We looked at each other, marching through these gestures of sympa-thy; we did not know what else to do. She checked her watch. "I'm late for work—"

Mrs. Jefferson also worked the evening shift at the Macy's per-fume counter, spraying innocent bystanders and inquiring politely if they wanted to buy Obsession or Happy. She sprayed with more abandon, she said, as we got closer to the EOG tests, particularly if her class was ill-prepared. She had developed a tic in her left eye over the last year, which she confided to me was easy to hide at the fragrance counter because she could pretend she got perfume in her eye. I had spotted the whole sixth-grade faculty hawking shoes after school hours at Shoe Carnival, and the art teacher bussing dishes at Ruby Tuesday.

"You can do it, too, hon," she said. "You're a cute little girl. I'll put in a good word. For the holidays—"

We all needed the money. What if someone had said, "No thanks, I don't need a second job, I have enough! I'm heading to the gym now." That would sound rude to us, frankly.

Mrs. Jefferson hoisted her purse onto her shoulder; she wanted to get out of here. "How do you have the energy?" I asked her.

"I don't," she said. "The Lord helps me teach these children. He gets me through the day."

She said that, merrily, though I had seen her at the perfume counter, one Saturday after I was on my own and I convinced myself to get out and walk around the mall. I saw her, clutching the spritzer bottle, aiming at customers with determination. She got everyone in her path. You buy perfume. You. You. I saw her hold out an exquisite bottle to a customer, a bottle designed to make anyone feel like a queen. Each bottle, a path. I will buy my diabetic daughter medicine and keep her from eating Ho Hos.

"You, it's just you to take care of," said Dolores. "You could work perfume and women's wear, you could rack it up."

The sounds of the sirens drained away. It was just me to take care of. It was an easy thing to say. Hal had left four months before. We had moved here, to North Carolina, his idea. We had just graduated college, we did not know where to throw ourselves, so we tried each other. It was a way to be, imagining that we loved each other, and for a while, we did. I'm not sure what happened. His body beside mine was a fortress, but then it was a jail. It happened when we decided to get engaged. I knew that if I went through with it, I would not be able to breathe. There was no good reason. I said no, I waffled, I was not the team player he had wanted. And then he moved out.

Each morning, I woke and had a moment when I saw the pale morning sunlight brightening the floor, and I forgot everything that had happened in the last few months. Perhaps Hal was in the next room, perhaps I still thought I loved him. The morning began with a pure, calm moment of nothingness, of boredom, even—that luxury—before I remembered what was true. Then, sometimes, I had a sensation that my body was disappearing; I was starting, somehow, to vanish. It wasn't a good feeling. So I got dressed in a rush, ate breakfast, got out of the apartment, for I needed to get to school, to set the crayon baskets on the tables, to hear the voices of the teachers and students.

Now I stood on the cement walkway in front of the school. The sun was warm and brilliant, but I was shivering. No one had come for me; not that I had expected it. But the soles of my feet were cold; I had never felt that before. I had to get out of here, but I did not know where to go.

Someone tugged on my jacket. It was Keisha Jones. She was chewing the tip of one of her brown braids. She wore her eagle mask, on the top of her head like a hat.

"Are you okay?" I asked.

She shrugged.

"Who's picking you up today?"

"I don't know."

"Your mom? Your dad? Your aunt?"

She raised her shoulders and dropped them; "I don't know."

We made our way through the police back into the office, where the secretary was sitting, typing an announcement, and weeping softly.

"Keisha Jones? No pickup again?" She handed me the phone contact list. I called her home.

"Who's this?"

"This is Miss Samson, Keisha's teacher. We wondered who was coming to pick her up."

Silence.

"Shit," said her aunt. "Oh. Sorry, I guess it was supposed to be me—"

"Is her mother around?"

"She's on second shift at the hospital. Not back until late—"

"Is anyone else there who could pick her up?"

"I can't drive, or I did, but—"

"Can you get on a bus?"

"I broke my foot, miss, and I can't walk."

"I'm sorry," I said.

"I can't walk." Her voice was rising. "Her mom's not coming home till late—"

"Anyone else I can call?"

"I don't know . . . her uncle, maybe, but, no, he's on till nine tonight, they're doing a big fundraiser at Chick-fil-A . . . they need him. Her dad's . . ." she paused. "I can't walk, honey, really, I can't—"

There were the various excuses we heard, the relatives who were assigned pickup but had been arrested; there were the family friends who had offered to do a good deed but were too depressed and forgot; there were broken-down cars, etc., but mostly the reasons people missed school pickup were dreary—the assigned person was at work. Everyone was always at work. The first job, the second job, etc. There was no car and there was a broken foot and there was another kid, waiting.

"I'll drive her home," said the secretary, rising from her chair. "If we go quick. Come on, sugarplum."

"No. Miss Samson," said Keisha, gripping my hand.

"I'll do it," I said. I didn't know why I said it. Keisha jumped up and took my hand.

"You know the way?" said the secretary, raising an eyebrow. "She's on North Ninth."

She said it that way because this was where the "free lunch" children lived; she thought I'd somehow be intimidated. "I can figure it out," I said, annoyed.

"Well," said the secretary. She regarded Keisha. "Keisha Jones, you turn in your signed permission slip for the trip tomorrow?"

Keisha looked at her, and her shoulders wilted. "I forgot," she said.

The woman shook her head. "Then you can't go."

Keisha stared at her. Then one tear, two, began to run down her face. "I want to go," she said. "This time, I got to go!"

"Rules, baby," said the secretary, patting her on the shoulder, and then Keisha turned and hurried out the door.

Keisha stood, crying noisily, in the corridor. I knelt down and hugged her. Her sobs were loud, and then softer. Then she stepped back.

"I want to see a sea turtle," she said. Her voice rose. "I *want* to! Now."

Her voice echoed inside me. I heard her. I knew that tomorrow she would be sitting at a desk in the fourth grade, where they had some extra seats, probably coloring in sheets on a marine theme. Someone in the sadistic school bureaucracy would think this was a way to include her, but obviously this would just make her feel more left out. I hated the whole world, for a moment.

"Okay," I said, quickly.

I was a kindergarten teacher, which meant that I was not an impulsive person. But she was one of those students who seemed to have decided I was good. It was a silly, rash decision; I had done nothing but give her a little attention in class. We sat and sounded out words together. *I see a c-at. The c-at is s-oft.* She was the best one in class, my speed reader. *The cat is soft. The cat jumps. I see the cat.* Done. Next book. It was the rare, divine dance between teacher and student, in which I helped her locate what she already knew.

"Okay?" she asked, her voice trembling.

"Yes," I said, deciding. "Now, let's go."

I signed her out. She set the mask back on her face again, in an attempt, perhaps, to look fierce, grabbed my hand, and did some long leaps to the car, the way an eagle might, if it were trying to take off into the air.

I HAD A CAR SEAT IN THE BACK FOR TIMES I HAD TO CHAUFFEUR children home. She buckled herself in. She removed her mask and surveyed my car. "Messy," she said.

"I know. Sorry about that," I said. The backseat was basically a museum of fast food wrappers. I swept them onto the floor and tossed my cell phone into the glove compartment. Keisha gingerly settled into a seat.

"It smells," she said. I was both ashamed and offended and opened a window.

"How's that?" I asked.

"Okay," she said.

I started the car. We sat there, in silence. She kicked at some of the crumpled wrappers on the floor.

"Why'd he shoot Mrs. Hill?" she said. "She was nice."

I glanced in the rearview mirror; she was rubbing the gray feathers of the harpy eagle mask against her lip.

"I thought he was going to shoot me," she said.

"Oh, no," I said, though I couldn't answer this—why Mrs. Hill? Why anyone?

"Why did he shoot her?" She had put on the eagle mask, but incorrectly, so she resembled an eagle with a human mouth.

I swallowed. There was no reason. Oh, some religious types would put it somehow into "God's plan," the gun-control advocates would say it was because we didn't have any gun laws, but truly there was no reason I could give her. So I said nothing. The cars in front of me fled to their glimmering futures.

"He needed a time-out," she said.

My hands felt like limp flowers on the steering wheel.

The classroom was one place where it seemed that the world could be explained; I sat in the tiny seats beside the students and showed them: This is an *A*. It begins the word *apple*. This is a 1. If you add another 1 you have 2. You didn't have to believe in anything but these facts, and the students started, at various paces, to absorb them. But what did you do when you were crouching in the classroom, listening to gunshots outside and not knowing where to run? The teacher's best trick was that she appeared to know everything. But that afternoon, in that room, it was clear that I knew nothing, and that made me deeply ashamed.

I leaned forward; it was hard to see. The late-afternoon sun was so bright the cars in front of me resembled hazy, pale elephants moving into the day. I had that sensation that I had sometimes waking up, that somehow I was about to vanish.

Left was the direction of her apartment; my hands turned the car to the right. The sea turtle hospital was about a twenty-minute drive; if I drove fast, we could get there and back to Keisha's house in no time, and I could blame any delay on traffic. Keisha petted the feathers on her mask. She did not notice the turn at all.

WE DROVE. THE CITY FLASHED BY US. PEOPLE LIVED THEIR LIVES. They were lining up at the Hardee's and getting money at the drive-through ATM and joining the army of cars in the Target parking lot. It was impossible to see anyone's expressions from the car, but everyone moved through the day as though they believed there would be another minute, as though they believed there were more and more and more.

"Miss Samson," she said, "am I your favorite?"

The children sniffed this out, the teacher's preferences, with great and accurate stealth. You were to deny it, always, but there were ones you loved more than the others, it was true.

"Keisha," I said, "I love you and all of your classmates."

"I want to be the favorite," she said, firmly.

"Well, you are the best reader," I said. She nodded, firmly.

"I know," she said. She looked around for something to read, to show off. "Ex. It. Exit," she said.

"Good!"

"Cook. Ay-ee," she said, looking at a sign on a store.

"Cook. Eee. Yes."

"Here," I said. "Read these." I had a bag of picture books in the front seat. I handed her one: *Sea Turtles: Wonders of the Ocean.* At a red traffic light, I read her the facts: They nested at a beach not far away. I read: "Nesting occurs May through August. Turtles lay about 120 eggs in a nest. After the hatchlings come out, they head to the sea. Only a lucky few survive; some people estimate 1 in 1000 survive the first year, and about 1 in 5, or 10,000, become adult turtles. No one knows why."

The pictures showed the turtles swimming; they resembled hunched old men, flapping small fins in clear aqua water.

I drove. It was May, and the sky was bright and burning and young, a faded blue rimmed with pink, barely any sense of darkness behind it; abundant, golden clouds moved through it, and light fell through the clouds in a column, translucent. I had not noticed the sky's beauty in a while; as I looked at it, not with astonishment as much as restlessness, I wanted to run toward those clouds, that burning, gorgeous light, wrap my arms around the clouds and consume them, taste their salt and sweetness; I wanted to drag them as walls around the classroom so no mean thing would get in; I loved the clouds, the air, so deeply my skin felt thin.

Keisha flipped through the book quickly. Then she tossed it onto the floor.

"I want to see one," she said. "Now."

IT WAS 4:00 PM. I WAS A TEACHER ON A MISSION; I WAS GOING TO show her the sea turtles, something miraculous and new. The light was escaping from the sky so that it was now a golden pink color like the inside of a shell. Keisha sat in the backseat of the car. She slipped the rubber band over her forehead and rubbed her fingers along her eagle face as she looked out the window.

I thought of what she had asked me—why Mrs. Hill and not her? Or me? The drawings, the footprints made of blood. I didn't want Keisha to remember that today. My hands trembled on the steering wheel; I didn't want to be wrong or unreasonable, but I wanted Keisha to see the sea turtles; hell, *I* wanted to see one now, see these animals with their grand, hard shells floating dreamily in their tanks. I wanted us to have something new and gorgeous in our minds.

The coast passed by us, barely visible through the haze, the ocean wrinkled silver sheets. I parked at the beach just next to the sea turtle hospital. She leapt out, running into the sand.

"Keisha, you need to take off your shoes!"

She looked puzzled. "I can be barefoot?"

"Yes! That's what you do at the beach."

"I *know,*" she said, regarding me skeptically. Then she removed her shoes. There was no public bus from her neighborhood to the beach; the city council of the wealthy white beach community kept claiming they were not "zoned" for a route here. Keisha poured the sand out of her shoes, handed them to me. Her eagle mask was dangling from her wrist, and she put it on. She had drawn the mask with the bird's eyes wide open, so she appeared to be very surprised. She started running across the sand. I did too, and we ran toward the ocean, the sand rising up around us, a pale glittery haze. The waves came down, clear blue cylinders, rising up from the flat plain of gray. The roaring was tremendous, as though it could fill every corner of the world.

"It won't stop," she said.

She stood in the tide a few minutes, the water pooling, foaming around her ankles. She was perfectly still. The wind riffled through the feathers she had pasted on. She nodded, briskly, every thirty seconds or so.

"Why are you nodding?" I asked.

"I want the wave to go down *now,*" she said. "And now. Now."

We stood for a moment, and the waves came down at our

command. Now. Now. Now. The endless, cold expanse of water. She lifted the mask off her face and handed it to me.

"You want to be it?" she asked.

"Keisha," I said, surprised. "Sure."

I slipped the damp mask over my face. Now I was the harpy eagle. What was I supposed to feel? She watched me, a bit bemused. I stood, staring at the crashing water, the wanting a huge hole in me—wanting to be more than myself, wanting to know what would happen to any of us. I waited, listening to the roar of the water. The mask stuck to the heat of my face. I slipped the mask off my face and handed it back to her. She clutched it but did not put it back on.

"I don't see turtles," she said.

"They're somewhere out there, swimming," I said.

"What're they doing?"

I tried to imagine what a sea turtle might be doing out in the ocean. "Swimming. Catching fish. Flapping those flippers."

"Why can't I see those ones?"

"They're too far out. But we can see them at the hospital now."

We crossed back along the sand to the parking lot of the sea turtle hospital. The promotional materials made the place seem much more significant than it was. I thought it would be an actual hospital, two stories, with a lobby and such, but the hospital was a small vinyl-sided building, almost like a ranch-style house. A woman in her fifties with a short gray bob was sweeping the parking lot. Keisha and I hurried up to her.

"Hey," I said. "We just wanted to take a look. Can we come in?"

The woman stared at us. "We're about to close," she said.

"Just for a second. My student really wants to. Just for a sec."

I was speaking a little too quickly. We had to get in. The woman looked at us, and I wondered what she saw.

THE HOSPITAL WAS A SINGLE ROOM THAT HELD ABOUT TEN ENOR-
mous bathtubs. I stuffed a couple dollars into a box marked
Donations and walked toward the tubs. They were about the size of
Jacuzzis and were surrounded by walls that were four feet high. The
room had a dour, greenish, marine odor. Keisha held her shirt over
her nose. There was a low roar of a water filter in the corner.

"Come meet our patients," said the woman, who wore a name
tag that said *Melissa*. Keisha stepped onto a stool beside a bathtub
and peered into it. She let out a wispy, astonished breath; there was
a turtle, the size of a carry-on suitcase, floating very calmly in about
three feet of water.

"This is Holly," Melissa said. "She was hit by a propeller, and it
opened her shell. You can see the marks where it happened."

There was a big chart marked *PATIENTS* on the wall. It featured
a list of unlikely turtle names, such as Bing, Snow, Honey, Maxine,
Warren, Spike, Hugh, and others, and a list describing an illness or
injury—*fracture, carapace*; *cold, stunned*; *viral*; *hook, entanglement*.
The last column described the outcomes: *Released* or *Died*.

"How do you treat them?" I asked.

"Each one is different," said Melissa. "We get here by 7:00 AM
and get the food ready for each turtle. Some of them are sort of picky.
We have to scoop the tanks a lot and clean and wash towels. Each one
has special needs—"

I watched Keisha. She was both intrigued by the turtles and
maybe a little disappointed in them. Depending on the angles and
the shapes of their beaks, they all looked eager or philosophical or
disapproving. Snow peered at us, with his small, almost eagle-like
head, and shrugged his shoulders, the wrinkled shoulders of an old
man. There was Bing, who had a hook stuck in his ear; there was
Maxine, who had run into a fishing boat and seemed perpetually
shocked, staring at us with her unblinking black eyes.

"Our goal is to release them back to the sea," said Melissa, and she showed us a poster containing photos of energetic people cradling the enormous turtles and gently placing them in the tide. One photo, titled "Local Humans," showed a group of volunteers cheering as a turtle made its way to sea.

"It's the greatest feeling," said Melissa. "You know? When you know it's where it needs to be, when it pushes the water with its flippers . . ."

I admit, I was jealous of those turtles, of the care the volunteers took, of the force and purity of the love shown by the "Local Humans." Keisha gazed at Melissa with interest, the way children do when adults speak with great enthusiasm about something; it was as though the girl was trying to interpret what the woman was really saying about the world.

"Can I touch Snow?" she asked.

"He's a little grouchy. How about Hugh?" said Melissa. She walked us to the largest tank, where a turtle swam around. He seemed to be in a hurry, but he kept bumping into the sides, turning, swimming, and bumping again.

"What's wrong with him?" I asked.

"Hugh," said Melissa, and she stopped for a moment. She looked as though she were about to cry. "Hugh's in good health, but he's blind. He was caught in a fishing net, and a fisherman banged him on the head so hard he can't see."

"Oh, no," I said.

"He's good-natured," said Melissa. She snapped her fingers against the tub. "Hugh," she said. The turtle turned and swam in the direction of her voice.

"So how long will he be here?" I asked.

"Turtles can live over a hundred years," she said. "He'll outlive us all."

I could not breathe for a moment after that statement. "Really?" I asked. "He could live for a hundred years?"

"I don't know who will take care of him. We can't just let him out again if he can't see. He'll get eaten." Melissa paused. "This is where he needs to live for his whole life."

We watched Hugh, who had stopped and seemed to be listening to our voices. I thought of him paddling away in the dark, bumping into the same walls over and over. The thought made my insides feel trembly, hollow.

"Can I touch him?" asked Keisha.

"Sure," said Melissa. Keisha stood on her tiptoes and lightly touched Hugh's shell. I reached over and put a hand on his shell, too. It was wet and slick and very hard, a shell that appeared to offer great protection. I thought Keisha would think it was unpleasant, but she stroked his shell very sweetly, and Hugh, amazingly, held still.

"He's quite sociable," said Melissa.

Keisha lifted her hand, and Melissa squirted hand sanitizer on it.

Keisha stared at me. "This wasn't in the book," she said. "Save him."

"Me?" I asked.

"He needs a better tub!" said Keisha, her voice rising. "A bigger one. So he doesn't bump his head!"

"Well," said Melissa, now looking alarmed, "donations have trickled off, and with more funding—"

We looked at Hugh, who began to paddle away. It felt like he was judging us, with his rapt, wrinkled face, but he knew nothing about us except the pressure of our hands on his shell.

Keisha began to cry. "He's so cute," she said. She stepped back from the tub and kicked the ground, hard.

"Let's go," I told Keisha, using my firm teacher's voice. I took her hand and began to lead her from the tub. She broke away from me and ran out the door into the parking lot.

"Wait!" I called, running after her.

"Is everything okay?" asked Melissa, hurrying after us.

Keisha ran from the sea turtle hospital, and she could have kept going, through the parking lot, my god, onto the road, but she didn't; she stopped. When I reached her, she was crying, breathing hard.

I knelt in front of her. This was not what I wanted to happen. I had hoped that she could see one thing that was good.

The air was starting to cool.

"It's okay," I said, softly, "It's okay—"

She took a large gulp of air, and her sobs stopped.

"Tell me," she said.

"Tell you what?"

"Tell me what kind of tub he should get."

I told her what kind of tub Hugh should get, and then she got back into the car, and I drove her home. We both were tired, perhaps me especially, and I gripped the steering wheel harder, with more conviction, for when I had retrieved my cell phone from the glove compartment, I found ten missed calls on it. Keisha's aunt, her aunt, her aunt, and then her mother. It was just 4:30 PM when I pulled to the curb of Keisha's apartment on North Ninth Street. Keisha waited for me to come around the car and grabbed my hand, put her eagle mask on again, and we started walking toward Apartment 3A. There were a lot of cars parked in the lot outside her apartment, including one police car. I didn't feel like I was vanishing then; I was aware of every cell of my body—my hands, my face, my legs—every part both sacred and sad. My heart banged away in my chest, and my throat was turning to ice. A door to 3A opened, and a young woman burst out. "Keisha!" she exclaimed. A large group of people gathered at the door—there was her mother, off early, in her blue hospital scrubs, raising a Kleenex to wipe sweat off her face, and there was her aunt, leaning on a crutch—all of them staring at me.

I remembered what I had told Keisha when we were standing in the parking lot of the sea turtle hospital. The type of tub I wanted to build for Hugh would be big, a mile long even, with slides and curving parts in certain places to make it fun. It would have special pools with rocks so that Hugh could imagine he was in a tide pool. Maybe there could be other nice turtles in there that would be his friends. Slowly, Keisha had stopped crying. Maybe, she had said, a smart doctor might invent special drops that could cure his blindness and then Hugh could paddle out to sea. Maybe, I had said, we would all gather at the shore and watch him swim out, and he would take in the sea with his perfect new vision, he would remember how to swim, and he would feel the buoyancy of the waves under his fins as he floated into the deep blue water. Floating, she had said. He would like that. Floating, I had said. He would swim, strong, into the waves; he would swim and swim into the sunlit water. She had nodded. The sky above us had seemed weighted, holding back something invisible and enormous. I had knelt in the crumbling asphalt while her small hands gripped mine, and I had waited for her to tell me the next thing.

Free Lunch

Our story was the usual sad story of our current era.

We had not expected to land here. People ended up in New Brunswick, North Carolina, a glazed sprawl of about fifty thousand people, after they were fired or got divorced or wanted to end their lives somewhere warm. Many had a dazed quality, walking around, blinking, in the clear air that smelled, oddly, of a swamp. They were thinking: *Is this where my life has led? Where do I go now? How long do I have to live, anyway?*

I had spent seventeen years of my life at a desk at Hugo Resources, a shoe-manufacturing firm on East Thirty-fourth Street in Manhattan, as an associate vice president of marketing. I didn't love my job, and I didn't hate it, but it was what I walked out of the house to do each day, it helped fill our children's stomachs, and it was my one small glory, my use. One day, the head of Human Resources appeared at the door. We thought he was coming to tell us more depressing news about our benefits. No more dental? No more contributions to the 401k? This time, the news was worse.

—Let me talk to you, he said, taking us each into a window-less office.

He offered me a donut. I took a glazed. I should have taken a fancier donut. I should have taken eight. I was, along with twenty others, fired, dismissed, gone. They didn't want to pay us anymore. Not pay us? Why not?

I had worked at my company for seventeen years. I had a title that sounded good if you said it fast. I took it all badly. Some of us stumbled out, sobbing. One woman threw up into a wastebasket. Others had a gift for looking on the bright side. They imagined more time with their children, pottery classes, walks in the park. They were brave! They were flexible!

I was not.

I wanted a job. I wanted my title. I wanted, let me add, the money. All of a sudden, our family income was halved. I actually felt dizzy when I understood this. I liked having money. Not much, but enough so that we could walk into Target and I didn't have to cringe when the children asked for things. Not a new iPod, but a DVD. A pretty shirt. A watch. I wanted them to feel part of the community of consumers. I wanted to keep our apartment. I tried to calculate the numbers we needed each month in my head. I realized that every store would be a battle in this way, every withdrawal from the ATM a cause for shortness of breath.

—No offense, said the head of Human Resources, —but we have to let you go.

I WAS PACKING UP MY PERSONAL BELONGINGS, TRYING NOT TO CRY, wondering why Diane Moran across the hall was allowed to stay, what made her so special. I packed beside my coworker, Lionel Solang, who had been dismissed after fifteen years, and he was batting back the same tears. We were both forty years old and crying like babies. It seemed that someone had died, but really it was a part of us. We were standing in the employee lounge by the vending machine. Lionel Solang worked in—or had worked in—accounting. He strode around the office with that accountant's crisp certainty, that pride in calculation, budgeting, and now he looked frightened, adrift, lost without anything to calculate. We stood in that small, sweaty room, the yellow vinyl couch where I had taken breaks, that luxury, a break. Now everything would be a break. The vending machine, stuffed to the gills with its scary, salty products, glowed.

—I gave everything my all, he said.

We were prone to clichés now.

—Me, too.

—What did I do wrong? Can you tell me? he said.

—I don't know.

—You were good at this job. You were an integral part of this company.

—You were, too.

We looked at each other with the deep bond of people who had been similarly abandoned to the extravagant boredom of the world. The fluorescent lights burned. Lionel's eyes were the green of an ocean. I noticed this.

—Really? I was?

—It's all totally unfair.

—We'll show them.

—Yeah. Someday.

—Now.

He looked at me, that sort of look.

—I'm scared.

We stood there, listening to that. Scared? How did that sum up anything? We had just been swiftly, absolutely erased.

—Don't worry, he said. He touched my arm.

He touched my arm. What was this? I was married. I had imagined this, idly, to pass the hours, but not with Lionel, not with anyone real. I did not know what to do. My skin was cool, suddenly. He leaned forward. There were those eyes. The world was a boat, and I was falling off it. There was the light shock of his lips on mine, and then we were comforting each other, not just with words then, but with our mouths, our hands; there was that wave we both rode, that surf, those hands and arms I grabbed; we were not invisible, we were not. I was trying to unzip my skin and get rid of myself; he was, too.

—Come here, he said.

We went into one of the conference rooms. We locked the door.

WE DID NOT DO MUCH, BUT WE DID ENOUGH. AFTER WE FINISHED, I could tell he wanted to slink away and cry. That was the more compelling emotional choice at the moment, self-pity. I knew we would not do this again, and I did not want to. But groping Lionel was the most honest thing I could have done right then. Why do we believe that strangers tell us something more honest than our dearest ones?

With that goodbye, I took my personal belongings and left.

I TOLD MY HUSBAND ONLY ABOUT THE FIRST THING. THE FIRING. The other fact, my involvement with Lionel in the conference room, was a stupid, rotting secret. They say that people will do anything to avoid shame. At that moment in the lounge, I did not care about guilt; I wanted to avoid shame. When I fell asleep that night beside my husband, whom I loved, I did not relive the moment the Human Resources person told me I had to leave; I thought of Lionel's lips on me in the lounge. They were, somehow, protection against a falling into a chasm that went on and on.

There was nothing then but numbness and résumés. Trying to

figure out how fast we could keep from sinking. Could we dream money and see it show up in the checking account? How little could we spend, eat?

I tried to be good. I shopped at the cheap market. I tried to encourage everyone to eat cheap foods. Let's all try lentil chili! We tried to appreciate the small things. Going on walks. Sunsets and the like. The decibel level in the house rose.

My husband's hand touched my back.

There was nothing but numbness and résumés.

Then my husband's company started behaving in a peculiar fashion. He was summoned into another windowless office. They offered to move him to this town, New Brunswick. He would have a contract for a year, and that was it. No more promises, his head guy said, as though my husband were a whiny five-year-old. We can offer a year.

IT WAS AT LEAST SOMETHING. WE LIVED IN A PECULIAR TOWN, A town that seemed to have arisen with the invention of Walmart, the housing developments resembling vinyl stage sets in which suburban mothers would run amok. The entire town fled into the local churches Sunday mornings, to soccer practice Saturday mornings. We chased them, trying to figure out where to go. We drove the wide, empty streets, we looked out the windows at the parking lots, we ate, slept, swept the floors, tried not to buy things, talked, ignored each other, waited. We tried to feel at home. We called people we met in the park, but they never called back. We sat in the apartment we were renting, alone, trying to keep the air-conditioning off because we didn't want to pay the electric bill, sweating, mostly, lonely, arguing.

I sent my résumés out. Nothing. Nothing. The phone only rang with calls from telemarketers, who seemed a bit desperate, themselves.

—What is going to happen to us? I asked my husband. I had

taken to asking him questions like this. I wanted him to be an authority on something. I wanted someone to be.

He wiped the sweat off his forehead. We were both always sweating now.

—I don't know.

—What are the children going to think?

The children were mostly sad. They wanted only to eat sour-cream-and-onion potato chips and stare at alternative worlds on screens. Any extra energy was reserved for demands that could not be met, that seemed, in a way, nostalgic.

—I want a Wii.

—I want a Barbie head to put makeup on.

Nope, nothing, don't even ask. It felt almost like a relief to not be able to buy this stuff, any stuff, but the problem was that others still seemed to be able to buy it; we watched.

—Why doesn't anyone invite us over?

The kids looked at us with new, critical eyes. They sensed we had failed them, but they did not know how deeply. Some nights I dreamed of Lionel Solang, not because I wanted him, but because that moment in the conference room was the last time I felt any sort of power. Who was I? I thought, looking at my husband, who slept fitfully, containing his own crimes and sadness. Sometimes he cried out in the night.

—What's going to happen? I asked my husband in the middle of the night. He lay beside me, naked, pale, both of us large, bewildered animals huddled under our thin Walmart sheets.

—They'll go to college, he said.

—Not for a while, I said. —And what are we using for payment?

—Uh, he said. —Maybe you'll dream what we should do.

We closed our eyes.

SO WE WERE HERE, IN THIS SMALL SOUTHERN TOWN, AND ONE PLACE where everyone invited us was to church. Come over to First Baptist! Presbyterian! St. John's! Come worship Jesus with us! We said thank you but no, because, actually, by the way, we were Jews.

Oh, they said. Oh.

We were Jews in the most superficial way. In our former city, we went to Temple maybe once or twice a year. But here, we were odd enough so that people mentioned this about me in a cursory description. There is Donna. She's new in town. By the way, she's Jewish.

We wouldn't call ourselves Jews ordinarily, but now we were, supposedly, Jews.

It was, in this new state of affairs, something.

OUR SON HAD A TALENT FOR SPOTTING THE TOWN'S CHASIDIC RABBI striding down the streets. The rabbi walked down the creamy, hot streets, in his long black coat and top hat, his wife with her ankle-length dresses and her extremely convincing wigs. He walked, his glasses steaming up beneath the branches of the glossy-leaved magnolia trees, the lacy pink crepe myrtle, the deep green, erotic foliage of the South.

—There's Rabbi Jacob again.

The rabbi and his wife had a purpose. They wanted to locate any Jews in town and convince them to do Jewish things. The recession was apparently not harming them. In fact, maybe it was good for their business. He loved us. We were it. We could be holy if we wanted. The rationale for this was not clear to me, but I did know that we were like catnip to him, and that after he had located us, one month after we moved to town, he came knocking at our door. He brought us homemade challah one Friday afternoon. Then he came by to blow the shofar for us at Rosh Hashanah. In his mind, these visits were not startling intrusions but kind and welcome gifts. He came in and blew the ram's horn, that long, bleating sound flooding our pine-walled, orange-carpeted rental. The walls were so flimsy we knew our neighbor's TV-viewing schedule by heart. The shofar interrupted *Anything For Money.*

—What the hell is that sound? our neighbors shouted. —My God! Can you turn it off?

The rabbi and his wife had been sent here on a mission. They could have ended up in Bismarck or Petaluma or Mobile; they landed here, in North Carolina. Part of their job was to spread their version of wisdom. And they wanted to spread it to us.

Rabbi Jacob kept inviting us to his apartment for a Shabbat meal. He was like a suitor who could not be discouraged. There was, I will admit, something flattering about the attention, even if we thought a lot of what they believed was, well, misinformed. Why did the men and women have to sit on separate sides of the temple? Why couldn't they have sex with each other when the woman had her period? On and on. My husband was desperate for some kind of friend here, anyone. I was not.

—It's free food, my husband said. —Because we're Jews, we get free food. We don't even have to bring anything because it won't be kosher enough. We're totally off the hook. When else do we get a deal like that?

At least he was practical, and it wasn't as though we had money for dinners out. He was right. It was something I loved about him.

So, finally, one day in April, we trudged over to the rabbi's apartment one warm Saturday for a free Pesach lunch. That was the main reason we went; our own desperate loneliness and a free lunch. Perhaps that was why anyone dipped a toe into religion. I didn't eat breakfast so that I would be particularly hungry for this event. I felt guilty that these were not really appropriate reasons, so I insisted that we pretend we were observant and walk there instead of drive. It was a mile-long walk.

—Why are we walking again?

—They don't drive on Saturdays. So we won't today.

—Why not?

—They just don't. It's their rule.

Of course, as we pretended to be observant, Lionel Solang was in my head. Of course. He came into my mind at inopportune moments; he stamped on me when I was trying to make some new start. Lionel was the only one who knew me, in a way. He knew how far I had fallen.

We wound down a street named, sadly, Confederate Drive, to Plantation Estates, a slapped-together development of townhouses where the residents looked unemployed or as though they were about to be. We knocked. The door opened. There they were, Rabbi Jacob, in his black top hat, and his wife Aviva, with her convincing wig.

—Hello! Hello! Come in!

They were absurdly delighted, the sort of joy reserved for relatives greeting infants; perhaps that was what they thought we were.

—Come meet Joshua and Adam!

Their children were four and three. There was a newborn sleeping upstairs. Aviva beamed at us. The table had been set beautifully, the silver gleaming. The rental condo was not in such good shape; it looked like there had been a flood in one corner, as the ceiling had a large, cloudy stain. There were suspicious dents in the wall, as though someone had been kicking it.

—Welcome! said Aviva.

We walked inside to the heavy, wonderful odor of stewed meat. The kitchen walls and counters were completely covered in tinfoil. The room resembled the silver wrinkled interior of a Jiffy Pop container.

—Was there a fire? I asked.

—Oh, we cover everything in foil for Pesach. So nothing leavened will touch the counters.

—That must take forever, I said.

—It was easy, she said.

Joshua and Adam stood, staring at us, clad in their tefillin and *kipas*. They looked cute, miniature versions of their father. Our son reluctantly donned a *kipa*; it kept falling off.

—Go play. They've been waiting for you, said Aviva.

Joshua and Adam ran into an area with a rust-colored carpet that appeared to be buckling. Aviva had made several salads. She picked up a lettuce head, lifted each leaf, and peered at it fiercely.

—What are you looking for? I asked.

—Bugs. Not kosher. If I find one, I have to throw the whole thing out.

—The whole salad? I asked. I wondered if we could intervene and take it home.

—Yes.

Our son emerged from the den.

—He hit me, he hissed. —That little guy.

—Uh, I said.

—He also threw a truck against the wall.

—Maybe it was a mistake, I said.

—I don't think so, he said. —I want to go home.

—Let's eat first, I said. I was too hungry to intervene in disputes. My son gave me a look. Adam and Joshua blurred by us, heading upstairs. Our son and daughter followed them.

—Where's the baby? I asked Aviva.

—She's asleep upstairs.

—She can sleep through all this?

—She's a good sleeper.

I looked at the immaculate table, the three different salads in crystal bowls. Aviva did not seem at all stressed, with her two small children and a newborn and her main activity, which was inviting

Jews over and making them an elaborate kosher dinner! Every week! This was her work, coming to a town and absorbing us into her tribe. It wasn't that different from the churchgoers who kept inviting us to First Baptist or St. Mark's.

—Why aren't you tired? I asked.

—I don't know. I sleep when I can.

I heard a commotion upstairs, the ominous rumblings and *thwap*s of children's play.

—Is the baby okay? I asked.

She was squeezing lemon juice into a bowl.

—She's fine.

There was a thump from upstairs. The rabbi came into the kitchen. He was beaming at the sight of me and my husband, here in their tinfoil kitchen, actual captive Jews! I wondered how we ranked on the mitzvah tally. Four of us, and they probably thought I was good for a couple more kids. Ha. Perhaps this was the sort of day they waited for.

—We are getting a shipment of handmade matzah next week, he announced. —Did you know that my cousin is a matzah supervisor in Brooklyn? He times the matzah-making from the moment the water hits the flour—eighteen minutes. That's what they have. Then they have to throw the whole thing out.

—Eighteen minutes? My husband asked, trying to understand some deeper meaning. —Why?

—Because it is, the Rabbi said.

The Rabbi seemed pleased, excited by this information. I found myself becoming irritable. Why? Why was there more throwing food out? Why cover the kitchen in tinfoil, why time the matzah production? I was having unsupportive thoughts. There was so much energy, so much flurry, and I wondered, for what?

I was very hungry.

Did you know, Rabbi, I wanted to tell him, *that it felt good when Lionel put his hand on my breast, it felt good when he pressed his lips against mine, because he, too, had been cast off. I was crumbling. I had done all the right things, Rabbi, I had, truly, and it still did not matter; they did not want me anymore. They still let me go.*

Aviva smiled at me; she was shiny with the exuberance of someone who believed she was on the right path in life. I probably had the same shininess ten months before. How quickly I had lost it; I feared I would never get it back.

There was another crash from upstairs. This time, the ceiling shook.

—Wow, I said, concerned. —What are they doing up there?

—Just playing.

—Do you want to check? I asked.

—They are fine.

—I'm going to check, I said. —Be right back.

I climbed the stairs to the second level. I was curious to see how they lived. There were two bedrooms. There were no real beds; mattresses were set on the floor with some blankets crumpled beside them. The lack of housekeeping skills was a little bit disconcerting. Did they not care how they slept, or were they simply too busy? In one room were Joshua and Adam. My children were standing by the wall, watching. Joshua and Adam were wrestling on the bed, rolling across it like dogs. Joshua picked up a metal flashlight and began to hit it against the bed. Adam laughed, watching him.

—Where's the baby? I asked.

My children looked at me, blank; there was a baby here?

—Where's the baby? I asked.

Adam lifted the sheet. Right on the mattress, beside her wrestling brothers, the newborn infant was sleeping. Her arms were over her head as though she were celebrating. At the sight of her, my children gasped. Bless them; they had, in some ways, had a decent upbringing.

—Here she is! Adam said, and he jumped on his brother again.

Quickly, I scooped up the baby. She was so small; she barely filled her pink terrycloth onesie. Her shining blue eyes fluttered, and she rested a cheek on my shoulder.

She was a baby, and I held her to me, her breath, frail as a butterfly's, against my heart.

—Boys, I said, wondering if I would get in trouble for disciplining them, —careful on the bed!

They looked at me, stunned. They were totally getting a pass because of their outfits. They were little Chasidic ruffians, I thought. This could not go on.

I cradled the baby in my arms. She was so small, nearly weightless; it was almost difficult to believe she was alive.

The children followed me downstairs. Aviva was bringing the bowls of salad to the table. She looked up, saw me carrying the baby, and smiled.

—Oh, she's up? Aviva held out her arms, and the baby melted into her. —This is Shana, she said.

I looked at her holding the small, light baby, and I felt heat ripple through me, a feeling I had not allowed myself.

—The boys were wrestling on the bed, I said. —They were hitting it with a flashlight. They almost rolled on her, I said. —Do you know what could happen then?

I tried to make my voice even, but I was mad. She looked at me, hearing this.

—You went and got her, Aviva said.

—Someone else should have, I said. —Maybe you.

—God sent you, said Aviva.

—No one sent me, I said. —I just went.

—Thank you for getting her, she said.

She kissed the top of the baby's head, very gently. Adam and Joshua were bobbing around her now, and Adam reached forward and kissed the baby's pink foot. The moment had shifted from potential childcare disaster to a scene of familial love; it was sweet but unnerving.

I was still hungry. Starving.

—Everyone, said Aviva, —it's time for lunch.

We all sat down at that beautiful table, the silver candlesticks gleaming, the tablecloth a spotless, pure white, the table spread with crystal. The rabbi called each one of us to wash our hands three times and say a prayer before we ate, and our son asked why, and the rabbi said because we were told to do it. It was not a good answer, but sitting there, knowing what I knew, sitting in this strange town because we had been kicked from the jobs we had held for seventeen years, not knowing what would happen next, knowing I had betrayed them, knowing I would hold this inside me my whole life, I understood that there were no good answers. None.

And we ate an enormous lunch—which, may I add, was free—for no reason except we were Jews, sort of, and that they wanted us to do what they did, for no reason but that it was written down in a book thousands of years before. They liked us, and we wanted to be liked. Aviva was a good cook. It was a good lunch, and we talked about the matzah supervisors and ways to avoid leaven, and we weren't planning to follow any of this; I knew that we would go home after and rebelliously eat bread. I could already picture the muffin I would attack when I got into our kitchen. But we sat there, nodding, pretending. The children went into the other room until mine came back and stated that they'd been hit again by Joshua, who claimed that he was just playing with a truck.

I did not believe that God had sent me, and I hoped Aviva would not leave her infant daughter loose in the bed again, and that her daughter would not be accidentally smothered or worse by her wild sons. I hoped that we would find jobs that would not make us so eager for this free lunch, and I hoped we would find friends that would make us less eager for any sort of company. I hoped that we could find something in common with Aviva and Rabbi Jacob, because they were, in fact, nice. I kept thinking of her baby, the sight of her sleeping, tiny, loose, on the bed. It was all I could think about. We kept eating and eating, and at the end of lunch, we helped her bus the dishes and stood with her in the humid, tin-foiled kitchen. I thought of that tiny baby lying on the bed, sitting there like a toy or a shoe, revealed by her brothers under the sheet, and then I loved that baby, that tiny perfect being, loved her as though she were my own.

As Aviva said goodbye, the baby was cradled on her shoulder. Shana opened her eyes and stared at me. My heart jumped.

—Bye, we said to Aviva and Rabbi Jacob.

—Bye, we said to Joshua and Adam.

—Bye, we said to Shana. We turned and walked out of their townhouse onto the sidewalk, and when I turned around, I saw Shana still looking at me, with her clear bright eyes, and I felt those eyes on me as we went on into the day, under that blazing, empty sky, my family and I, to our own particular uncertainty.

For What Purpose?

This is what they did: they handed over their IDs and boarding passes, they answered questions about their destinations, they took off their shoes, they put their belongings in the plastic bins, they surrendered liquids over three ounces (or they didn't and then were sent for questioning), they collected their belongings, they walked through the scanner, they lifted their arms, they stood, frozen, like dancers or criminals, arms raised, while the scanner took its picture, they walked through the scanner. The light, in the general area, was a dim blue. It made everyone look holy or sick.

I was usually the first one they encountered. I stood at a podium and asked them questions. I had been trained in behavior detection. I looked at the brief quirk of an eyebrow, the tension in a lip. I looked at how long their hands scratched their faces. For a short time and with purpose, or longer, for no reason. They told me where they were going.

For what purpose? I asked.

Always, there was the brimming hope, the expectation that we would find someone, the liar, the criminal. There was the hope that we would find someone who was dangerous.

That was our job.

I had worked here for three years.

We had four people in my family. Then we had two. My parents, gone, suddenly, eight years ago, car crash on the way to the opera. My sister did not believe it when I had to tell her. I did. That gave me a power that I did not want.

THE NIGHT MY PARENTS LEFT, MY SISTER AND I SAT IN THE LIVING room while my parents got ready. It was the first time they had ever been to the opera, and our father was, as always, in a hurry, afraid he'd miss a parking place; our mother was slower, buoyed by a sense that she deserved this: not just the opera, but some grand thing to nourish her.

My father got tense when mother wanted to stop and get ice cream before; I suggested a caramel Blizzard at Dairy Queen. It was just an idea I tossed off, unthinking, but she looked at me as though I had seen right inside her and said, "Yes." My sister wanted to get in the game; she suggested that my mother stop at a department store and buy a new purse. My mother shook her head. It would take too long, my mother said. Maybe tomorrow. My sister deflated, a limp balloon. Our parents walked out of the house, my father rushing ahead, my mother touching his shoulder with her fingertips, the two of them tense and determined, imagining they would walk into a room full of sound.

And they were gone.

In the long tradition of life after death, it seemed that nothing was affixed to anything—refrigerators and dryers hovered over the linoleum where they sat. That included my sister. She was mad that no one had listened to her idea about the purse. There was no proof that ice cream had been the cause of anything. We watched each other as we got the house ready to sell. My sister and I moved through it, deciding who would get what. This clock. Those earrings. That rug. We would negotiate each item with absurd calmness. We each wanted everything, wanted a safe haven for each item. Mostly, we each wanted our parents to walk through the door again.

Then my sister couldn't take it anymore. She couldn't hear the sound of my voice; it didn't say anything that would comfort her. She clapped her hands over her ears and refused to listen.

"You told her to get the ice cream," she said. She was a small, tense girl who burrowed firmly into any ideas that came to her and then refused to come out. She moved, swiftly, to Malaysia to teach English and hear any language but her own.

I was left here, with no plan for myself; I knew that I was supposed to live. I felt like I was made of sand. No one was watching me, and I had duty to nowhere. But I wanted to be of use. I took a plane to a small, unremarkable city and decided to settle in. I went through security and watched the agents do their work. They stared at the X-ray machine, they patted passengers' sides and shoulders, they fixed their bright, tense gaze on the crowd. I was drawn to them, beautiful, standing in their dark blue uniforms, scanning the crowds for something suspect, something that you could stop. Their faces were serene, enviably remote with understanding. I wanted to inhabit that knowledge and suspicion. I wanted to stop something, everything. I applied for a job in airport security, and they placed me here.

I began by screening the carry-ons. Looking for the sharp item, the explosive in the luggage. I saw the ghostly outlines of the passengers' shoes, jewelry, slacks, lingerie, cameras, the harmless items they tried to sneak through, like a bottle of wine or jar of mustard or jam, and the stupid items, like the scissors and knives. I was good at finding things. I was relentless. I wondered if the passengers ever thought of me as the planes lifted, wings cutting brash into the blue sky, as they gripped the plastic arms of their seats and let out a breath, looking down at the earth through the clouds. If they ever believed in some part of themselves that I had, perhaps, kept them safe.

WHEN I WASN'T PEERING AT LUGGAGE, I MADE MY ATTEMPTS TO construct a life. I watched the rest of my crew, who had spouses and coffee tables and cars. We had trained together, six of us, all walking into the multi-purpose room that held the session, all of us sitting under the sickly blue light, watching videos, power points, droning narration describing graphs, gestures, behavior, telling us who might bring harm.

They were the first people I had gotten to know since the accident; I was, just then, vulnerable to kindness, and they were generally kind to me. Getting to know them, I lost the need to meet anyone else. Also, each one reminded me of a member of my family. Lester had dark, spongy, lichen-like hair, the same texture as my father's. Deanne walked briskly, like my sister did when she was planning some sort of coup. Joanne sometimes squeezed my shoulder the way my mother once did. It was as though my family had, like spies, slipped under their skin. We spent our days standing in the bluish airport security area, but between flight times, we became friends.

Each month brought some new announcement. Lester was engaged. Deanne was pregnant. Joanne's son was graduating from college. There were showers, for brides, babies, there were cards circulated and donations taken for gifts. There were consultations about renovations; there were suggestions for mechanics and schools and what sort of covered dish to bring to church. Someone would drop some groceries by when I was sick, or lend me gardening tools, or help me fix my TV. There was a general sense of accumulation that was dumbfounding and strange and sweet.

MY APARTMENT HAD A BALCONY WITH A FEW POTS OF ROSES ON IT. I tended them; I bought frozen food and defrosted it for dinner; I watched comedies at night on TV. I had tried, a few times, to make inroads into the world of love, gone out with men whom I chatted with on the Internet. I had met a few of them, sat across from them in restaurants; they were desperate to be liked, the ones I met, and their chattiness about their virtues was depleting. Maybe that was why I didn't want to go out with any of them more than once.

My fellow crew members were the ones I knew. They had staggered into the airport terminal from their own disasters, of various ilk: bad marriages, drug-addled kids, tumors, depressions, embezzling relatives, early deaths, the rest. We all said I'm sorry to each other; everyone had an individual mountain to scale. That was it. We were here to guard others. I felt useful when I stood with my crew at the security gate—that was what pulled me through my day, that sense of usefulness. I was grateful for it.

We all took our work seriously. Lester assumed a dignified, alert expression when he gazed at the X-ray machine, always locating the object that needed to be removed. Joanne was efficient, precise at patdowns. Estelle was good at helping people organize their possessions in the plastic bins. When I worked with them, I secretly tried to find the parts that seemed to have been sent to me. Lester's hair. I watched the way he smoothed his hand over it, the way my father had done when he thought about his clients. Deanne's walk. I waved her over, sometimes, when I did not need her, so I could watch her heels hit the floor, hard, the way my sister's did when she needed to tell me something. And Harvey and Fernando and Joanne, each harboring their own treasures—Harvey pointed the way my father did when he was excited; Fernando's mouth resembled my sister's; Joanne let out a cackling laugh that my mother sometimes had. I didn't love them, but I sort of did, if love is being mesmerized by the mere fact of others, and the way they trick you into believing that they contain the other people you have known. It was the sort of love I owned now, and I just lived with it, though I tried to remember what it was to have the love others did. I had those moments of jealousy, looking over the passengers streaming through the gateways—those passengers, strapped into their seats with the luxury of boredom and desire, waiting for their beverage service, believing that they would walk down the Jetway into the rest of their lives.

I went to work, balanced on my life, this tiny platform. Sometimes, heading to work, I felt like I was going to slide off of it, sparked by a small sight—a gardenia bush like the one that bloomed outside of our house, a blue Mercury driving by. But this usually faded when I entered the terminal, when I took my place at the podium, when my gaze was supposed to locate any hint of mishap in the world.

ONE DAY, JOANNE READ US ALL A MEMO; BUDGET CUTS WOULD NOW go into effect. We were not all necessary to preserving national security. One of us would be let go.

Joanne read this to us; it just had been emailed to *ALL STAFF LOWER ATLANTIC REGION.*

"What did they mean, go? To another airport?"

"No, go. They don't need us. One of us."

I looked at them. Joanne cleared her throat. Fernando tapped his foot. A harsh deodorant smell came off Deanne.

"How are they going to decide?"

"I don't know."

"Then what?"

"One of us is let go."

While she was reading this, the second email came: Lester would decide. He had started here a year before the rest of us, and he had, as we all knew, stopped that guy with the steak knife in his sneakers the month before. He had six weeks, and Regional would abide by what he said.

I found it difficult to breathe. Would someone protest? No one did. We were weirdly passive in the face of this announcement. Our dark blue uniforms, so official, so comforting in their way, suddenly seemed nostalgic, with the flimsiness of Halloween costumes; Joanne fingered her collar with a tender gesture that I had never seen before.

"Everyone, stations!" said Joanne, and we took our posts.

WE WENT OUT TO RUBY TUESDAY A COUPLE TIMES, BUT NOW IT WAS different. Lester sat in the middle of the red booth, and everyone observed what he ordered. A crab-dip appetizer. Some mozzarella sticks. We all looked at one another. Joanne complimented him on his appetizer choice. She leaned toward him, asparkle with admiration.

"Crab dip. Good choice. I always loved its creamy texture."

"Thanks, hon," Lester said, dipping in a piece of garlic bread.

Suddenly, everyone was ordering crab dip, even those who, I knew, hated it. Several bowls of crab dip sat there, mostly untouched. I ordered one too, immediately. Everyone seemed both tender and monstrous. All anyone wanted was to stay, to be viewed as worthy of inclusion. It seemed the deepest desire, to be acknowledged, to be deemed worthy of remaining here, with the rest of us, and we sat around the table, eyeing the crab dip, hoping.

I noticed that the crew was acting a little differently now. The fact of our potential vanishing from this group freed everyone to reveal other elements of themselves. Now I noticed the things I didn't want to remember about my family. Joanne suddenly switched from a brisk, efficient worker to a compulsive flatterer, something my sister tended to do. Deanne became a flirt, which my mother did with cashiers at the market when she was bored, and Fernando sat up taller and claimed the mozzarella sticks in a bossy way, the way my father made grand, bullish gestures when he was annoyed with all of us. My heart thrummed with panic. The ground felt like sky.

Perhaps I should be more flexible. I knew this was just a job that gave us money, and we could walk out of the terminal to become something else—a waitress, a manager at Subway, a security guard at a bank. But this was where I had wanted to be. It seemed absurdly arbitrary. Why did anyone decide to hitch his or her feelings to anything? Why one place more than another? All of the crew members wore amiable expressions, smiled at one another, dipped garlic bread into their crab dip, and looked away.

I imagined my coworkers taking my arms and escorting me out of the airport; I could feel their grip on my skin. I sat with them around the table and wondered—*What would happen if I were escorted out of the airport? What would happen to me?*

A PASSENGER I HAD NEVER SEEN BEFORE CAME THROUGH THE SECU-rity line. He handed me his driver's license. He was handsome in a bland way. "John Comet," I said, and then I looked at the name again.

He laughed. "That is my name," he said. He was a slight, wiry man, and he was wearing a dark blue suit. It was a little limp around the collar, like an old flower petal. He had very white teeth. He had lush, uncombed brown hair, as though his normal mode of transport was running through wind. I noticed him first because he looked me in the eye. Not like a passenger, but a person. Just looking at who I was.

"Where are you going today?"

"Cincinnati."

"For what purpose?"

"Business."

"What kind of business?"

This was not a necessary question; I did not know why I was asking it. But he glanced at my badge, absorbed it, and answered.

"I am involved in the marketing of custom luggage."

"Oh," I said. He paused. I handed him back his ID.

The others usually picked up their boarding passes and hustled on, removing their shoes, lunging for the plastic bins. He did not move. He stood there, waiting.

"Sir?"

"What do people say when you ask them, for what purpose?"

A question. I regarded him.

"What do you mean?" I asked.

He cleared his throat. "Where do people say they're going to go?"

"People like to visit other people. Or vacations," I said. "They like to get away from their home. And conventions. There are conventions for everything."

He stood, his foot softly tapping as I spoke.

"Don't be scared," he said.

I looked at him.

"Why do you think I am?" I asked.

He smiled. It was normally the sort of comment that should have gotten him hauled over for questioning.

"I don't know," he said. "I'm just a sales guy. I know things sometimes."

He was right. I was scared. But somehow his asking made it fade for a moment.

"Are *you* scared, Mr. Comet?" I asked.

He shoulder twitched, just slightly. He was.

"No," he said. "Just travelling."

There was a sorrow in his voice that sounded exactly like I felt. I was surrounded by liars. He had nothing to gain by my fear. We were two planets floating, separate, in the blue air. Oddly, that stirred me.

He smiled at me, those bright teeth, and then he walked on to his destination.

HE SHOWED UP AT THE AIRPORT THREE DAYS LATER, AND THEN three days after that. I could see him from far away, his gait quick and clipped as he went through the airport; he slowed down when he began to approach me. Each time, he handed me his ID and asked me a question. The second time, he asked me, "Why do you think people like those conventions?" The third time I yawned when he approached me, and he asked, "Ms. Orson. Did you miss your coffee this morning?" Passengers had to be careful when asking questions, so as not to seem too interested in how this place operated. He seemed merely to believe I had something he wanted to hear. When I answered him the third time (yes, I had missed coffee, in fact), he nodded, his eyelids flickering, and I was startled, for I thought I detected something else about him: he wanted to know who I was.

THERE WERE TWO WEEKS LEFT BEFORE LESTER MADE HIS DECISION. I walked into the airport in the morning, past Deanne, past Joanne, past Fernando, past Harvey, past Lester. I wanted to talk to them but did not know about what. Our conversations had become oddly cheerful and stilted, so that no actual information was being conveyed. Today they were extremely fascinated by their various procedures and for some reason were having trouble looking at me. Joanne leaned forward and brushed my shoulder with her hand. Tenderly.

"How are your roses?" she asked.

It seemed strange to even ask a question; the roses weren't the point at all. Civility was a form of distraction.

"Great," I said.

She nodded. Then she got to the point.

"You notice how Lester's been walking around us?" she said.

"Yes," I said.

"He's been spending more time near you," she said. "We've discussed it."

My throat felt cold.

"What did you discuss?"

I could see a smile in the crease of her eye; it crushed me to see it.

"I can't say. There was consensus."

Joanne stood, arms crossed, sheathed in the armor of this alleged consensus.

"Why were you talking about me?" I asked. Softly.

"We're trying to help you," she said. "We're trying to give you a heads-up—"

"How nice. A heads-up," I said.

She stepped back, her face reddening. Joanne! I stared at her, noticing the mole on her left cheek, the patch of grayish hair above her forehead, parts of her I had never quite seen before. When had they become part of her? Then I glanced at Fernando, and I saw a birthmark on his ear, and I saw Harvey limp in a way I had never noticed as well. I shuddered. What else had I missed? In them, in my family? Had I missed some flaw in my father's driving, so that I had let them go to the opera when they should not have gone? Had I made a mistake in telling my mother to get ice cream? Who had we been, truly? I worried that I was having difficulty remembering them. My parents had fought, on and off, during my childhood, trading off in their bossiness; my father's realm concerned time, his need to be punctual. My mother wanted mostly to treat herself, with pretty shoes and desserts with clouds of whipped cream—those were the ways each one disappointed the other. Sometimes they walked through the house and their words sounded like metal lids pressing down on steam. That's when my sister liked my voice, when we went into the yard and came up with names for the roses that grew there: the Orange Queen, the Tropicana, the Snowburst; the roses seemed parental in their way, watching us.

But I remembered, too, the moments when my parents loved each other, when their shared hunger for the world was such that they decided to take us somewhere new. Sometimes, we jumped in the car and went to a random place—a donut store in an alley, a tarnished merry-go-round—and they walked beside us, holding each other's hand.

I didn't know what about them to remember. As I thought about that last night, my parents became cartoonishly diminished, my father blind, my mother rushing, me oblivious to it all because I just was. Then I remembered getting off the phone and telling my sister that there had been an accident, and not being able to tell her the next fact, my mouth dry, bitter, until I did, and I wondered what she had heard in my voice then, or after, what I had done, ever, that made her fly so far away.

"Why are you telling me this?" I asked.

"I don't know," said Joanne. She looked frightened, of me? Of herself? "Don't ask me; ask the consensus."

I did not want to believe what she said was true.

"I have to protect our country," I said, softly, and I went to my station.

I WENT FOR COFFEE WITH JOHN COMET. WE MET AT A DINER NEAR the airport. I had never had coffee with a passenger before. The table, the silver forks on their paper napkins, the hill of white sugar in the canister, everything seemed shiny and theatrical. We had been guard and passenger, and now we regarded each other warily, now something else. I ordered coffee, and I got an English muffin, as he did.

"Why are you this? A security agent?" he asked.

I told him what had happened to my family. And then how I had felt, walking through an airport. I wanted to wear that uniform and stand at the security gates; I wanted to feel how it would feel to be the gatekeeper, to decide whether or not it was safe to allow them to walk through the scanner, to shepherd them safely to their planes.

At work, the last few weeks, I had been holding everything in, every nuance of feeling. Now John Comet was sitting here, completely innocent, and I wanted to unload everything onto him. His hand reached up and smoothed his light brown hair from his face. With purpose. A blameless gesture.

"So that's what I've been doing," I said. "For three years."

"Well," he said. "I see."

We were not exactly great conversationalists. The silver sugar canisters glowed in the sun.

"How did you get into custom luggage?" I asked.

"I'm in marketing," he said, leaning forward slightly. "This company hired me and said, what do people really want to take with them when they're going somewhere? Some people bring lots of, you know, toiletries, other people say screw that, I just need my tennis shoes. We aim to please everyone. We give people ways to carry things. Anything."

He spread more butter on his muffin, vigorously.

"My wife didn't like luggage," he said.

"Your wife?" I asked.

"Ex. She took one bag when she moved out. With our son. Louis. She left all his stuff. His toys, his Pokémon cards, etc. I knew he'd want it. I had to bring it to him."

"When did she move out?" I asked.

"Two years ago. And a month. She's waiting tables in Miami. Married a new guy. Louis is in third grade. "

His voice was coarser than I had expected. He had a slight accent, maybe New Jersey. He stirred some sugar into his coffee, gently, and then a bit harder.

"So," he said, his voice softer, "I tell my customers you need lots of pockets."

We talked about nothing. How I grew roses on the deck of my apartment. A few of them, yellow and pink and cream, their fancy faces turned toward the sun. He owned rare beetles, a unique specimen that was usually found in Brazil. His voice became soft, wistful as he told me about them. "I was on a tour when I saw one. Sitting on a leaf. It had green, purple wings that looked like glass. It looked like it had come from another galaxy. But here it was. I wanted it. I had never wanted anything like that. I wasn't supposed to bring it back. But I did. I have four of them. They live in a custom-made cage by the refrigerator. They eat lettuce and carrot shreds." He whispered so that his words felt like a treasure bestowed on me.

We ordered more from the menu, from the breakfast side, bacon and French toast and scrambled eggs, and the dinner side, pot roast and fettuccini Alfredo and steamed broccoli. There was nothing so special about him; he was just a luggage salesman, not even really a handsome one. He wanted to be caught. He tried to conceal nothing. His face was just his face. I knew that he could see everything in mine, the raw haggardness of wanting. I did not feel like a security agent. When his hand reached for mine, it made me feel like god.

THE NEXT DAY, I TRIED TO LOOK PAST THEM ALL, TOWARD THE LINES of passengers, toward John Comet. I saw him again and again, coming toward me, but it was not him; there were hundreds of not hims, marching toward their destinations. They walked, clutching their briefcases, their faces damp, to New York, Philadelphia, Boise, Las Vegas, a crowd of people to be questioned, searched, waved on, or detained. My heart was a hook; it was reaching toward John Comet.

He came along, finally, dragging another piece of luggage with many compartments. He seemed to be a candle, glowing through the airport's blue dimness, though his incandescence was invisible to everyone but me.

WE MET IN THE SAME COFFEE SHOP AGAIN A FEW DAYS LATER. HIS presence before me as a regular human was startling and almost disappointing; it was as though he were a ventriloquist for the John Comet I saw, glowing, in my mind. We ordered what he had before, and also Jell-O and a salad of beets.

He told me about his son. "Halloween," said John Comet. "I've never been able to take him around for Halloween."

"Why not?"

"His mother makes up stories about me."

I took note of his face. It was not the face of a liar; a liar's face was speeded up. His face was still, which was hard to do if you were pressing something down.

"What sort of stories?"

"Oh, like I didn't watch him. He ran into the street."

"Did he?" I asked.

"No!" he said. He said it so sharply I believed he was honest. "Not when I was there."

I leaned forward, watching; I understood that he wanted to spend time with me partly because he wanted to be judged.

"Why did she say this about you?" I asked.

"She wanted to get away," he said. "She loved someone else."

He clasped his hands. He was sitting there like a cup of coffee. Looking at him, his square face, his dark eyes, his salesmanishness, you couldn't tell he was someone who had slid off the surface of his family into nothing.

We left the coffee shop. This time we drove to his apartment. It wasn't what I expected, but was a worn-out, motel-like place, with stucco walls and a red rippled roof. At the door of his apartment, we started to kiss. He tasted dark and sour, of coffee and salt, and I wanted to follow that taste into the rest of him. His fingers held onto my shoulders. I had never noticed everything this way. The lights from the streetlights were long, radiant bars.

Then his body rustled, and he stepped away from me.

"They're awake," he said.

The window was open. Inside his apartment, right beside the window, was a large wire cage. It held four beetles. Their shells resembled glass, purple and green and iridescent, the colors so deep everything around them was shameful, blanched. The beetles were almost braggy in their gratuitous loveliness. We stood, faces almost touching, as the beetles made their way across the limp shredded lettuce with their fragile black legs.

"Let's go inside," I said.

I felt his breath on my ear, his body pressed against mine. I longed for him so much my fingertips hurt. John Comet paused. "Not now," he said.

"Why not?"

"They're eating. We can watch them from here."

I wanted to go in now. I wanted to touch those shells that resembled glass but weren't. But mostly, I wanted John Comet. I wanted to press our bodies together, run my hands along his arms, his chest, walk through him like a door to my salvation. Instead, we stood for a long time, looking at those beetles, gleaming.

THE NEXT DAY, I WAS STATIONED AT THE END OF THE BIN CONVEYOR. I was the last person passengers would encounter before going onto their flight. Lester came up to me.

"You're on questioning today, Sally," said Lester, brightly.

"Yes sir," I said. Lester had taken to carrying around clipboards, taking absurdly copious notes. If I slipped up, the decision would be easy.

I was, in my porous state of longing and fear, highly effective. I found items of interest: a Swiss army knife, art deco scissors, a package of firecrackers.

And here was John Comet, pulling along his luggage. His face set in its same expression. He was off today to Philadelphia. No sign of what we had done the night before, or what we hadn't. He stood in the body scanner, arms lifted as the machine whirred. He was highlighted under his right arm.

"He needs a patdown," said Deanne, looking around. "Is there a man available?"

There was not.

John Comet looked at me, his face blank as milk. "She can do it," he said.

Deanne looked at me with eyebrows raised, like, *Do you want to touch this weirdo?*

I stood very still.

"You good with this, Sally?"

"I'm a team player," I said, crisply.

We went in a corner.

"Lift your arms, sir," I said.

He raised them into a T. I could search him however I wanted. I began to slide my hands down his arm. His arm was surprisingly taut and thin in the airport light, as I pressed down the sides for any metal objects. He stared straight ahead, at nothing.

"Done?" he asked.

"Not yet, " I said.

I squeezed the other arm. Sometimes people set off the machine for no reason. A slight move, a radiance, a ghostly threat only the machine could see. I stood, official, wearing my uniform, but I did not want to let go of his arm.

He let out a breath. Of love? Desire? Annoyance? Did he just want to get on with his day? I lifted my hand off his jacket. Slowly. A fingertip, a palm, the thin material of his suit. Each moment was sorrowful, releasing him. I missed each inch, each cell slowly. Slowly. I let go. Then I stepped back, back into the world of only me.

"All clear," I said. "You may proceed to your destination."

His eyelids fluttered. I didn't know what that meant. He nodded at me, and smiled, a beautiful smile, and took hold of his luggage and walked onto his gate, and I stood in the light, as he went away.

JOHN COMET CALLED ME TWO NIGHTS LATER. HE HAD JUST GOTTEN off his plane. He wanted to see me. Now.

We met in the diner. He wasn't hungry. He wanted to walk out of the diner into a park. He had the worn, dazed presence of someone who'd crossed a time zone—something had been lost. His hair was damp and sticky. His body had the stale smell of airplane air.

He pressed his mouth to mine the moment we walked into the park. The park black, the grass glistening under the grayish fluorescent lamplight. He kissed me hard, slowly, as though trying to inhale some important element inside of me. Gold. We fell together onto the grass. We were velvet and water and arms and lips, and we were no one, and that was what we wanted, to climb into another person and stretch out into their lovely darkness. To believe another could make room for you, could perhaps keep you safe. That had to be the answer, for I did not want to contain only myself, my rotten sadness.

His arms were thin and steely, and the earth was hard and damp under us. We were alive, weren't we? Didn't this prove we were alive?

Suddenly, he rolled away. I lay, breathless, beside him.

"I saw my son," he said.

"Good," I said. Now, on with it. He stretched beside me, a bar of candy.

"From the street. He ran toward me, and then he was mad."

"Why?"

"He said I missed all his baseball games."

He stood up against the starry streetlights.

"I wanted to go," he said. "How could I convince him? She didn't tell me about them. She wanted Raymond to go with her. The asshole. Not me."

He began pacing, as though he wanted to run now, to some other future, as though he could not bear this moment where we were housed.

"Maybe you did something," I said, a little irritably. "Think for a minute. Maybe you did."

He stopped and looked at the sky. His face held one feeling. He was distraught. He loved his son, I could tell that. "What?" he said. "Can someone tell me?"

I thought of my parents, leaving the house for the opera. I thought of the last time I had seen them alive. I thought of every gesture they made, one after another, each one leading to the final disaster. Or was each one random? What did any single action mean? I watched them put on their coats, my father's black wool coat full of holes, changing it for a brown one he didn't really like, my mother walking around, always ready to leave before he was, and looking at my sister and me and saying, "I have to stop to get something to eat."

I looked at John Comet, standing there. The earth like a cracker under his feet.

"I can't tell you anything," I said. "You can kiss me now."

I stood up and grabbed his shoulders. I could feel his breath on my face; I wanted to taste it. He took my hand, and we walked out of the park to my car.

He stared at me; his face was utterly familiar to me. Fear.

"Oh," he said.

We stood, examining each other. He did not move.

"I," he said. It was a breath, a softness—I. I what? I want to? I don't want to? I am afraid? I can't? There was an expanse of air between us. What was the purpose of this? Love? My skin was as thin as silk; it barely contained me. He rubbed his hands over his face and stepped back. I stood perfectly still as he walked away from me.

THE NEXT DAY, WE WERE ON ORANGE ALERT. THE PASSENGERS WERE quiet, obedient during orange, looking at us with a damp-eyed gratitude that we would protect their little beating hearts.

Lester stood, looking official, perhaps knowing already who would go. The rest of us didn't. I stood with good posture in my uniform. I tried to imagine what I could do to convince him that I should stay. The others schemed in a similar fashion. Everyone was very polite, as though their old selves never existed, as though none of us had ever met.

"Can you pass me some new gloves? I do appreciate it."

"I'm happy to do X-ray till noon if that would help you out."

The best manners. Smiling. Who the hell were they? Clouds rolled across the airport, filling the runway with mist. Flights were landing, unloading their passengers back to earth. I saw the passengers, feet just touching the ground, rush out, to their loved ones, that most earnest of gestures; I did not know how I would be part of that eager, massing crowd.

Lester was walking around, looking at his clipboard. He walked over to me.

"Sally," he said. "Can I talk to you for a sec?"

A sec.

We walked over to a corner.

"Well," he said. He coughed.

I waited. One sec. Then two. My hands froze.

"It's you," he said. He coughed again.

"What?" I asked.

"I'm 90 percent sure. I can tell you end of day. You do a good job. I don't know why anything happens."

What am I? I thought.

"End of day, I'll give you the final answer." He coughed again and walked away.

I walked out from behind the screen. I noticed the others watching me. I did not know what else to do. I went to my post.

John Comet. I could not stop thinking of him. On the grass in the park the night before. It was better to put my mind there, the wet muscular darkness, our breath, to be somewhere other than here.

And then there he was. His luggage rolling behind him. A different suitcase today, one I had never seen. Many compartments.

I tried to look professional, for the last time.

"May I see your ID?"

"Certainly."

He smiled, his beautiful bright smile. It made me ache to see it.

"Where are you going?"

"Today, Philadelphia."

"For what purpose?"

He took a breath. "Not sure."

"Sir," I said. "For what purpose?"

He looked at me. He blinked.

"Family," he said.

I handed him his driver's license.

"Proceed," I said.

So he walked on. Barefoot by the conveyor. Trudging on to somewhere. His innocence was illustrious and galling. My whole body was a question mark. About the mechanics of everything in the world.

Lester was looking at us. I followed his gaze. He was watching John Comet, who was standing, like anyone, while his luggage went through the X-ray machine. The lines were slow today, people somber, trembling. Everyone thought everyone else would blow things up.

And now Lester was standing. He was walking toward the X-ray machine. He was putting his hand on John Comet's shoulder.

"Sir, can you step here for a moment? We want to take a look at your bag," Lester said.

John Comet's face was white. "Why?" he asked.

"Sir, we're on orange alert," said Lester.

John Comet walked with Lester to a corner. I stood at my podium. I could see Lester start to unzip the bag. There were many compartments on the outside to unzip. One. Nothing. Two. Nothing. John Comet stepped forward. Three. Lester lifted a baggie full of lettuce and examined it. John Comet shook his head. Lester opened the baggies and sniffed the lettuce. He opened the main suitcase and lifted the lid. John Comet stepped forward and held his hand over the suitcase, as though to warm his palms.

"What the hell?" Lester said.

The beetles were inside the suitcase. I could see them, the four large ones, their shimmering shells, the almost dainty way they made their way across the suitcase. There were not just four. There were more, there were smaller ones, dozens, all of them moving like a shimmering square of purple/green silk. The other passengers stopped as they walked by. There were gasps. Some of the beetles started to crawl out of the suitcase, gliding green jewels. They were beautiful in their gaudiness, their pure beetle-ness, but others didn't think so. A woman shrieked. Lester slammed down the lid.

"Agriculture!" called Lester. "For God's sake. Get them on the phone."

A man placed his ID on the podium. I did not take it.

"Miss?" the passenger said, annoyed. "I have a flight to catch."

I looked at him. I stepped away from the podium, leaving the passenger standing, boarding pass in his hand. I was running. "No," I shouted. The word pierced the air; no one was supposed to shout here. I wanted to shout more. John Comet was looking around the security area. His eyes were burning, and his face reddened; now it was all over, for he looked as though he were going to burst. Lester. He was going to remove him, in a moment, he was going to apprehend his luggage, take the beetles, charge John Comet with god knows what. John Comet was looking for me. I knew this.

I thought of my parents just then, how they rushed through the door to the car that night; I thought of John Comet, standing, collar limp with heat, on a sidewalk in Miami, watching his son from across the street. I thought of how I did not know how I would be able to walk out of this airport now, how I would go on to the next thing.

And then I was running to John Comet, before they arrested him; I was running through the security area so fast the others looked up. I wanted to reach him before they took his suitcase full of the beetles he loved, those puzzled, glimmering creatures, before I could reach forward, before I could rescue them.

What the Cat Said

It was two in the morning when the cat spoke. It was raining again, great pale thunderclouds moving like ships through the sky. The bedroom flashed with white light. The children, earlier that evening, had tried, for the first time, to run away.

Now the cat was pacing the room. He was full of anguish. We were all trying to sleep. That was, in itself, a joke. No one slept very deeply, ever. Our boy was up the most. "My blanket fell off," he said. "It's hot." He stood by the bed. "I need to find my Yankee card." He paused. "Now."

He did not want to leave the day even after it had left him. It was a touching sentiment, though, for us, tiring. It was the gray hour of the morning when nothing seemed alive, the hazy moment before the march through our lives started again, before the sun was up and the dreary race continued, to eat, to be educated, to fill the wallet.

"I love you," the cat said.

The words sounded almost choked, as though the cat had been holding this in a long time.

I thought my husband had said it, or our son. The cat looked at me. The room whitened with lightning, then went black again.

I did not love the cat. His name was (horrifyingly, and chosen by the children so it could not be changed) Cutie. His gray, matted hair floated through the house. He had the bad judgment to bring leathery, half-eaten lizards to us as gifts. I did not like his guttural yowl, his desire to jump into my lap. He had his sweet moments, but at the end of the day, I had nothing left for him. And it had been my idea to admit him to the family, to pretend I had more tenderness inside of me than I did, to test myself, though of course I said it was for the children.

"Was that the cat?" my husband asked.

The cat sat and stared.

We all had a bruising night. Our son, eight years old, was experimenting with disdain. "I want to run away," he had said. Before he went to bed, he had packed up what he needed: chewing gum, a small golden trophy from T-ball, some autographed cards of Derek Jeter and Mickey Mantle and J.J. Putz, because he liked to laugh at his name. His sister looked at him, absorbing his tactics. She packed a Hello Kitty bag with a plastic comb, a pink crayon, and a pack of Smarties so old they had petrified.

"We are going to join the poor," our son said.

They put their backpacks on their shoulders and marched, with great and sorrowful dignity, downstairs. He opened the front door and stepped out onto the porch. They looked out into the great pulsing blackness of the night, the grinding machinery of cicadas. They stood, nobly, on the concrete edge of the porch.

No one stepped out into the darkness.

My husband laughed, unkindly.

"Don't," our son said, running back in and slamming the door, enraged and relieved that he would not have to negotiate the wet black maw of the night. They were stuck with us. They slapped uselessly at their father's big legs. They were so small. But so intent and full of plans.

They had been denied. Our boy had been disinvited from a playdate with Gary Snow. Gary Snow had a trilling laugh, hair as light as sunlight, and an exhaustive collection of baseball cards that he housed, oddly, in a casserole dish. Gary Snow had invited our son to his house and then had been invited to John Meyer's birthday party and suddenly, cruelly, cancelled.

The girl had also been betrayed. She had found the cat gnawing on one of her My Little Ponies. The cat lolled back, eyes glittering like a drug addict's, the pony's tiny pink leg in its mouth. The girl screamed as though the cat were murdering a living thing. "I hate Cutie," she said. Now she peered into rooms to check to see if he was there first; she woke from bad dreams in which he tried to eat her.

The children had numerous and passionate complaints. The complaints both deflated and excited them. They wanted to find solutions! Their solution was to ask for more TV. They would watch TV until their eyes crusted over. They wanted candy, candy, candy. They lay on the floor in their underwear, their bare, summer-brown skin aglow in the false blue light. They were so beautiful, I wanted to eat them. All of us adults were vampires of their sweetness.

They knew.

They were staring at the television, eyes half-drooping. Something gorgeous was in the bright glare. They were straining to see it. That thing was adulthood.

They wanted everything, and we could only give them so little.

I heard the rustling; soon they would see through our grubby lies. Our pathetic attempts to shove them off to sleep at 9:00 PM so we could have sex. Our insistence that more than half an hour of TV a night during the week would curdle their brains. My attempt to convince the boy not to do Little League simply because I didn't like the other parents. They would recognize our lameness, our failure—and theirs—to live forever.

"When am I going to die?" the boy had already asked.

We mumbled, looked away, scratched our legs.

"When?" he asked, searching our faces.

Soon, in a big huff, they would pack up and move out. Trailing stuffed animals, baseball cards, My Little Ponies, the objects that they had coveted and which, at seventeen, would make them feel naive and small. They would head off armed with rock posters, black T-shirts that boasted scary sayings, green hair. They would think they were starting anew! They would have better lives than we did! Soon they would be disappointed by sex, or thrilled by it; soon they would feel things—sexually, emotionally—that we never had. Or they would feel less. We believed we had beat out our own parents on this score, but there was no knowing, really. No one said. We lay in our bed, the sheets damp with the chemical smell of spermicide, breathing hard.

"I don't like your toes," my husband said. "How they rub against me."

"Why?" I asked, alarmed.

"I don't know. I'm just not a fan of them."

I contemplated this. What was this new change? Should I be understanding? Or mad?

The cat sat there, a gray and hairy beast.

"I love you," said the cat.

Did the cat love me? Or—more likely—did he just want dinner? I had forgotten to give him dinner. I felt bad about it, but not that bad. He was so fat his stomach dragged against the ground.

If the cat was saying I love you, and he was saying it to me, what was my responsibility to him? Did I have to pet him more? He seemed to need nothing. He awoke several times a day, stretched, checked his food bowl, trotted to the front door, went out, came in, and over and over. He had been allowed into the house because he was the one with no longings.

The rain began to bang against the house. The cat sat there, with immense patience.

"Was that the cat?" my husband asked.

"Yes," I said.

"He can talk now?" asked my husband wistfully.

"He said, I love you."

"To you or to me?"

I said, trying not to brag, "I think he said it to me."

"How do you know it wasn't to me?"

"I just assumed," I said.

Cutie was apparently done speaking. He would just gaze upon the wreckage.

"Why couldn't it be me?" I asked.

"Who did you say it to, Cutie?" my husband asked the cat. "Me or her?"

The cat stepped forward. My husband petted its head. Now he was pandering. Cutie rolled over on his back. He was large; his gray fur smelled of wet grass; there was a leaf stuck to his underside. He was a wild animal. We had innocently invited him into our home. We had even joked to the children that he was the third sibling. They liked that, someone they could push around. "He is your furry brother," we said. But he was really no better than a possum or a rat. He assumed the fragile mantle of a household pet, nibbled politely at the kibble, rubbed against your legs, posed adorably with a ball of yarn, but up close, he smelled of damp earth, and his hot breath had the metallic undertone of blood.

He rolled on the bed, his legs trembling, splayed out, in a

shameless erotic display. His belly was pale pink, rimmed with translucent white fur.

What did he feel when he watched us?

My husband petted him. "It was me, wasn't it," he murmured. His arm was covered in curly hair. He looked brutish. He was sexier now than when we first met, when he was just thirty, a raw-faced boy. Why didn't he like the way my toes rubbed against him? What other mistakes would we find in each other? But we loved new things, too. My husband had put a freshly washed plate into the cabinet with a tenderness that moved me. In what corner had he found this gentleness in himself? Would he find other things to love about me? We were peculiar mirrors for the other, and we were each long, stubborn walls; the pressure of marriage was trying to crack through them, to own the gorgeousness that we believed lurked inside. It was a lifelong task to distract us.

"What do you want, Cutie?" I asked. "What? Tell us."

We wanted an answer. The pressure in the room was unbearable. Nothing would break it, not speech, not sex, not sleep.

Cutie writhed under my husband's hand and then nipped at my wrist.

He was prone to this sort of casual savagery.

"No, Cutie!" my husband said. "Be nice!"

This was what we were used to—it was comforting, actually. We were more frightened by the idea of the depth of his feelings. Cutie meowed, a regular catlike sound.

"Ignore him," my husband said, now annoyed.

Cutie leapt off the bed.

Credits

"Reunion" appeared in *Ploughshares*, Fall, 2007.

"Theft" appeared in *The Harvard Review*, Spring, 2005, and was reprinted in *Best American Mystery Stories 2006*.

"Anything for Money" appeared in *Zoetrope All-Story, Fall, 2001*, and was reprinted in *Zoetrope All-Story 2*, 2003.

"The Third Child" appeared as "The Visiting Child" in *Granta*, Fall, 2005.

"The Loan Officer's Visit" appeared as "The Visit" in *The Harvard Review*, Summer, 2012.

"Refund" appeared in *Ploughshares*, Summer, 2005, and was reprinted in *Pushcart Prize XXXI, Best of the Small Presses, 2006*.

"This Cat" appeared in *Narrative*, October 2013.

"A Chick from My Dream Life" appeared in *The Iowa Review 1992* and was reprinted in *Pushcart Prize XVIII, Best of the Small Presses, 1993*.

"Candidate" appeared in *Ecotone*, Spring, 2007, and was reprinted in *New Stories from the South: The Year's Best, 2008*, and also in *Astoria to Zion: Stories of Risk and Abandon from Ecotone's First Decade*.

"The Sea Turtle Hospital" appeared in *StoryQuarterly*, February 2014.

"Free Lunch," under the title "Sent," was one of *Narrative* magazine's "Top Five Stories of the Week" in 2013.

"For What Purpose?" appeared in *Guernica*, October 2014.

"What the Cat Said" appeared in *The Harvard Review*, Fall, 2008.

Acknowledgments

Enormous thanks to those who supported these stories over the years, in so many ways, especially: Christina Thompson, Don Lee, Adrienne Brodeur, David Hamilton, Paul Lisicky, Bill Henderson, Meg Wolitzer, Tom Jenks, Olga Zilberbourg, Ian Jack, ZZ Packer, Andrea Barrett, Martin Espada, Otto Penzler, Scott Turow, Danzy Senna, Jacquelyn Mitchard, and Douglas Soesbe; to Eric Simonoff and Claudia Ballard for constant belief in my work and guiding these stories to a good home; to the wonderful team at Counterpoint Press, especially amazing editor and life coach Dan Smetanka and dynamic publicist Megan Fishmann; and, with love, to David and Meri Bender, Suzanne and Aimee Bender, Natalie Plachte-White and Michelle Plachte-Zuieback, Frances Silverglate, Sean Siegel, Perrin Siegel, Margaret Mittelbach, Jennie Litt, Jenny Shaffer, Katherine Wessling, Timothy Bush, Amy Feldman, Hope Edelman, Deborah Lott, Eric Wilson, Rebecca Larner, Rebecca Lee, Dana Sachs, Malena Morling, Virginia Holman, Sunny Xuemei, and Norma Varsos.

And, of course, to Jonah and Maia for their beautiful, essential Jonah- and Maia-ness, teaching me something every day, and to Robert, for being my dear partner in everything and for sharing the best words.